It was cr *couldn't let her walk out of his life.*

He knew he shouldn't be feeling this way about a complete stranger he'd met at his brother's grave. But this woman was a puzzle he intended to solve.

"Wait. Please. I just want a chance to get to know you." In the dim light, he saw the lines in her forehead deepen. "I don't know anything about you. I don't even know your name."

She looked down and took several long, full breaths. "I'm Sergeant Laurel Tanner, Crystal Cove Police Department."

Sergeant Laurel Tanner. The name hit Scott with the impact of a bullet. The shock of her revelation numbed his limbs and his tongue, but his mind raced forward, filling with anger.

This woman, this beautiful woman who had his insides tied up in knots, had shot and killed his twin brother....

Dear Reader,

Welcome to another month of top-notch reading from Silhouette Intimate Moments. Our American Hero title this month is called *Keeper,* and you can bet this book will be one of *your* keepers. Written by one of your favorite authors, Patricia Gardner Evans, it's a book that will involve you from the first page and refuse to let you go until you've finished every word.

Our Romantic Traditions miniseries is still going strong. This month's offering, Carla Cassidy's *Try To Remember,* is an amnesia story—but you won't forget it once you're done! The rest of the month features gems by Maura Seger, Laura Parker (back at Silhouette after a too-long absence), Rebecca Daniels and new author Laurie Walker. I think you'll enjoy them all.

And in months to come, you can expect more equally wonderful books by more equally wonderful authors— including Dallas Schulze and Rachel Lee. Here at Silhouette Intimate Moments, the loving just gets better and better every month.

Happy reading!

Leslie Wainger
Senior Editor and Editorial Coordinator

Please address questions and book requests to:
Reader Service
U.S.: P.O. Box 1325, Buffalo, NY 14269
Canadian: P.O. Box 1050, Niagara Falls, Ont. L2E 7G7

HARD
EVIDENCE

Laurie Walker

Published by Silhouette Books
America's Publisher of Contemporary Romance

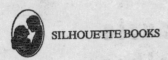 SILHOUETTE BOOKS

ISBN 0-373-07564-2

HARD EVIDENCE

LAURIE WALKER

was born in Killeen, Texas, and raised in Costa Mesa, California, where, at age fourteen, she met the man of her dreams. She admits it was actually "hate at first sight" in their case, but "second sight" blossomed into love, and they've been married for over twenty years. Along with their teenage son, they make their home in the forested foothills of Oregon's majestic Mt. Hood. When she's not writing, she enjoys skiing, motorcycle riding and giant roller coasters.

Laurie worked for eighteen years before she quit her day job to become a full-time writer. Less than a year later, her gamble paid off when she won the Romance Writers of America's Golden Heart Award for Romantic Suspense and subsequently sold her first novel. She hopes to inspire others to pursue their dreams.

In loving memory of my mother, G. Nauvelle Hale, who faced death as courageously as she faced life. A part of her will live forever in my heart and in my heroines.

Prologue

Sgt. Laurel Tanner crept to the end of the old brick building, her .38 caliber revolver clasped tightly in both hands with the barrel pointing upward. Responding to a last-minute tip from a less-than-reliable informant was a risky business, and she held her breath as she pivoted around the corner. A damp coastal fog tumbled down the alley, obscuring her vision. Her heart pounded fiercely, acknowledging the increased danger. The stillness and quiet did nothing to dispel the bad feeling brewing inside her.

Slowly, she moved forward.

Deep, muffled voices carried dully down the concrete alley in her direction. *Damn,* she thought. The buy was going down out *here,* not inside as her informant had indicated. Gary Boyd, her partner, would be at the far end of the building, waiting. The voices grew louder. Hair prickled at the back of her neck. She knew she should retreat and wait for backup, but she couldn't risk losing the creep who'd been supplying drugs to the local high school kids.

A tall, dark figure stepped out of the patchy fog and into view. Laurel recognized the man, and the shock immobilized her. Standing before her was someone she knew all too well, Deputy District Attorney Brian Delany, son of Judge Raymond Delany.

A black leather briefcase dangled from his right hand. In his left hand he held a semiautomatic pistol.

As he caught sight of her, an angry scowl twisted his face. He started to raise the gun.

"Police. Don't move." She delivered the command with strength and confidence learned through her years on the force. Nothing in her speech or actions gave away the emotional upheaval churning inside her. Brian Delany. God, how she wished it had been anyone but him. In the dim light, she watched his features soften as he recognized her. His shoulders slowly relaxed. From a few yards away, she could see the transformation as he slipped into the charismatic persona she'd seen in the courtroom and in the newspapers. She remembered how foolish she'd once been to trust him.

"Laurel." He said the name fondly, but his sly grin belied another motive, as it had two years ago when he had assumed the dinner he'd paid for included a night of sex.

She wouldn't succumb to his trickery. But she couldn't let him walk this time. She had to play it by the book.

"Let me explain." He extended his arms out slightly from his sides in a gesture of openness. The gun pointed off to his left.

"Lower the gun to the ground. Slowly." She kept her eyes fixed on his, though it was difficult to read his intent in the diffused light from a nearby street lamp. Gary would be inside the building now. She was on her own.

Brian started to lower the gun. "Okay, honey. You win— again."

Laurel saw the flash from the muzzle of Brian's gun at the same moment the blast rang in her ears. A white-hot pain exploded in the left side of her chest.

She got off one round before she fell backward into blackness.

Chapter 1

Laurel drove through the open gate to the cemetery. Ornate headstones cast long shadows across the neatly trimmed lawn. Apprehension welled up inside her, but she couldn't turn back. The conversation she'd had a few hours ago with her captain had left her frustrated, hurt and undeniably angry. She had to say her piece, even if the words would only be heard by a dead man.

The cemetery was quiet and empty, much as her life had been since the shooting. She'd awakened in the hospital nearly a month ago with a bullet hole in the upper left side of her chest. The bullet had missed her heart. Her adversary had not been as fortunate. Ballistics confirmed the single round she'd fired had pierced Brian Delany's heart and taken his life.

The nightmare hadn't ended with Brian's death. She'd relayed the details of the shooting to Captain Larson from her hospital bed. She would never forget the look on his face when she'd finished, or his words after he'd informed her of

Brian's death. "There's more," he'd told her, stroking his fingers over his salt-and-pepper mustache as he always did when he was worried. "When Gary found you, Delany had no briefcase and no gun."

She'd been stunned. Her confusion mounted when forensics revealed no powder tracing on Brian's hands. Pending the outcome of an investigation, the captain had put her on suspension. Four weeks later, she was still suspended.

Laurel continued down the narrow paved lane that wound through the cemetery. She expelled a heavy sigh that tugged at the scar tissue near her shoulder, reminding her that her body had yet to heal completely.

Dusk lingered in the crimson glow of the July evening sky as she parked her red Mazda and stepped out onto the freshly watered grass. The searing heat of the previous weeks had dropped to more tolerable highs and comfortable lows.

She wore wash-faded jeans and a gauzy pink shirt belted at the waist. As she walked up the hill, water droplets oozed over her sandals and between her toes, but she didn't mind the coolness. It helped to calm some of the anger she'd been forced to contain while speaking to her captain.

In the weeks that followed the shooting, her informant had mysteriously disappeared. The local newspapers had practically canonized Brian Delany, saying he was an innocent gunned down by an overzealous cop who'd panicked and shot the first thing that moved. Obviously, Judge Delany had had a hand in that report. She could live with the bad press, but ruining her professional reputation hadn't appeased the judge's anger. Captain Larson had just explained that if she didn't recant her statement about Brian Delany, Judge Delany would go after her badge.

She couldn't bear the thought of permanently losing her job. In recent years, she'd begun to think of the department as her family. Walking beside the neatly spaced headstones reminded her of how much it had hurt to lose a family member.

She had no trouble locating Brian's grave. From pictures in the newspaper, she knew the Delany family plot occupied the uppermost portion of the hill. A huge single live oak shared the sacred spaces. As she approached the grave, her steps slowed.

A dozen fresh yellow roses lay beneath the newly placed stone marker. "Beloved Son and Brother." She read the inscription aloud as she touched the cold marble.

It hit her with a force she'd never suspected. Her bullet had taken the life of Brian Delany. Tears she'd held in check, tears she'd been unable to release, flowed freely down her cheeks. Her shoulders shook with the force of her sobs as she silently prayed for forgiveness, from God and from herself.

She'd thought she'd been prepared to make the deadly force decision, but she'd been wrong. It wasn't supposed to be this way. It wasn't supposed to be someone she knew— someone she'd once cared about. She looked at the dates engraved beneath his name. He would have been thirty-four last week—if he'd lived.

Laurel's certainty of Brian's guilt did little to ease her aching grief at the needless loss of life. She believed all life was precious. Her job was to bring criminals like Brian Delany in for trial, but this time he'd forced her to respond to his threat. Knowing she'd done the only thing she could didn't stop her from feeling she had failed.

Her tears gradually stopped. She hadn't sobbed like that since she was eight years old and her father had broken the news of her mother's death. A teenage boy had shot her mother when she'd entered the local market during a robbery. Now, wiping her cheeks with the back of her hand, Laurel realized she felt a little better. Perhaps Dr. Perry, the department shrink, was right after all. Maybe the healing process could finally start.

The hour had grown late, past time for her to be on her way. Laurel heard a muffled noise behind her, sending a chill up her spine. Her instincts took over. She felt for her gun, then remembered it had been taken, along with her shield. The sound was unmistakable—footsteps fast approaching from the direction of the big oak tree.

As she turned, Laurel saw a tall, dark figure step out from behind the tree at the top of the hill. She took a defensive stance.

The man kept coming toward her.

She ignored the hair prickling at the back of her neck. "Don't come any closer," she ordered.

His face was still in the shadow of the tree. He held his arms out from his sides, empty hands displayed in a gesture of openness as he took a final step, which brought his face into the light.

Laurel felt the blood drain from her face. A chill traveled through her, but she couldn't fight it, couldn't move. The muscles in her legs went limp. As the ground started to tilt, she found herself staring into the eyes of Brian Delany.

Damn, Scott thought. *She's going to faint.* As her knees bent, he lunged forward to catch her, but his leather-soled shoes slipped on the wet grass beside his brother's grave. He made a diving roll to his back, wrapping her protectively in his arms as they both tumbled to the soggy ground.

The cool dampness of the grass soaked through the back of his white dress shirt as he loosened his grip on the woman. The air he pulled into his lungs smelled of fresh-cut grass and something infinitely sweeter. Long wispy strands of golden brown hair fell across his cheek. He inhaled again.

From the moment he'd seen her at Brian's grave, he'd felt there was something compelling about her. Like the unspoken communion he'd shared with his identical twin, the feeling was as fascinating and creepy as it was uncontrollable. He'd tried to convince himself it was simply the appreciation of a beautiful woman, but experience told him it was something more. The swell of attraction grabbed him too quickly and held him too tightly to be dismissed so easily.

When they were younger, he and Brian had an uncanny knack for falling for the same girl at the same time. The problem carried over into their adult lives, as well. Unfortunately, the complicated relationships had always ended in disaster.

Was this Brian's woman?

Scott shifted uncomfortably on hard ground. As she lay sprawled on top of him, her supple body conformed to his contours as if she were made for him. He knew he couldn't keep lying there holding her, smelling the sweet, elusive fragrance that clung to her skin, without his body reacting the way nature intended. Slowly, he tried to turn to his right side so he could lay her on the ground beside him. It wouldn't do for her to come to in their current position, especially after he'd nearly frightened her to death.

He wrapped his right arm around her shoulders, carefully supporting her head as he moved. Her right leg fell between his own legs, the front of her thigh brushing intimately against him. His physical response was immediate. He sucked in a deep, unsteady breath.

A second later, her eyes flickered open. Thick, wet lashes swept up in surprise as she pushed against his chest, levering herself away from him.

Scott sensed he was in trouble. He released her immediately, but her actions pressed her thigh more tightly against him. He knew the second she identified his arousal, as the stricken look on her face immediately changed to outrage.

"I'm sorry, but you—Ahh!" His apology ended in a long cry of agony as she brought her knee to his groin and rolled off him.

Scott saw her scrambling away on her hands and knees as he lay on his side gasping for air. "Wait." He tried to get up, but the pain was too intense. "I'm Scott Delany. Brian's brother. I didn't mean to frighten you."

She was on her feet, but his words made her stop and turn around.

With one hand clutching what was left of his masculinity, Scott reached his other into his pocket, pulled out his wallet and tossed it at the woman's feet.

He closed his eyes while she flipped through his identification. The pain gradually eased up. Scott remained quiet, with his eyes closed, until he heard a thud on the ground by his head. He didn't look at the wallet, but kept his gaze fixed on the woman before him.

"Your license is expired."

Stunned, he took a few seconds to form a reply. "Is that all you have to say?"

She had a stubborn lift to her chin he hadn't noticed before.

"You've got a lot of nerve." She paused, rather thoughtfully, Scott observed. "But I guess that shouldn't come as any big surprise, should it?"

"What the hell does that mean? Never mind," he quickly added. He'd lived with his father and Brian long enough to figure out the insult. She still didn't know how they'd both ended up entwined on the ground. Scott slowly raised himself to a sitting position. "As I started to say—" he gave her a long, potent stare "—I'm sorry if I hurt you. You started to faint, so I tried to catch you. Only I slipped on the wet grass and, well..." He felt an unfamiliar warmth in his cheeks. "You know the rest."

"Apology accepted." She nodded, but under her watchful gaze he had the sensation of being dissected and catalogued.

Scott got up slowly, calling on all his reserves to stifle a moan. He brushed himself off as best he could, keeping well out of range of her lethal knees.

"Sorry about your clothes," she said, glancing sideways.

What a perplexing woman Brian had found. That thought caught Scott off guard. He wanted to know who she was and what her relationship to Brian had been. The instant attraction he felt for her disturbed him. Somehow he sensed that the chemistry between them was as dangerous as it was potent. He sure didn't want to repeat mistakes of the past, but he had no mind for logic tonight.

Behind her wary expression, he caught lingering traces of the vulnerable woman he'd first seen. He resisted the urge to reach out and brush the wayward lock of hair from her face, but he couldn't seem to pull his gaze away.

As he'd gotten older, he'd learned that nonverbal communication between identical twins was common. He and Brian had often found themselves thinking the same thing or wanting the same thing at the same time. Sometimes it had felt as though they'd had a single identity. Though he and his brother had not spoken in four years, Brian's death had definitely left him with a sense of incompleteness. At first he'd assumed it was because Brian had died leaving their problems unresolved. Now he was intrigued because he'd expected the strange urges and compunctions also to have ended with Brian's death. How then could he explain his compelling awareness of this woman he'd never seen before?

If he had truly lost part of himself when Brian died, something in the eyes of the woman standing before him made him want to get it back.

As she combed her fingers through her shoulder-length hair and brushed tiny blades of grass from her jeans, he noticed she had a unique kind of beauty. His need for answers grew steadily as he followed her movements. It boggled his mind to think about the complexities he'd witnessed in her over the course of a few minutes—her vulnerability as she'd wept beside the grave, her strength and determination as she'd fought to protect herself, and then the wariness as he'd revealed his identity. One thing was certain: she thoroughly intrigued him.

"Were you a good friend of Brian's?" He hoped his voice sounded casual, but the idea seemed absurd after their earlier intimacy.

"I...I knew him." Her eyes were puffy and swollen from crying. She didn't quite meet his gaze. Instead, she looked down at the patch of grass stains on the elbow of his shirt. "You ruined your shirt."

"That's okay...." He waited for her to supply her name. She didn't.

"I—I have to be going." Her composure faltered for a moment.

"It's late. I'd better walk you to your car." *Oh, brilliant line, Scott. The woman took you out in two seconds.* He gritted his teeth and forced himself to face her again. The corners of her mouth turned upward and for a moment her clamp eyes sparkled as they reflected the light from a nearby lamp. Scott swallowed.

"That's not necessary." She smiled. "Really."

God, she was beautiful when she smiled. He didn't even mind that she was laughing at him. He smiled back. "True, but we could pretend long enough to salvage my ego."

The warm brown of her eyes reminded him of something, but he couldn't quite recall what.

"You haven't told me your name," he said, forcing himself to speak calmly. She still didn't respond. "I could go on calling you Sleeping Beauty if you'd prefer. It seemed appropriate for a while there." He didn't mention the urge he'd felt to awaken her with a kiss, but his gaze drifted to the sensual lines of her mouth.

"Laurel," she said.

Her smile was brief, but very nice. He felt the tightness return to his body and fought to control it. "Well, Laurel, I guess Brian neglected to mention he had an identical twin."

She stared at him the way so many others had stared at him before. With the exception of his father, Scott had never cared what other people thought about him. It was crazy, but this time he very much wanted to know how he measured up.

"I was sitting under the tree when I heard you crying." Panic flashed in her eyes and he immediately regretted his words.

"I didn't mean to eavesdrop," he quickly assured her. "I was pretty upset myself. I just found out about Brian a few days ago. I've been in Europe for the last four years. My family…" Scott sighed. He didn't want to bring up the past. He was trying hard to put all the hurt feelings behind him so he could mend his relationship with his family.

Laurel's expression softened. She cocked her head slightly to one side and looked up into his eyes as if hearing what he had to say was the most important thing in the world.

The tightness in his throat eased a bit. "We had a falling-out and didn't keep in touch." He'd thought a lot about Brian and his parents in the last few months. He'd even planned to contact them when he made the business trip to

Los Angeles this month. Unfortunately, it was too late to mend his relationship with Brian. But learning of Brian's death had convinced him to put aside his pride and make amends with his father while there was still time. He looked at Laurel. "This is the first time I've been back, the first time—here. I guess it didn't really hit me until I stood there beside the grave."

Her body stiffened slightly. Scott grew impatient with himself. He wasn't usually this clumsy and inadequate. If he only knew more about her—who she was, what her relationship to Brian was—he'd know what to say.

"I've got to go." She lifted that stubborn chin, but her voice quivered.

Scott didn't want her to go. The idea of not seeing her again caused a knot in his stomach. As she took a step back, he got an uneasy feeling. He noticed the way she never quite took her eyes off him, though he suspected she didn't return the same kind of interest he felt for her.

He shoved his hands deeply into his front pockets, fighting an intense and irrational urge to hold her elbow or place his hand on the small of her back as he walked beside her to her car in the dimly lit cemetery. He sensed a tension in her, as well as a readiness to act on that tension. She'd been caught off guard once. He didn't think she would let it happen a second time. Her defenses were up and in full working order. He had to bring them down and he didn't have much time.

It was crazy, but Scott knew he couldn't let her walk out of his life. And he couldn't shake the attraction he felt for her. If Laurel had been Brian's lover, he knew he shouldn't be feeling and thinking this way about her. But he didn't know, and he couldn't stop himself from wanting to find out. She was a puzzle he intended to solve.

When they reached the red sports car, Scott stood on the passenger side while Laurel walked around the front. She seemed to be favoring her left side slightly and he felt a pang of guilt for his clumsiness back at the grave.

She opened the door. His heart pounded as though he'd run a marathon. "Would you like to go somewhere for coffee?"

"No." Her bluntness surprised them both. "I'm sorry. That's not . . . I just can't."

Scott heard the unmistakable tone of regret in her voice this time.

She started to get into the car.

"Wait. Please." He breathed deeply with relief when she paused. "I don't want to make this harder for you. I'd just like to get together and talk." In the dim light, he saw the lines in her forehead deepen. He knew he was pushing his luck, but after having successfully negotiated a truce with his father this morning, he was feeling very lucky. "I know this sounds forward, but I can't help it. I want a chance to get to know you. I don't know anything about you. I don't even know your last name."

She remained silent.

"Were you—" He paused to think of a delicate way to phrase his question. "Were you Brian's girlfriend?"

Instantly, he saw the repulsion in her expression, and for some perverse reason he didn't fully understand, that pleased him. She looked down and took in several long, full breaths before lifting her face to look him squarely in the eyes.

"I'm Sgt. Laurel Tanner, Crystal Cove Police Department."

Sergeant Tanner. The name hit Scott with the impact of a bullet. He couldn't seem to force air into his lungs. The shock of her revelation numbed his limbs and his tongue, but his mind raced forward as it filled with thoughts of anger and betrayal. This woman, this beautiful woman who had his insides tied up in knots, had shot and killed his twin.

Chapter 2

Laurel forced herself to drive slowly out the cemetery gate
and down the road. The expression on Scott Delany's face
stayed with her. When the shock had faded, she saw his un-
masked pain and disappointment. Her hands trembled as
she clutched at the steering wheel and tried to make sense of
her mixed emotions.

The horror of seeing Scott for that first second kept re-
playing in her mind—she had been both relieved that Brian
wasn't really dead and terrified by the enormity of the cover-
up that would have been required to fake his death. When
Scott announced his true identity, it caused a whole new set
of emotions.

An identical twin. She could hardly believe it. It was difficult enough picturing Brian Delany as someone's child or
brother, but she'd read the engraving on the headstone and
accepted it as true. The special relationship she'd witnessed
between her own half brother and half sister taught her how
close siblings could be if they wanted to.

Suddenly, all the stories she'd heard about twins came back to her in haunting detail. She'd seen television shows about how some twins communicated in strange and complex ways. One show told of how a woman living in the Midwest was badly burned and her twin living in California felt the pain instantly. She recalled a case from her earlier days on patrol when she'd encountered a woman who had been raped and severely beaten. When they'd gotten her to the hospital, they'd found her identical twin had been brought in for a sudden, inexplicable attack of pains on her right side. When it was discovered that the twin who had been beaten had a ruptured right kidney, her sister's pain disappeared.

Laurel frowned as she lifted one hand from the steering wheel to massage her left temple. *Had Scott shared anything like that with Brian?* She remembered the pain she'd seen in Scott's eyes and the fresh yellow roses on the grave. He seemed so sincere. Recalling how she'd once been taken in by Brian's facade of charm and sensitivity, she reminded herself of the need for caution.

As she pulled into her parking space and turned off the engine, she closed her eyes and tried to envision the differences between Scott and Brian. Naturally, being an identical twin, Scott had the devastatingly handsome looks Brian had possessed. She remembered how Brian could draw the gaze of every woman in a crowded room. Scott had those same deep blue eyes lined with thick, dark lashes, and dark brown hair so rich and full she could imagine its texture between her fingers. Scott had the same sharp jawline and prominent cheekbones, too, but she sensed something was different about him, though she couldn't put her finger on it.

Brian had boasted the aura of a carefully polished politician, no doubt a position for which he'd been groomed by his father. Brian had used his thespian skills both in and out of the courtroom, letting people see only what he chose to show them. On the other hand, Scott's every emotion could be seen in his face.

She remembered his concerned expression when she first opened her eyes. But she remembered more than his face—the firm texture of his body beneath hers, came clearly to her mind. Now able to attribute his actions to Scott instead of Brian, she felt a latent warmth push upward from her belly. Her reaction brought with it a burst of self-recriminations.

Laurel, you've been a cop too long. You've really lost it if you can react physically to a man who looks exactly like the man you shot, a man who has every reason to hate you. Besides, if he's exactly like Brian on the outside, who's to stay he'd be much different inside?

As Laurel went inside and locked the door behind her, an unwelcome truth formed in her mind, bringing forth a laborious sigh. She hadn't been a cop too long . . . she'd been *alone* too long. The longer she stayed on the force, the more convinced she became that her line of work and any kind of long-term romantic relationship were mutually exclusive.

Exhausted both mentally and physically, she took a quick shower, brushed her teeth and climbed into bed. As she stared at the shadows and listened to the hum of cars on the street, she found she couldn't get Scott Delany off her mind, couldn't erase the look of betrayal she'd seen on his face when he learned who she was.

She knew it was crazy, but she felt this compunction to make him understand her side of the situation, what had really taken place in the alley that night. She wanted him to know she was a good cop who had responded to the situation in the correct way, the only way she could. But how could she convince Brian's twin when she couldn't even convince her own department?

As she closed her eyes against the shadows, part of her realized she was being idealistic. Despite the physical intimacy of their meeting, they were strangers. He probably had about as much use for the truth as his father did. Lord knew Judge Delany wanted no part of it these days. She had no reason to think Scott was any different.

Laurel spent a restless night dreaming of two men with one face. The same handsome features at times expressed a small degree of shyness and uncertainty, creating an endearing image of masculine vulnerability. Then they would suddenly mutate into a glassy-eyed demon with a wide, phony smile and four pawing arms.

She knew what had brought on the image. For a moment yesterday, when she'd first opened her eyes and thought she saw Brian, it had not been the armed assailant she'd faced in the alley that she recalled, but the Brian she had struggled with here in this apartment two years ago.

She'd accepted a dinner invitation from the deputy district attorney with mixed feelings. She'd definitely been attracted to him on a physical level. Her handsome companion remained charming and polite throughout dinner and during the drive to her apartment, just as he'd been the entire time they had worked together on the antidrug project. When she didn't invite him inside, he smoothly took the key from her hand, glanced around at the open windows in the apartment complex and said, "I just want to kiss you good-night without an audience."

He hadn't waited for her to agree. As soon as the door was open, he stepped inside and pulled her into his arms with the determination of a man used to getting his own way. It wasn't the gentle good-night kiss she might have expected. His fingers wound tightly through the long strands of hair at her nape. He was fully aroused, unfazed by the pressure of her hands pushing at his chest.

At first, she was annoyed, because he either was totally ignorant of the fact that she didn't return his feelings or thought she didn't know her own mind. When he ignored her direct order to stop, her annoyance changed to shock and then fear. He turned and pinned her against the wall, pressing himself against her. "You want this as much as I do. I've seen the way you look at me. Don't deny it."

When she yelled for him to stop, he chuckled wickedly and said, "No way. I've waited too long already." At that moment, she realized he intended to rape her.

That realization forced her to get a grip on herself so she could respond as she was schooled to do. He was a lot bigger and stronger than she was. Had she not been trained in martial arts, he might have succeeded.

Sitting at the kitchen table, Laurel shivered so violently at the memory that her coffee sloshed over the side of her cup. As she wiped up the mess, she thought of the contrast between Brian and Scott. Yesterday, Scott had immediately released her and, she realized in retrospect, acted with courtesy and respect. Whether it was an act or not, she couldn't be sure.

Under the circumstances, she couldn't very well walk up to Scott's door and start explaining what had gone through her mind and why she'd reacted the way she had when she came to, lying on top of him on the ground. She hadn't told anyone about the incident with Brian in her apartment and she never would.

Why Scott had shown an interest in her, she couldn't imagine. She'd looked her worst since she'd gotten out of the hospital. She hadn't worn any makeup or done anything with her hair. If that wasn't bad enough, her eyes must have been red and swollen from crying. Yet he had seemed genuinely interested in her.

A warm tingle filtered through her body. Laurel pushed it aside. Any interest he'd felt had surely died when she'd told him who she was. She recalled the look of abhorrence on his face once he realized she had killed his brother.

It wasn't just Scott. It always happened that way. As soon as most men found out what she did for a living, a shutter fell over their face. The few times they continued to pursue her, she knew they just wanted to add a cop to the notches on their belt buckle. She should be used to it by now. The idea that there could ever be anything between her and Scott was clearly ridiculous.

She got up from the table and headed for the bathroom. As she scrubbed herself in the shower, she made several decisions. First, she had to prove her story on record for her own self-esteem. It had absolutely nothing to do with wanting to wipe that look of revulsion from Scott Delany's face.

Second, now that her body had healed, she couldn't sit on her hands while her future hung in the balance. Detective Sergeant Polk, from homicide, had turned up nothing in Brian's car, home or office to corroborate her story or to connect Brian with the drug dealers. Nor had anyone had any luck finding her informant, Donald Cooper. Despite the captain's warning, it was time to begin some serious investigating on her own.

If something didn't turn up soon, they would be forced to make a decision about her future based on what evidence they had. If the man killed in that alley had been almost anyone else, she would have felt more secure. Usually, the powers that be would take the word of a police officer. But Brian Delany wasn't anyone else. He was a respected member of the district attorney's office and the son of a rich and powerful judge. She was slowly learning many people would let her rot in jail before they'd take a stand against the judge.

The third decision was the hardest. She knew she had to start at the beginning. She had to go back to the alley where she was shot and deal with what had happened to her. The idea of returning to that place, even in broad daylight, made her shiver. She knew she had to conquer that fear in order to get on with her life, and she had to start today.

Laurel put on a light touch of makeup and pulled her hair into a ponytail to keep the thick mass off her neck on what promised to be another scorching day. She selected a white eyelet sundress to combat the heat, but frowned as she realized the thin shoulder straps and low-cut neckline would not hide the puffy red scars near her left shoulder. Instead, she slipped into a lavender cotton dress with a dropped waist and chose a pair of white sandals. A quick check in the mirror made her feel better. She needed all the confidence she could muster to go back to that alley and face her ghosts.

Laurel got into her car and drove to the street where she and Gary had parked the patrol car that night. After pulling in behind a bright yellow Camaro, she sat, trying to remember every detail she could from the night of the shooting. She didn't realize how nervous she was until she reached up to turn off the engine and saw her hand shaking. A slow, deep breath helped.

Laurel had wanted to be a cop for as long as she could remember. She wanted to see that criminals like the one who shot her mother were brought to justice. If she couldn't face what happened here and put it behind her, she couldn't do her job. She'd be putting not only herself at risk, but the lives of the officers she worked with, as well.

Today a quiet serenity engulfed the neighborhood. The only sound, aside from the occasional passing traffic on the street, was that of her own footsteps on the concrete. Laurel looked around as she walked, taking inventory of the surrounding buildings, windows that might look onto the alley, and the distance and location of the nearest street lamps.

As she approached the corner of the building, she felt a tightness in her throat. She closed her eyes and took another deep breath. Returning to the place where she had been shot and had taken a life was proving more difficult than she'd imagined.

Lost in her thoughts, she didn't hear the approaching footsteps until the two boys came upon her. Automatically, she made a mental note: white males, sixteen to seventeen years old, dark hair and eyes, five-eight and five-ten, wearing the dress of the day, black Levi's jeans, black Nike high-tops and black T-shirts. One also wore black leather gloves and a purple bandanna. Something about him struck her as odd, but before she could figure it out, she saw the fear in their expressions. They glanced over their shoulders as if they were running away from something, something that scared the devil out of them.

Laurel battled her instinct to stop them for questioning; she no longer had the authority. However, she could try to find out what had spooked them. With her breath coming in short, fast gulps, she walked quickly to the corner and turned behind the building. She took two steps forward and froze as her gaze shot to the face that had plagued her dreams. Though this time she knew it was Scott and not Brian she faced, her initial shock registered in a shudder throughout her body.

The grimace on Scott's face said he'd noticed it, too.

"What..." She cursed the high, unnatural quiver in her voice. "What are you doing here?" Though she felt totally unprepared to deal with Scott, she stepped closer.

His gaze traveled the length of her.

She was certain the warm flush in her cheeks had come from the shock of seeing him here.

His lips separated into a brief smile before he forced them into a hard line. "I should be asking you that question."

Disappointment registered first. She must have imagined his smile. Why was he here? And why, for heaven's sake, was her heart pounding like a schoolgirl's? She found her own feelings too bizarre to contemplate so she focused her attention on her task. "I came here to see if I could find anything the other officers might have missed or—"

"Or what?" he asked with grim accusation.

"Or to see if there was anything I might have forgotten about that night," she answered with a steady voice.

"You mean like seeing the real criminals you were after when you shot my brother?" Disgust filled his eyes.

His censure stung to an unreasonable degree. "I meant exactly what I said, Mr. Delany. I know what I saw that night." How could she ever forget that moment of horror when she'd realized Brian had actually shot her?

"So tell me, Sergeant Tanner, was Brian the first man you killed?" Then he added with a snarl, "In the line of duty?"

"Yes." Her voice sounded stronger than she'd expected.

Scott shifted his gaze to the ground, then back to hers. "Is this..." He choked up for a moment. "Is this where Brian was standing the night you shot him?" He looked down at the ground again and she thought she saw hatred in his eyes. "Is this Brian's blood, Sergeant?"

Laurel swallowed hard before she let her gaze drop to the ground. She fought the wave of dizziness that came over her when she looked at the blackened patch of concrete. Taking in a deep breath, she raised her head and forced the words out with a practiced calm. "No, Mr. Delany. That's my blood. Brian was standing over there."

As she pointed to a spot a few yards behind Scott, she saw the shock register on his face.

"I... Your..." He couldn't seem to finish a thought.

Laurel felt another wave of dizziness as she looked down. She stepped back and reached for the brick wall to steady herself. The memories came back so swiftly she staggered. The barrage of unconnected thoughts fleeting through her mind in those few seconds of consciousness after she'd been shot suddenly clarified. As she'd faced death, she remembered thinking of her mother and the special relationship they'd had. Laurel had also thought of the sons and daughters she herself would never have, and an odd sense of bereavement had overcome her.

While all this raced through her mind, she had responded as she'd been trained to do. She'd squeezed the trigger after he'd fired at her. But had she seen Brian's body fall to the ground? She wasn't sure.

Scott muttered a curse, then stepped to her side and slipped his arm around her shoulder. "Come on." Despite the annoyance she heard in his voice, he carefully supported her as he propelled her back toward the street. Once they turned the corner, he stopped. She saw a mixture of concern and anger on his face. She was still shaking, surprised to feel tears running down her cheeks. She thought she'd expended them all yesterday.

With an exasperated sigh, Scott pulled her into his arms. "I'm sorry. I didn't mean to make you cry." His voice was low and husky. He cradled her head against his chest. His heart thumped a rapid beat under the soft fabric of his shirt. The warmth of his hand seeped through the fabric of her dress to her skin.

She closed her eyes and shut out Brian, the resounding echo of gunfire, the spilled blood on the concrete, and the memories. She shut out everything but the sound and feel of the heart beating beneath her cheek. The comfort she drew from this man surprised her.

Along with the reassurance, a special warmth surged inside Laurel. She had to stop it now, had to pull away. This was crazy. She shouldn't be feeling this way—not in the arms of a Delany.

"I didn't know." A thin edge of resentment carved through the honesty of his words. "No one told me."

She felt him swallow. When she looked up she saw pain creasing the skin around his eyes.

"Where?" His voice cracked.

Something inside tugged at Laurel. Keeping her eyes focused on him, she pointed to the spot on her chest where the bullet entered. "It went in here and straight through." The entrance wound was smaller and less ragged than the exit wound on her upper back. She found no reason to tell him the bullet had missed her subclavian artery by less than a quarter inch.

"Does it hurt?"

"Not anymore," she lied, fighting for the courage to pull back from his embrace. "Please." She pushed lightly against his chest. His arms dropped, causing more confusing emotions—like emptiness and disappointment—to emerge.

Laurel struggled to piece together what he'd told her. She couldn't believe Judge Delany hadn't even told him that she'd been shot that night, too. Frustration and anger brewed inside her as she thought about the futility of her situation. The full weight of the judge's influence reached a lot farther than his family. People believed whatever he said. In recent weeks, reporters had willingly accepted his story without probing more deeply for the truth.

She looked up at Scott's face and found some of her own anguish mirrored there. He was staring at her, his eyes giving away the fact that he hadn't been told the whole story. She could tell how desperately he didn't want to believe her. Believing her meant accepting that his father had been less than honest with him. She knew it wasn't Scott's fault he hadn't known—he'd had no reason to doubt his parents' story. The more she thought about it, the more evident it became that if anyone was going to right this situation with the truth, it would have to be her.

She swallowed and hugged her arms to her chest. "Look, Scott, I'm sorry, too." She paused while he brought his gaze to hers. "I didn't want to shoot your brother. I realized last night that the department psychologist was right. I've been very angry at Brian because he made me shoot him and then I felt ashamed for being angry at someone I had killed. That's why I was crying at his grave yesterday."

Scott's jaw clenched tightly.

She shook her head. "I'm sorry. I shouldn't involve you in this. And I'm sorry for hurting you last night. Why don't you go home and try to forget you ever saw me."

She turned her face away, afraid of what she'd see in his eyes. When he moved, she thought he was going to do as she said, but he surprised her by stepping closer. He took her chin in his hand and gently turned her face to his. "I can't do that." The turmoil in his eyes touched his voice.

A slight tremor shook her body as his fingers moved lightly over her chin before he withdrew them. She watched his lips shape the words that frightened and excited her. He was a Delany. She didn't want a reason to like him.

"Tell me what really happened that night," he commanded gently.

She admired the painful determination in his voice as she thought about his question and the courage it took to ask it. "You may not want to hear it."

"I want the truth." As he looked into her eyes, he spoke with an intensity that told her he meant what he said.

She nodded, then turned to pace a few feet before him. "My partner, Gary Boyd, and I had been going around to various schools and youth groups talking to the kids about the drug problem we have here. We tried to be straight with them. We suspected there was someone—some kind of an authority figure—involved because of the way the kids we arrested reacted to some of the questions put to them. By making personal contact with these young people, we were trying to give them someone they could go to who they knew wasn't involved with their drug suppliers." Laurel crossed her forearms in front of her and rubbed her hands up and down her arms as she paced.

"Just before we were to go off duty that night, I got a call from an informant. He gave me the address of the building in front of the alley." She indicated the direction from which they had come.

"He said the guy who was supplying drugs to the school kids was there and if I hurried, I might be able to catch him, or at least find out who he was." She thought back to that night. The special assignment they'd been on, and daytime temperatures that reached the nineties that week, had caused her to leave her protective vest in her locker, a stupid and nearly fatal mistake she would never make again.

She told Scott everything leading up to the moment she faced Brian in the alley.

"If the fog had already rolled in, are you sure he saw you? He might not have known you were a cop."

"He knew."

"He could have been here looking for the dealers, as well." Scott's voice held a note of accusation. He was obviously groping for some small shred of evidence to protect his brother's reputation, but even as he did so, she could see the doubt in his eyes.

She couldn't blame him for trying. Brian was his flesh and blood, while she was an outsider. For a second, she found herself envying Brian. Even after his death, he had what she longed for—a sense of belonging. He had a family and friends who stood by him and supported him.

"How can you be so sure?" Scott made one last attempt.

In more ways than she could count, she regretted what she had to say. "He... He spoke to me... called me by name before he raised the gun and pulled the trigger." Laurel tried to control the tremble in her voice. She didn't tell Scott about the satisfied smile on Brian's face. That would only cause him more unnecessary pain.

A muscle quivered in Scott's jaw as he stared into her eyes. His body tensed visibly.

"So...you really did know him. Personally, I mean." His gaze bored into hers, asking much more than his words.

"We worked together on a youth project two years ago." Laurel prayed her cheeks didn't give away her discomfort. If anyone were to discover the truth about her relationship with Brian, she'd have one hell of a time trying to explain it to the captain and the homicide detective. "You believe me, don't you?" she said. She saw the answer in his eyes, whether he wanted her to see it or not.

For a second, Scott's shoulders sagged, then he reached one hand up to massage the back of his neck. "I believe that's what you think you saw that night."

The tightness in his jaw and the tension she felt in him told her he was fighting his gut reaction. Early in her law-enforcement training, Laurel had learned the value of listening to her own gut feelings and instincts. She suspected Scott believed her, even though he didn't want to.

"I know this must come as quite a shock to you," she said, reaching out to place her hand on his forearm. The muscles beneath her fingers tightened, but he said nothing. "Scott, I'm sorry Brian is dead. I really am. But I know what I saw. If Brian wasn't the drug dealer we were looking for that night, he was at least involved with something illegal or he wouldn't have shot me."

For a moment, she thought he was going to say something, but then he closed his eyes and she knew how hard he was struggling inside. Her own eyes started to burn. She reached out to touch him again, but he pulled back, using his open palms as a shield to keep her away.

The gesture stung immeasurably.

After leaving the alley, Laurel drove up and down the streets in the neighborhood where her informant usually hung out, determined to chase thoughts of Scott from her mind. She had no luck, but it wasn't for lack of trying. When she rid her mind of his image, she recalled the inner turmoil she'd felt as he held her and stroked her back. The distraction annoyed her.

She cruised the high school parking lot and adjoining streets. Although Donald Cooper had dropped out of high school a few years ago at age sixteen, he still had friends there. Some of them were probably attending summer school in order to graduate. She rolled slowly to a stop abreast a small gathering of students, one of whom she recognized. "Hey, Derek," she called out. "You seen Coop lately?"

Derek shook his head. "Not for weeks."

She gave a slight nod toward the others.

"You guys know where Coop is?" Derek asked the other boys.

They all shook their heads. One said, "No, man. He's gone."

"Thanks." Laurel started to pull away, then paused. "If you see him or hear of where he might be, give me a call." She sighed in defeat as she drove away. Having come up empty again, she decided to go home.

She took a long, leisurely bath and lay down on the bed for a short rest. Apparently her body had not healed as completely as she'd thought, for she found herself easily tired and slow to recover from exertion. After a short nap, she planned to eat dinner, then get back out on the streets again. She'd never get wind of Cooper's activities by sitting around her apartment.

She closed her eyes, and Scott Delany filled her mind. A strange disquiet surfaced inside her. There was something in their last encounter she'd overlooked. She struggled to remember their conversation and what had prompted this feeling. Suddenly, the answer came to her. Scott *had* believed her when she told him what happened. She'd recognized it at the time, but not the significance of it.

If Scott believed her word, that of a stranger, over the word of his father, he must have had a good reason. And why had he not kept in touch with his family for the last four years? He had to know something incriminating about Brian, something in his past or in his personality, that would make her story credible.

Despite the stab of pain she felt every time she looked at Scott, she knew she had to see him again. She had to find out what he knew.

...

Chapter 3

Scott walked into the formal dining room where his parents sat eating the special dinner prepared by Maggie, the family cook of some thirty-odd years. The silver-haired couple turned in unison as he entered. Other than the color of his hair and a few wrinkles, Raymond Delany showed little physical sign of his age. The combination of a strong body and a determined face added to his air of authority.

Scott met the disapproving gaze in his father's eyes, tightening the knot already in his stomach. It wasn't so much that he'd again earned his father's contempt—it was the memories that look evoked of years past, when his father's approval had been so important to him.

He focused on his mother's gaunt face as he went straight to her chair, bent down and touched his lips to the soft, slack skin on her cheek. "Sorry I'm late, Mother. The time got away from me." He didn't elaborate that he'd walked for hours trying to digest the information Laurel had given him. She was a complication he hadn't anticipated. He couldn't help but wonder how she was going to affect his new and tenuous relationship with his father.

From the moment Scott first heard the news of Brian's death, a powerful conviction had compelled him to end the silent feud between him and his father. He knew the judge would never make the first move to end their long and bitter conflict. As he'd expected, his father had not made it easy for him. That he'd gotten this far surprised him. When he looked into the older man's eyes, Scott knew his father wished that *he* had died instead of Brian.

Scott stabbed at the salad on his plate. He realized he'd inherited his own stubborn streak of defiance. When he'd left for London, he'd been determined to prove to his father that he could make it on his own. He worked hard, made friends easily and never lacked female companionship when the need struck. It had taken most of his four-year exile to learn that money and success had little meaning for him without his family.

His years of struggling to turn a floundering telecommunications business in London into an international success had taught him the importance of knowing when to stand firm and when to repress his ego and pride for the good of the company. Yesterday he'd undertaken his most difficult task ever, when he'd asked his father to put the past aside in the interest of family unity. The truce they'd struck consisted mostly of concessions on Scott's part, but he'd known the sacrifice had been worthwhile the moment he'd seen the joy on his mother's face. Though he and his father hadn't resolved their differences, they were at least speaking to each other.

In the last few hours, he'd asked himself a hundred times why his father had left out so many important details about Brian's death. Scott understood it was more than wanting to protect his own honored reputation on the bench. From the time Scott and Brian had entered grade school, until the final argument that had severed Scott's ties with his family, his father had never allowed himself to believe Brian could do any wrong—unlike Scott, who never seemed to measure up.

How many times had Scott been tempted as a boy to expose Brian's antics to their father? Always, that special intangible bond that existed between them kept him silent. Scott knew Brian had used that bond—used *him*—but he had let him do it. Perhaps if he had told on Brian, let him suffer the consequences for his actions, Brian might still be alive today. Scott had thought long and hard about that theory this afternoon, though it brought him a great deal of pain and anguish.

"Brian came by every Thursday night for dinner, no matter how heavy a caseload he had," his father said. "He never disappointed your mother." His father spoke with a melancholy tone. As if to negate the emotion, he plopped a succulent chunk of Swiss steak into his mouth and chewed it as though it were jerky.

Scott clenched the napkin in his lap and bit back the comment on the tip of his tongue. A glance at his mother's sallow face reminded him he had to keep a tight hold on his temper. Forcing himself to remember the loneliness they'd all endured during his four-year exile, he reached for the Waterford goblet and took a long drink of the chilled water.

"Brian also never passed up a free meal," Sarah Delany said. "Especially one of Maggie's specialties. She made your favorite tonight, Scott. Try it."

Scott smiled at his mother and gave her a quick wink. She'd always been the peacemaker of the family. Tonight he appreciated her efforts to defuse the situation between him and his father more than he could convey.

"Now that you've proven yourself as a successful entrepreneur," she went on, "I was hoping you'd given some thought to the idea of moving back here again." She raised a baby carrot to her mouth and took a delicate bite. The strain of Brian's death and the subsequent rumors had added years to her face.

The wireless-communication business he shared with Hershal Saxton, a longtime friend and partner, had flourished since the deregulation of British Telecom. "I've considered the possibility." Yes, he'd thought about moving back to the States, but not for the reason his mother indicated. "If we purchase the telecommunications company in Los Angeles as planned, it could happen."

In truth, he'd thought more about a woman with light brown hair and honey-colored eyes. *Honey.* That was it. That was what her eyes reminded him of: pure sweet honey. A smile tugged at his mouth. When he looked up, both his parents were staring at him.

"It's not a decision I can make in a day—or a week, for that matter," he said, hiding his wandering thoughts. His mother's face lit with undisguised hope, while his father's response remained more difficult to read.

"Does that mean you'll be staying for at least a little while longer?" Relief animated her voice and brightened her eyes.

He smiled as he nodded, realizing he was as happy about the prospect of extending his stay as his mother seemed to be. He'd missed her terribly. That she'd been caught in the middle of his fight with his father and Brian had caused him a lot of guilt.

"Orange County has a lot to offer," his father stated matter-of-factly during a lull in the conversation.

He knew the comment was probably as close to an invitation to stay as he would get from his father, so he accepted it graciously. It was certainly a hell of a lot more than he'd gotten four years ago.

Scott's gaze fixed on a diamond-and-emerald brooch pinned to his mother's silk blouse. It was exquisite, but not in keeping with her normal understated elegance. "That's a beautiful brooch, Mother. Is it new?" Scott watched her face cloud at his compliment. She stroked the jeweled pin lovingly with the tips of her fingers.

"Brian gave it to her for Mother's Day," his father quickly interjected.

At first, Scott felt as though his father was chastising him for the time he'd been away, for the holidays that had passed without a word from him. After more careful consideration, he realized his father was explaining the stricken look on his mother's face and warning him not to pursue a subject that would add to her distress. Despite his father's gruff and distancing mannerisms, Scott knew the love his father had for his mother was genuine.

He said nothing further about the brooch, but wondered how Brian had managed to pay for it on his salary as a deputy D.A., given the expensive style in which he lived. Scott didn't like the conclusions taking shape inside his head.

They spent the rest of the meal catching Scott up on the news he'd missed over the last few years. Finally, his mother admitted she was tired and wanted to retire early.

Scott followed his father into his study. Dark mahogany walls, which had once given the somber room an eeriness, now seemed coldly elegant. He shut the door behind them.

His father looked back over his shoulder at the sound of the door closing and raised an eyebrow before stepping to the bar and pouring two glasses of brandy. He handed Scott his drink and settled into a soft leather chair. "Well, spit it out, Scott."

Why did his father always make him feel as if he were ten years old? Scott set the brandy down untouched. "I was wondering why you didn't tell me a cop was also shot the night Brian died."

"The cop didn't die in that filthy alley," his father replied.

Scott's chest constricted at the thought of how close Laurel had come to doing just that. And he wondered if Brian had fired that shot as she claimed. He wanted to believe that there was some sort of misunderstanding, that the police would find evidence of Brian's innocence and discover that Laurel had made an honest mistake. But he had that deep nagging feeling he used to get when they were kids and he knew Brian had gotten into trouble. "She says Brian had a gun and that he shot her first." He watched his father's gaze narrow on his own.

"You've talked to that woman?" Accusation laced his father's words. "Why, Scott? How could you?"

"I wanted to hear what she had to say," he answered.

"Did you really expect her to come out and say, 'Gee, I'm really sorry. I panicked and shot the first thing that moved.' For God's sake, Scott. Grow up." His father's voice rose slightly, but not so much that his mother would be able to hear it. "She screwed up. Did she call for backup? Did she even tell her partner where the real deal was supposed to be taking place? No, she had him carefully out of the way so no one would witness her incompetence."

"That's the most ridiculous thing I've ever heard," Scott yelled back, despite his silent vow not to provoke another argument.

"Is it? And just why do you think that? My God, Scott. She's using you to get to me so I'll have the charges dropped." His father's face wrinkled with disgust.

Anger swelled inside Scott. He'd been used before, and the idea that he could let it happen again sickened him. But the last time, Brian had done the using. And that time it had been too late to do anything about it but leave.

"There's not one speck of evidence to corroborate her story," his father continued. "I would think you'd be just the least bit concerned that someone is out there telling the world that your brother sold narcotics to children!"

"Of course I'm concerned." Conflicting emotions tore at Scott. He couldn't bear to think of Brian doing anything so horrible and destructive to children. As much as he wanted to prove to his father once and for all that Brian wasn't the perfect son the judge believed him to be, he was worried sick that there might be some truth to what Laurel had told him.

"It's not as though Brian can stand up for himself and deny those accusations, either. We're all he's got." His father's voice broke. "We've got to be united on this."

Scott wanted very much for the fighting between them to end, but he had to ask himself—at what cost? Laurel's incarceration? Her future? He looked levelly at his father and wondered how far the man would be willing to go to protect Brian. His thoughts tumbled out uncensored. "But what about the truth? What about justice?"

His father slammed his hand down on the arm of his chair. It was the closest Scott had ever seen his father come to physical violence.

"Don't you dare sit there and lecture me about truth and justice. I've dedicated my life to it." His father's voice trembled.

For the first time, Scott saw the glossy sheen of tears in his father's eyes, and he regretted his outburst. He, too, had aged from grief. "I'm sorry, Father. I know you have." He also knew it was true. Except for the blind spot he had where Brian was concerned.

* * *

Laurel awoke to the ringing of the phone by her bed. She discovered the bright light coming through the crack in the drapes and instantly sensed something was wrong. Looking at the bedside clock as she reached for the phone, she mumbled an unladylike curse.

"Hello." She propped herself up on one elbow, now fully alert to the new day.

"Sergeant Tanner," the captain's voice boomed, "I want you in my office by nine sharp."

"What happened? Did you find something?" Laurel could barely contain her enthusiasm.

"No, Laurel. I'm sorry. I'll explain everything when you get here. Don't be late." He hung up before she could ask any more questions.

Laurel had one of those sinking feelings she usually got when she was on a call and things were about to go sour.

She showered and dressed in a simple navy suit with a white, collarless blouse, then added a gold chain and earrings as she slipped into her navy pumps. She wanted to look professional and confident when she went to the station. Something told her she was going to need all the help she could get.

Later, as she started up the steps to the front entrance of the station, she understood the reasons for her concern. Exiting the building about twenty feet in front of her was Judge Raymond Delany.

Her heart hammered in her chest as their eyes met and locked. Strength, as well as stubbornness, hardened his gaze. She had no idea how long the contest of wills would have continued if it had been left uninterrupted. But, fortunately, fate intervened.

Laurel sensed Scott's presence before he appeared in her line of vision. He moved between her and the judge, his broad shoulders effectively ending the silent challenge. As she took in a deep breath, her gaze traveled from the already familiar cut of Scott's dark hair to his purposeful stance beside his father. She couldn't hear their conversation, but when Scott turned to face her, she knew it didn't matter. The regret in Scott's eyes alone sent a chill spiraling through her.

She glanced at the glass doors ahead and wanted to run straight for them. Despite the sense of dread consuming her, she summoned all her courage and walked over to where Scott stood.

Lifting her face to meet the judge's eyes once again, she spoke with conviction straight from her heart. "I'm terribly sorry for your loss. Your family has my sincere sympathy, Judge Delany."

"Your sympathy is not what I want, Sergeant." The depth of contempt in the judge's eyes struck a touch of fear in Laurel.

Respectful of his bereavement, she lowered her gaze and turned away. Scott muttered something as she departed, but his words were lost in the clatter of her heels on the steps.

Inside, Laurel took in a long breath of the cooled air to calm her down. She passed the desk and went straight to the squad room, counting on the familiar setting and supportive faces to help her out. The smell of strong coffee wafted under her nose. As she passed by Alice Johnson, her friend gave her a hug and whispered into her ear, "Keep your chin up. We're all with you."

Two other officers, Pete Dickson and Sam Ladd, greeted her warmly, but several others looked away or pretended not to see her. She hid her disappointment behind a cautious smile as she rapped lightly on the captain's door.

Her paranoia blossomed into reality as soon as Captain Larson began to speak. He didn't mince words. "The grand jury hearing will be next Tuesday."

Usually the proceedings were carried out in secret, with the grand jury hearing testimony only from witnesses and victims, and being presented with all the physical evidence the police had gathered. In this case, though Laurel was the accused, she was also both witness and victim, therefore her testimony was required.

"It's not looking good, Sergeant. Your testimony is all we've got. We haven't come up with a shred of physical evidence to corroborate anything you've said. To make matters worse, your own partner's statement and our forensic report will be used to refute your story. You knew from the start what we were up against."

Yes. She knew. The judge's influence and Brian Delany's being a respected member of the district attorney's office were a potent combination. The accusations she'd made didn't sit well with anyone, especially since they were uncorroborated. If the D.A. did nothing, it would be as if they were admitting Brian's guilt. Some might say they were sacrificing a dead man to protect a guilty cop.

The captain ran his fingers over his mustache, and regret deepened the lines in his forehead. "I know you, Laurel. I don't believe for one moment that you fired your weapon in a panic as the press and a few others say. But you haven't given us anything to go on—no evidence, no motive, no means."

Her whole body tensed. "The bottom line, Captain?"

"The district attorney isn't very happy with the shadow you've cast on his office. He's pushing for involuntary manslaughter and misconduct."

Laurel felt as though all the air had been sucked out of the room. When she finally found enough breath to speak, she discovered she had nothing to say that hadn't been said already.

One of her reasons for loving the force so much was the camaraderie she'd shared with her fellow officers. Cops stood up for one another. How many times had she seen that network of support in action, been a part of it? She hadn't felt so betrayed since the day her father and stepmother had brought her half brother home from the hospital and she'd heard her father say, "Now we're a real family."

Laurel looked at the captain, all the emotion drained from her voice. "I saw the judge leaving the building on my way in."

"Damn it, Laurel," he said. "No one likes what's happening here, least of all me, but the D.A.'s got a damn good case. Let's go over it one more time, and don't leave anything out."

And so she told the captain one more time. Every detail, except the part about her date with Brian Delany.

When Laurel got home, the phone was ringing. She let it continue to ring as she pulled off her heels and went to the refrigerator for a can of diet Coke. "For Pete's sake! Go away!" she yelled at the device as the monotonous ringing continued. She didn't feel like talking to anyone.

What if it's Cooper trying to contact me, or someone with a lead on him? she thought. "Damn." She picked up the receiver. "Sergeant Tanner."

The moment she heard the sigh of relief on the other end of the line she was tempted to slam down the phone.

"Thank God you're home. I've been concerned about you." Scott's voice sounded edgy.

Laurel gave a cynical laugh. "Well, I guess I should be grateful you weren't all-out worried about me. I probably wouldn't be able to reach the knife in my back."

"Please, Laurel, I can explain."

"Funny, that's exactly what Brian said before he raised the gun and shot me." The silence stretched on, and Laurel cursed herself for letting her anger get the best of her. Usually she had more self-control, but her conversation with the captain had used up all her reserves.

Finally she sighed with frustration. "Sorry, that was totally out of line." She didn't have to explain what a bad day she'd had. Scott obviously had firsthand knowledge of the new charges threatening her.

"I'm sorry, too. I know this is asking a lot right now, but I've got to see you," he said.

Laurel remembered the pain and confusion she'd seen in his face when she'd told him the truth about what had happened in the alley. Her resolve weakened at the huskiness in his voice. "Why?"

"I think we both know why." His words were quiet, intimate. "Will you have lunch with me?"

She started to say no. She *wanted* to say no. She was still angry about this morning. So why did she feel this desperate need to see him? Dragging her fingers through her hair, she told herself Scott was her only link to Brian. She still had the gut feeling that he knew something he hadn't told her, something that might support her case.

"Okay," she finally conceded. Insisting they meet at a park in Corona del Mar in one hour, she gave him directions and told him to bring sandwiches and a pair of running shoes.

Laurel hung up the phone and sat at the table with her head resting on her arms. Her pulse was racing, but after what happened at the station, she didn't want to admit to the effect he still had on her.

Forty-five minutes later, she sat on a wooden bench atop a grassy knoll overlooking the ocean. Dressed in pink-and-gray running shorts with a pink top, she watched children playing in the tide pools down below and wondered about the sanity of her decision to see Scott.

She glanced over her shoulder at the row of houses lining the east side of the street opposite the small park. The houses were small, but well maintained and very expensive. Before her injury, she'd come here often to run or sit and watch the waves crashing onto the rocky points. She'd dreamed of someday owning a house on the beach, and of sharing it with a husband and children. But that dream seemed to be moving farther out of reach with each day the investigation dragged on.

In the distance, she saw a tall, dark-haired man wearing tan walking shorts and a light blue shirt. Though she'd always seen Brian wearing expensive Italian suits, the resemblance made her breath catch. Scott carried a large, white paper bag.

He turned from side to side, scanning the park with a guarded expression on his face. His step faltered for an instant when he looked her way, then his whole body seemed to relax as his lips parted in a smile that showed the contrast of his perfect white teeth against his tanned skin.

Her pulse rate escalated noticeably. As he approached, his gaze slid down to her feet. For a moment, all the problems between them receded. The appreciation she read in his expression made her skin tingle with an excitement she hadn't felt in a long time. She quickly stifled it.

"Hello, Laurel." He smiled and glanced around them. A number of people strolled along the walk or sat on the grass, but none were close enough to intrude on their conversation. "This was a great idea."

She wasn't so sure about that. Trying to keep her voice steady, she said, "It's one of my favorite spots to run or to just sit and think."

While staring at the ground to regain her composure, she noticed Scott's shoes; they looked brand-new. She smiled and invited him to sit down.

"Thank you for agreeing to see me." Scott set the bag between them.

Laurel sensed him staring at her, but shrugged off the implications. She felt uneasy about being there with him, partly because of the escalated pace of her heart when he approached her and partly because she actually wanted to be there with him. The intensity of that feeling and the strong physical reaction she had to him frightened her. It was at odds with the painful lesson she'd learned a few years ago. Relationships with men outside of law enforcement were complicated at best, and disastrous as a rule. Under the circumstances, it would be unwise for her to allow even a friendship to develop between them. He was a Delany, and she'd yet to discover the reason he'd wanted to see her. So, why did she still find it so hard to breathe whenever he smiled?

Scott unwrapped a thick turkey sandwich loaded with lettuce, tomato, Swiss cheese, avocado and sprouts. "Hope you like this. I wasn't sure what to get." He pulled out another sandwich, two large pickles and two diet colas.

Her appetite had dwindled since she'd returned from the hospital. The salty air and the aroma of fresh mayonnaise and Swiss cheese brought it back with a vengeance. She took a large bite of the sandwich as Scott watched her reaction. "Wonderful," she said, reaching for her napkin to wipe a drop of mayonnaise from her chin.

They ate without much conversation. When they were finished, Scott got up and took their trash to a can by the walk. A young woman wearing a skimpy white bikini passed in front of him on his way back. If he took any notice of her, it didn't show. His attention seemed to be focused solely on

Laurel, and though it thrilled her as a woman, the cop in her remained suspicious.

"Okay, ready?" he asked.

"Ready for what?" She looked at his outstretched hand.

He lifted one canvas-clad foot and said, "I assumed we were going to walk on the beach."

When she got to her feet, she pulled her hand from his and he didn't try to reclaim it. They walked across the park to a narrow path that led down the side of the steep cliff to a strip of sandy beach. The coastline was comprised of a series of small sandy coves punctuated at each end by rocky outcroppings that begged children of all ages to climb and explore. Laurel preferred this area to the more crowded swimming beaches farther north.

They investigated the colorful sea life in the tide pools, then climbed over the first group of rocks to a less-frequented beach. Scott held out his hand. She hesitated before slipping her fingers in between his.

As they walked, he said, "I'm sorry about what happened this morning."

She heard the tension in his voice and stopped to face him. "I know you're not to blame."

"Maybe I am," he admitted.

She started to pull away.

"Indirectly." He tightened his grasp on her hand. "I went to their house for dinner last night and I confronted my father about what really happened in the alley. He was pretty upset with me."

Laurel felt a lump in her throat. She had to be misunderstanding what he was saying—for the idea of Scott speaking out on her behalf to the judge was too much to hope for. He had to have another reason.

"When I found out what he was going to do, I tried to talk him out of it." Scott shook his head, a deeper anguish darkening his expression. "He's a stubborn man when it comes to anything concerning Brian."

Judge Delany was a stubborn man concerning everything. His "favorite son" would naturally top the list. Laurel thought about the often-quoted title Brian had acquired over the years and wondered if Scott realized it existed. If so, the implication must have been painful for him to bear. And it would explain the tormented look in his eyes.

Turning toward the ocean, she let the breeze push her hair away from her face. She looked out over the wide expanse of water and at the gulls soaring freely above. Laurel knew the moment had come to ask for his help, but suddenly the prospect made her very uncomfortable. She wished there was another way, but she had so much at stake—her career and now, possibly, her freedom. Thinking back to the morning she had met Scott in the alley, she recalled what he'd said about wanting to hear the truth. Now more than ever, she wanted to believe him.

"Scott." She swallowed. "I understand your reluctance to say anything bad about your brother." His fingers tightened on hers for an instant before he released her hand. "But I've had this feeling that you know something either about Brian or about what happened that night that could help us unravel some of the mysteries about him or what he was doing in that alley."

Laurel thought about the grand jury hearing, which was less than a week away, and how important her testimony would be. Her heart pounded harder as his silence stretched on. At least he hadn't walked away. "If I wasn't absolutely certain about what happened, and if my career and possibly my freedom weren't at risk here, I wouldn't ask for your help. But they are. So I guess I'm appealing to your sense of honesty and justice. You said yesterday you wanted the truth. Is that still what you want?"

Scott looked at her with a profound sadness in his eyes. He turned his back on her and ran his fingers through his hair. His withdrawal caused a flicker of pain in her chest.

"It's not that simple." Frustration sharpened his words. He gazed sullenly across the sand, then back to her. "I don't know anything about Brian's dealings or whatever he was into. I sure as hell am having a hard time believing he'd sell drugs to high school kids."

"But you're not surprised that he was involved in something illegal," she persisted, watching his expression closely.

A flicker of doubt passed over his face. "I don't know," he said in a voice filled with regret. "We hadn't seen each other in so long. Everything I hear about him seems to indicate he'd changed, that he was what my father claimed him to be—a fine upstanding citizen, a pillar of the community. Yet, I just don't know."

Laurel could see his turmoil reflected in his eyes. Her own turmoil was more visceral. "Scott, I'm going to find the truth one way or another. I don't have a choice anymore." She didn't have to add that that was because of his father's influence. They both knew Judge Delany had pressured the D.A. to take action.

Scott stepped forward and placed his hands on her shoulders. "What do you want from me?"

Laurel swallowed, but never let her gaze stray from his. Her mind reeled with the possibilities his question evoked. Her face grew warm at the thought of what they could share if things were different. She had to force her thoughts back to the business at hand. If she were incarcerated, she wouldn't be sharing anything with anyone for a long time. The prospect sent a chill down her back.

"I want to look at Brian's things." She paused only a few seconds. "I know the detectives have gone through his house and his office, but they may have missed something. They *had* to have missed something. Brian wasn't stupid. Whatever he was up to, he would have hidden it well." She placed her palms flat against his chest. "Can you get me inside? Will you help me find the truth?"

He stared at her for a long time before giving her an answer. "The first part is no problem. Brian named me his sole beneficiary. The house and all its contents belong to me now." A slight tremor shook his voice, revealing his sentiments at the sad irony of the bequest. "It's finding the truth that worries me. If you're right, this is going to devastate my parents. I don't know how much more they can take. Brian was always so special to them."

Laurel's chest constricted. She understood what his childhood must have been like. Though the circumstances differed, they shared the same emotions of rejection, of feeling left out or second-best. And yet, if Scott felt bitter about it, it didn't show in his voice. He was a remarkable man. If circumstances were different...

Looking into his eyes, she whispered, "I'm sorry."

Scott's gaze probed hers. "If you're wrong, we could find proof that clears Brian's name once and for all."

"I know," she said in a voice that sounded strangely weak.

"Okay, I'll help you look for the truth," he reluctantly agreed. "But I don't think we'll find anything."

Laurel heard more in his voice. She tried to read the expression on his face. She didn't understand the reason for the depth of her attraction to Scott, she only knew the truth in what she felt. Right or wrong, when he came near, her heart raced with excitement; when he touched her, her skin tingled. There was no sense denying it.

Scott had shown that he was attracted to her, as well, but she didn't think that was reason enough for him to put his father's wishes or his family's best interests aside. He'd said he'd help her. She should be satisfied with that, but it wasn't enough.

"Why, Scott? Why are you helping me if the truth could destroy your family?"

"Now that you've raised the questions, I need to find the answers for my own peace of mind. I wouldn't want anyone else to go to prison for something Brian did." His gaze wandered over her face before it rested on her eyes. "Part of me wants to prove that you're wrong, Laurel," he admitted with a husky voice as dark emotions crossed his face.

"And the other part?" she forced herself to ask.

His eyes darkened with a primal hunger that said more than words could convey. Anticipation rippled over her skin. Slowly, he lowered his mouth to hers. At the first touch of his lips, Laurel's confusion faded. His fingers curled through the hair at her nape, holding her close. Even without his gentle coaxing, her body pressed against his, satisfying the craving awakening inside her.

She wrapped her arms around him, moving her hands up and down the length of his spine. He was strong and solid beneath her touch, and that strength was too inviting to resist.

Scott explored her mouth with his inquisitive tongue. She lost herself in the delicious sensation, wanting it to go on forever. The crashing of the waves and cries of the gulls faded from her mind. Heat swirled inside her. She wanted more. She needed to touch him, and to feel his hands on her bare skin. When she thought their bodies were about to meld, he pulled her gloriously closer.

From somewhere nearby, a young male voice whooped, "All right!"

At the same time, the sound of a teenage girl's giggle penetrated the languid haze in Laurel's mind. Her head began to clear. Scott breathed raggedly against her cheek, still holding her close. She heard the pounding of her heart above the sound of the surf. After that kiss, she wasn't surprised. How could she ever deny her attraction now?

She pulled back slightly, puzzling over what had just happened, unsure what to say or do next. The relationship was developing so quickly between them, it left her unsettled. She risked looking into his eyes, and her mouth went suddenly dry. "This is going to be complicated."

He traced her bottom lip with his thumb. "It already is." After a moment, he looked away and said, "We'd better go."

Scott walked her to her car. "I'll take you to the house tomorrow. We'll go through everything together."

She nodded, but her mind was still on the kiss.

Chapter 4

Scott approached Laurel's apartment with equal measures of exhilaration and dread. The memory of the kiss they'd shared on the beach yesterday and the way she'd melted into him sent a fiery jolt through his body. He couldn't remember ever having such a strong reaction to a woman before, and that scared him. He rang the doorbell at the designated hour.

Laurel greeted him with a smile on her face and her purse in her hand. "I'm ready to go."

He spotted her feigned cheerfulness immediately, though he pretended not to notice.

She locked the door, dropped her keys in her bag and started for the car without saying another word. Nervous energy sizzled beneath her calm exterior as she walked ahead of him with purposeful steps.

Scott thought again of the way she'd responded to his kiss yesterday, the way she made him feel when she looked into his eyes. As she struggled to maintain the distance between them, he wondered if she regretted that moment of freedom or if she was simply uneasy about entering the house where Brian had lived. Judging by his own jumbled emotions, he guessed it was a combination of both. He'd certainly had second thoughts about staying in Brian's house when he'd first arrived from London less than a week ago.

As he drove the short distance to Newport Beach in the Saturday morning traffic, he glanced across the seat at the puzzling woman beside him. "If there's anything there, we'll find it."

She quirked her lips at him then. It wasn't quite a smile, but it was a start.

"I want you to know how much I appreciate this," she said hesitantly. "I know it must be very difficult for you."

Difficult didn't begin to describe his ambivalent feelings. He smiled. "No problem. I need to go through his things, anyway, before I decide what to do with everything. I still don't know why he left it all to me." Scott worried about that. Brian had never done anything without a reason. If he had intended to make Scott feel guilty, he'd succeeded. But could he also have been trying to ensure Scott's silence? Brian could have assumed Scott would protect him as he'd done in the past. But Scott had made it clear four years ago that he wasn't going to take the rap for Brian anymore, not so Brian could save face with their father—not even to save Brian's career.

Scott forced aside the unpleasant speculation as he pulled up in front of the narrow lot and parked the car. Real estate on the bay was so expensive, no one wasted space on amenities like driveways or yards. Brian had chosen an elegant two-story home with a private dock off the back deck.

Scott took a key from his pocket and opened the door. An alarm buzzed for a moment until he stepped around the corner to the panel and punched in a series of numbers he'd already committed to memory.

He reached for Laurel's hand. "Come on. I'll show you around." The marbled entry had a wide curving stairway, which led to a balcony and the bedrooms. He decided to start with the first floor. As they moved from room to room, he watched Laurel carefully. Her eyes seemed to take in each detail, classifying and cataloging the information in much the same way as she'd done with him that first night in the cemetery.

They moved quickly through the living room, dining room, kitchen and the laundry. When they got to Brian's study, Scott opened the double doors and let Laurel take her time assessing the place. It was the most obvious spot for Brian to keep records of any business dealings he had, legal or not. "The detective had someone in to download all his computer files," Scott said, "but I don't think they found anything. Brian always used to say, 'Never put anything in your computer you wouldn't want to see on the evening news.' He was pretty good with software, but he knew there was always someone better. No system is foolproof." He walked across the room and stood before a large seascape. "There's a wall safe behind that picture, but it contained only a few legal documents."

Laurel moved through the room, looking at Brian's things from continually changing perspectives. "Who's been taking care of the place?"

Scott glanced around the room. He hadn't particularly noticed the lack of dust on the large desk or file cabinet. "He had a cleaning woman come in once a week. She contacted my father and he told her to continue after the police finished with the place."

Laurel walked behind the desk and sat down. She put her hand on a drawer, then paused, lifting her eyebrows and looking directly at him.

"Go ahead, that's why we're here." He watched her go through each desk drawer. Her movements were quick but cautious. She was being careful not to overlook any detail. So was he. Only, the subject of his attention was a thoroughly enchanting woman.

He studied the shape and tilt of her nose, the curves and hollows of her cheeks. Finally, he walked over to a spot behind her, so that he could look over her shoulder in case they ran across anything he might find significant. With each breath, a fragrance as light as sunshine reached his nostrils. He watched her long slender fingers shuffle through papers and receipts. Her unpolished nails had a nice shape. For a moment, he allowed himself to imagine the feel of her nails trailing along his bare shoulders, down his back, clutching the tender skin of his buttocks to bring him closer....

Scott stood up straight and walked around the desk. He didn't even pretend he had no idea what had gotten into him. He knew exactly. Only it wasn't *what*—it was *who*. Laurel Tanner had somehow lodged herself under his skin so thoroughly he couldn't move or breathe or think without including her in his thoughts. He wanted her desperately. It was crazy, impulsive, and he wasn't given to impulse. He reminded himself this was the woman who killed his brother. But that insight didn't cure his attraction for her; it only made him feel guilty.

Facing away from her, he rested his elbow on the large wooden file cabinet and stared at a framed snapshot he'd previously overlooked. Dressed alike, he and Brian had been wrestling on the floor at age twelve when their mother captured the essence of their internal bond on film. They had joked about the picture's interpretation. Mother, in her imaginative pursuit of meaning, had thought it looked like one boy struggling to break free of his perceived self-image. He and Brian had known what it was really about. Scott shivered as the dark memory returned.

Laurel's hand on his shoulder startled him. The corners of her mouth turned down in a frown of concern. "Are you all right?" she asked.

He turned toward her and his heart slammed into his ribs. Automatically, he slipped his arms around her and the rightness of that feeling took his breath. He stared into her eyes. "I will be."

Unable to stop himself, Scott leaned down to brush his mouth against hers. At first, she passively accepted his lips, seeming a little unsure, then he felt her relax. The pliable warmth of her mouth entranced him. Instead of ending the kiss quickly, as he'd intended, he found himself seeking firmer contact. She tipped her head slightly to the side and returned the pressure.

Finally Scott forced himself to end the kiss. He held her close and felt the warmth of her breath against his face. "That was nice." He stroked her hair. "As much as I'd like to continue—"

She pulled back, her face flushed. "We'd better finish what we started."

He had to grin at her double entendre.

"I mean the investigation." She opened one of the file drawers and began searching it as though she had not been thoroughly kissed just seconds before. He watched the rapid rise and fall of her chest, but let her charade continue. There would be time later to continue their explorations of each other. He was sure of it.

She closed the first drawer and opened the next. The remaining drawers were empty. "Those would have been

Brian's files on his cases," he said. "I'm sure the district attorney took them."

"Did Brian have a passport?" Laurel asked.

Scott stopped and thought for a moment. The other officers hadn't asked him that. "I'm sure he did."

"Could I see it, please?" There was a distance in her eyes, and her voice seemed detached.

"It hasn't turned up yet."

"Safety-deposit box?"

"Not in there, either." What was she getting at?

She left the study and climbed the stairs. She looked in every bedroom and every closet. The closet in the spare bedroom was empty except for three suits hanging on the left side, two pairs of jeans and an almost-new pair of running shoes on the carpet beneath them. He watched Laurel rifle through the suits before her gaze dropped to the running shoes and color stained her cheeks. "Those are mine," he confirmed.

"Sorry," she muttered softly as she slipped past him, before returning to her cop mode.

The master bedroom had two walk-in closets. Expensive suits and shoes filled the first one. The other one seemed to be used for storage. No light came on in the storage closet when she flipped the switch.

"Must have burned out," Scott said. "I'll go downstairs and look for a new bulb."

"Wait." Laurel looked around the room. She went over to a chair and lifted it, then hesitated as if considering something and set it back down. "Can you reach the bulb?"

Scott tried. To his surprise, the bulb was not burned-out but merely loose in the socket. "How did you know that? And what difference does it make?"

"Maybe none." She paused at Brian's suitcases and looked inside each one. When she turned up nothing, she let out a small sigh. "Oh, well, it was just a thought."

"What were you looking for?"

"I don't really know. It just seemed as if he had gone to a little trouble to make it inconvenient to see inside this closet. Probably just wishful thinking on my part. Let's go back to the study." She turned and headed for the door.

Scott didn't follow. His mind traveled back a number of years to a conversation he'd had with Brian when they were in high school. Brian had asked out two girls for the same night, then talked Scott into filling in for him, unbeknownst to either girl. What was it Brian had told him? Something about always having a backup. He thought about the wall safe down in the study, and something clicked in his mind. He went to Brian's closet again and started moving his clothes aside.

"What are you doing?" Laurel asked from behind him.

"Either losing my mind or looking for another safe. Take your pick."

"Let me." She pushed him gently aside. "Go get a flashlight."

When he returned, Laurel had moved the empty suitcases from the other closet out into the middle of the floor. She moved shelves, tapped the walls and thumped at the ceiling. She got down on her elbows and knees to examine the floor. The fabric of her slacks molded to the shape of her bottom, a very nice shape, Scott thought distractedly. It took a chunk of willpower to redirect his thoughts.

"Hand me the flashlight again." She reached behind her with an open hand.

Scott placed the flashlight in her palm as if he was passing a surgical instrument, grateful she had not turned her head to catch him staring. Slowly, he lowered himself to the floor beside Laurel. He watched as she carefully lifted one corner of the carpet. She peeled it back to reveal a one-foot-square area cut out of the flooring and replaced by a loose piece of particle board. Under the board, they found the safe.

Astonished, Scott glanced over at Laurel. She turned her face toward him at that same moment. In her expression, he saw a mixture of hope and wariness. Experience had probably taught her to be cautious. He wondered about her past and if she'd had anyone with whom she'd been able to share those experiences.

Laurel released the flap of carpet and sat back on her heels, looking puzzled. He could see her tension in the way she held her head.

Scott's momentary elation faded as he began to anticipate what they might find inside the safe. What if they found proof of Brian's guilt? They could find evidence of something even worse than Laurel's story indicated. He looked over at her delicate profile and felt a raw pang of anxiety in his stomach. He thought about the other possibility and wondered how she would react if they found proof of his brother's innocence. He still believed Brian could have been doing some kind of undercover investigating on his own. The muscles in his shoulders began to bunch.

"You have any ideas about the combination?" she said.

He shook his head.

"People usually pick numbers that have some sort of meaning for them—a birthday, an anniversary of something special in their lives." Tiny wrinkles formed between her brows. "Can you think of any particularly special occasion for Brian?"

He shook his head again. "We could try our birthday, but what if the safe is wired into the alarm system like the other one?"

"I don't think so. It's my guess that he didn't want anyone to know about this one." She pulled the flap of carpet back again and eyed the tumbler. "Let's start with your birthday. Forward, backward, any combination that might make sense."

They continued working for nearly an hour. Scott's leg began to cramp. He flexed his foot and rubbed his thigh.

"Come on, let's take a break." Laurel got up and walked away from the closet. She stood next to the king-size bed, staring off into a distance unrestrained by the bedroom walls.

The cramping in his leg subsided. He stepped closer and placed his hands on her shoulders. "If I'd known that was what you meant—" he nodded to the bed "—I'd have suggested a break long ago."

She swung around quickly. The indignant expression fled quickly when she saw he was teasing her. "You're out of your mind, Delany." She laughed along with him, but she did step a considerable distance away from the bed to pace.

"There has to be something we're overlooking, some event or some person that had a special meaning for Brian," she said. "Please try to think back to the time when Brian bought the house. What was going on in his life then? Who was important to him?"

That was easy, Scott thought to himself. Brian was important to Brian. His very lack of consideration for Scott or anyone else had started their last argument. But looking into Laurel's eyes, honey-brown eyes that silently pleaded for his help, Scott forced his thoughts back in time.

He remembered the first time he'd been in the house. Brian had showed him everything, including the wall safe in the study. They had joked about Brian forgetting the combination like he did with his gym locker. Scott suggested he find a series of numbers he would never be able to forget.

Brian had said, "Then I'd better make the combination Susan Petroski's measurements." He and Brian had laughed heartily at Brian's reply. Susan was a beautiful young girl from high school with whom they had both fallen madly in love. *Madly,* he recalled, being the operative word.

Scott turned from Laurel and went back to the closet. Warmth tingled in his throat and face.

"What is it?" she asked.

"I'm not sure yet." He turned the tumbler clockwise to thirty-eight. "It's a crazy idea." Counterclockwise one revolution, continuing to twenty-two. "A joke, really." Clockwise to thirty-four. Something clicked. Scott looked up at Laurel, his throat suddenly dry.

Her chest rose sharply before she raised her gaze from the safe and nodded for him to continue. He lifted the steel door and placed it on the folded flap of carpet. Inside was a manila folder and Brian's passport.

Scott stared down at the folder as if it were a magical item that might disappear if he let his gaze slip. After a moment of silence, he felt Laurel's fingers on his forearm.

"Are you going to be okay?" she asked.

He nodded. The knot in his stomach tightened. "This is what we came for." He tried to give her an encouraging look, then picked up the folder. He opened it and thumbed through a few documents.

"What is it?" she said.

"Mostly business documents for some holding company." He had no idea what he'd expected to find—bags of cocaine or heroin, perhaps the fabled little black book with all the telling information neatly printed in alphabetical order. Scott wiped a hand down his face. "Let's take this to the table downstairs. I have a feeling we're going to be here awhile."

They headed for the kitchen, where Scott put on a pot of coffee. Laurel brought two chairs close together and opened the folder between them. "We'll have to read through these one at a time and see if we can figure out what they're all about." She paused, looking at the first document, then said, "Do you know an attorney in New York named Stanley Murdock?"

Scott's whole body tensed. At the mention of the name, a feeling of doom washed over him. "Murdock went to school with Brian and me. Later, he and Brian went to law school together."

Though he had tried to sound neutral, Laurel had picked up on his uneasiness and challenged him with an uncompromising stare. "Why don't you care for him?" she asked calmly.

Scott cleared his throat. "I'm not exactly sure. I just remember feeling very relieved when he decided to join his uncle's firm on the other side of the continent." He shrugged and sat down beside Laurel. He'd never trusted Murdock. "I hadn't realized they'd kept in touch."

They read and discussed the documents for over an hour. Laurel freely admitted her lack of knowledge when it came to the interpretation of business data. She questioned Scott extensively on the purpose and implications of a particular document each time she encountered something new.

Some recessive gene must have suddenly kicked in, because he felt an overwhelming surge of masculine pride each time she turned to him with admiration in her eyes and asked for his help. What really surprised and disturbed him was the fact that helping Laurel was first and foremost in his mind. He suffered a pang of guilt as a voice in his head told him he should be concerned with proving Brian innocent, not Laurel.

As he continued to study the documents, he realized the voice belonged to his father. Several documents referred to a New York-based holding company. Because Murdock was involved, Scott's concern multiplied. But he didn't want to say anything until he had something conclusive. He was still trying to make all the connections when he looked over at Laurel. She stared blankly at a piece of paper she held in her hand. "What is it?" he said.

Scott caught his breath when she turned to look at him, her eyes wide with shock. Though his heart melted with tenderness at the look of vulnerability on her face, the rest of him remained tense.

"A deed." She swallowed. "It's for the building next to the alley where... he died."

While she paused, Scott began to speculate.

"The holding company owned the building," Laurel said, confirming his speculation. "If Brian was an owner in the holding company..."

"You think that would give him a legitimate reason for being there," he guessed.

"Yes. At least as far as a jury is concerned."

"What about the time of night?"

She shrugged. "The district attorney would be more than pleased to tell the public how his dutiful deputies have to work long hours because of their heavy caseloads. Unfortunately, that's true."

"If he was an owner, then why haven't I heard of the holding company before? I don't recall seeing anything about it anywhere else. I admit I haven't looked carefully at his tax returns, but you'd think he would have kept this with his other records."

"You'd think," Laurel agreed.

They went through the rest of the file. Though they found no proof of anything illegal, Scott's hope for proof of

Brian's innocence dwindled. Despair clouded his thoughts. How could the brother who was so much like himself in so many ways have turned into someone so different? Scott pushed the file away, placed his elbows on the table and rested his head in his hands while he thought about what to do with the information they'd found. His first thought was to take the information to his father. The judge would see Murdock's name and read between the lines as he had. But it wasn't hard proof of Brian's wrongdoing. The deed would give him an excuse for being at the location and perhaps solidify the case against Laurel. The other documents would have seemed harmless enough had he not known Murdock was behind them.

He thought about Laurel and remembered what it was like to be on the receiving end of his father's wrath, whether deserving or not. She'd seen the concern on his face as he heard Murdock's name, yet she hadn't reacted with elation at the possibility of a breakthrough for her defense.

He felt Laurel's hand on his arm. He stared into her pensive brown eyes. God, he was confused ... and angry. Angry at his father. Angry at Brian.

She spoke softly. "As much as I want to get my job back and prove I didn't screw up, I don't want to hurt you or your family. I hope you believe that, Scott."

If Brian had appeared in front of him right then, he didn't know if he'd hug him or deck him. He felt torn in so many directions. He did know that he very much wanted to seek solace from his troubles in Laurel's arms. He wanted her to hold him and kiss him, to make him forget the turmoil behind him and ahead of him. He wanted to feel her mouth on his skin, hear her sigh against his ear. He wanted to let go of everything inside and make quick, passionate love to her, right here, right now.

But here was Brian's home and now was not their time. He stood and turned away from her before his resolve weakened. "I'd better take you home."

They made the short drive back to Crystal Cove in silence. He needed time and distance to clarify his thoughts.

When he pulled up in front of her apartment, she turned toward him. "What are you going to do with the file?" she said.

"I don't know yet."

"It's evidence. You'll have to turn it in." She lifted her gaze to his.

A heaviness settled in his chest. In effect, she had handed him a way out. If he chose to go directly to the D.A. and give him the documents, it would not be in her best interest, but she would understand. That kind of selfless gesture was so foreign to him, he felt all the more moved by it.

She reached for the door handle.

He grabbed her arm. When she paused, he wasn't sure why he'd done so. His heart was pounding, and when he spoke, his voice was husky. "I'll let you know before I hand it over. In the meantime, I'll hang on to it awhile." He wanted to do some investigating on his own before he brought in the police. Stanley Murdock was as smart as he was sly. Scott didn't want just any detective nosing around asking questions. And he didn't want Murdock to know he'd found out about the holding company.

He released his grip on Laurel's arm, slowly letting his fingers trail over her skin, skin as soft as her whispered thanks. If she had any idea of the potential trouble they'd uncovered today, she wouldn't be thanking him.

Chapter 5

Laurel spent the remainder of the day at home alone. She gave the apartment a thorough cleaning and got caught up on her laundry. While she worked at the mindless chores, she thought about Scott and the papers they'd discovered. In her own mind, she was certain the holding company would link Brian to some kind of criminal activity. But she wondered if the evidence had convinced Scott as completely as it had her. At least he was considering the implications. Otherwise he would have turned over the information to the D.A. immediately. It gave her pause to realize her first and foremost thought had been of convincing Scott instead of the D.A. She found the shift in her priorities unsettling.

Scott's decision to hold on to the documents for a while caused a ripple of excitement inside her she wished she could deny. He was battling with more than his disappointment in his brother today. She knew he'd felt something for her he didn't want to feel, because she'd seen in his face the same intense longing she'd felt herself. Every time she'd glanced up and discovered his gaze intent on her face, heat swirled within her. It had taken every bit of her strength not to accept his unspoken invitation to wrap her arms around him and hold him close and give herself up to the burning need he created. If she'd taken that next step, they both would have regretted it later.

Laurel sighed and tried her best to force all personal thoughts of Scott Delany aside for a while. It was difficult, but the desperate nature of her situation enabled her to do so. She had to figure out how to get a look at Brian's tax returns without spilling everything she'd learned to the investigating officers. She really didn't want to cause the Delanys more pain or embarrassment and she didn't want to ask for Scott's help if she had any other choice.

Her partner, Gary Boyd, might be able to get the documents she needed pulled from the evidence room. He was her only hope, but she hesitated, not wanting to get him into trouble. He'd already done so much for her. He'd practically lived at the hospital during her stay. Then he'd taken her home and checked on her twice a day for two weeks. He'd done her shopping and her laundry before she saw through him to the real problem.

Gary shouldered a large amount of guilt, as any officer did when his partner was shot in the line of duty. He'd been plagued by all the "if onlys" Dr. Perry had warned her about. *If only I'd gotten there sooner. If only I'd taken that side of the building.* She'd put an end to that kind of talk right away, but she couldn't help wondering if Brian might still be alive if any of those things had happened.

As the hour grew late, fatigue overtook her body. She finished her chores and climbed between freshly laundered sheets, still uncertain about how to proceed with her investigation of Brian Delany's affairs. Soon, a deep, sound sleep claimed her body and her mind.

She woke unusually late, feeling refreshed and eager to pursue her new leads. After she showered and ate breakfast, she called the station to talk to Gary. He had the day off, so she punched in his home number, only to hear his prerecorded message. Gary was at the gym practicing for the upcoming interdepartmental volleyball tournament—one more of her favorite activities from which she'd been excluded. Her frustration peaked when he failed to pick up the third time she called. She shouldn't be upset. Gary had every right to continue with his own life, regardless of her situation. He wasn't the one under suspension.

Laurel busied herself for a time watering her houseplants. She'd taken advantage of the green thumb she'd inherited from her mother by filling every available space with lush green foliage. The potted plants would have to do until she could manage to buy a home of her own. That goal was slipping further away from her each day. After the shooting and her subsequent suspension hit the news, her loan application had been rejected.

She stepped out onto her tiny patio to water her outside plants. Spotting Heather Jones, one of the teenagers from next door, she waved and called out, "How'd you do on your algebra test?"

"B plus! Thanks for your help," Heather returned.

"Way to go." Laurel gave her a thumbs-up sign. Anna, Heather's mother, was a single parent with three children in high school. Laurel liked them all, which was fortunate, since they would be neighbors for the foreseeable future. She stepped back inside just as her phone began to ring. She hoped it was Gary returning her call.

"Laurel, it's Scott." He spoke with a steady voice that exuded warmth. "I've done a lot of thinking since I left you yesterday."

"About the documents in Brian's safe?"

He hesitated. "That, too, but mostly about you."

Her skin began to tingle. It was a pleasant feeling she couldn't deny, much as she tried to fight it.

"Will you have dinner with me tonight?"

Her pulse leapt as it often did when she faced danger in her job. Her feminine instincts waged a fierce battle with her professional ones. The woman inside her wanted to see him again, to explore the feelings he stirred to life, but the cop hesitated. She had so many unanswered questions—why, for example, was he helping her, a total stranger? Years of relying on her professional training made her suspicious. She knew so little about him. He could have some hidden agenda. Lord knows Brian had had one.

"We could drive up the coast to Huntington Beach. There's a great restaurant by the pier." Scott made it all sound so simple. When she didn't speak right away, he continued. "Look, Laurel, I want to talk to you about Brian, but I'm not trying to blackmail you into having dinner with me." He paused for a moment. When he spoke again, his voice was lower, more intimate. "I think you know we have more than business to talk about."

Her heart hammered in her chest. It was pure foolishness to want to get to know him better. Nothing could ever come of it. Too many obstacles stood between them. Even if he didn't live in London and his family didn't hate her, he was a constant reminder of the human life she had taken.

As she listened to his voice, the feelings he'd inspired when he'd held her in his arms after learning she'd been shot came back to her in a rush. She remembered the strength he'd given her and the rightness she'd felt as his arms enfolded her. She remembered how he'd asked for the truth and then listened to what she had to say. But most of all, she remembered the spiraling ecstasy she'd discovered when he'd kissed her.

"Okay," she heard herself reply, despite the warning flags waving through her thoughts. They agreed on a time, and he hung up quickly before she could change her mind.

Doubt crept in to change her mind almost immediately, but she had no way of notifying him. Luckily, deductive reasoning came easily to her, and rationalizing was just a short leap away. She chose to forget what he'd said about not blackmailing her into having dinner with him. If she told herself she was going only to find out more information about Brian, the idea of agreeing to have dinner with him became more palatable.

She poured another cup of coffee and stood in front of the small garden window in her kitchen. The frustration surrounding her upcoming grand jury hearing had made her a little crazy. She'd struck out with every query she'd made regarding her informant, Donald Cooper. It was as though the guy had disappeared from the face of the planet. Without his testimony at the hearing, which was now only three days away, she would be in big trouble.

At the moment, Scott Delany was her only link to Brian and the subterfuge in Brian's life. Even if the documents they found had nothing to do with drugs or the reason he opened fire, the hidden assets would at least cast a shadow of doubt on Brian's otherwise impeccable reputation.

She'd also bet a month's pay that Scott knew something more about Brian's past that would help her case. His reaction to Stanley Murdock's name had been too strong. She wished she knew what he knew and why he was helping her. Perhaps this evening she would put his noble words to the test. Would he actually divulge secrets about Brian's past that would shed a corroborating light on her story?

The afternoon dragged by as she waited impatiently to hear from Gary. She finally gave up and started getting ready for dinner. She chose a simple black sheath. The soft fabric brushed loosely at her hips, reminding her of the five pounds she'd lost since the shooting. If her appetite picked up every time Scott was near, as it had in the park, she'd gain the weight back in no time. She thought about something she'd heard on a daytime talk show during her convalescence. The guest talked about women who used food to sublimate an unfulfilled sex life. She glanced back at her reflection in the mirror and shook her head. If that were her problem, she'd weigh five hundred pounds.

As she slipped into her black sling-back pumps with gold trim, Laurel noticed she was smiling. It felt strange after so many weeks of frowns and grimaces. She ignored the explanation that immediately popped into her mind. Her good humor had nothing to do with Scott Delany—she was simply looking forward to a rare evening out.

She walked over to her dresser and opened the top drawer, where she kept her jewelry. Her gold locket glistened in the light. With great care, she picked up the locket and fastened it around her neck. The tiny treasure had belonged to her mother.

Dressed and ready to go nearly an hour early, Laurel made a pitcher of ice tea and sat on the sofa reading a magazine article on the art of balancing babies and careers. The corresponding picture depicted a young woman in an expensive suit, with a briefcase in one hand and an infant in the other. A handsome man, who looked a lot like Scott, stood behind her with love and adoration in his eyes. In her mind, Laurel pictured a .38 caliber revolver strapped to the woman's hip and a nightstick in her hand instead of a leather briefcase. The image was so ridiculous she laughed out loud. "In your dreams, Sergeant."

The doorbell rang and Laurel found that she was not at all surprised to see Scott standing on her porch. In the short time she'd known him, she recognized he shared her penchant for punctuality.

She made herself take in a deep breath and let it out before she opened the door. He wore dark blue slacks, a white shirt that showed off his tan and a navy silk tie with a geometric pattern.

"Come in, please." She held the door open, but Scott didn't move. Instead, he slowly inspected her from her ankles to her eyebrows, causing a nervous flutter in her stomach.

"You look...gorgeous." His gaze settled on her face as he stepped inside. A smile spread his lips, attracting her attention to the line of his freshly shaved jaw and the faint spicy scent of his cologne.

"Thank you," she replied, a little irritated with herself because she felt both relieved and excited by his compliment. "You look very nice, too." She tried not to stare. "Would you like a glass of ice tea or a soft drink before we go?"

"Tea would be great. Thanks."

Laurel dropped a couple of extra ice cubes into her own glass when she got Scott's tea. The flush she felt in her face had nothing to do with the sultry summer evening. She sat on the sofa beside him, but not too close. Watching the movement of his throat as he took a long drink, she became suddenly thirsty and lifted her own glass.

"How long have you lived here?" he asked.

"About five years. It's small, but it'll do until..." She stared at the glass in her hand, not wanting to think about her unsure future.

"Until what?"

She looked up and found his gaze intent upon her face. "I'm trying, although not very successfully, to buy a house." She didn't mention her dream of owning a home on the beach; it was looking pretty ridiculous right now with her career in jeopardy.

"That's a big undertaking, considering the value of land in Orange County today. I'm impressed." He took another swallow of tea. "Why do you say unsuccessfully? Haven't you found what you want?"

Laurel tried not to stare at him as if he'd grown another head. Did he think it was simply a matter of making the selection? His background differed so much from hers! "My application for a preapproved loan was rejected after word of my suspension hit the newspapers." She tried to keep the hostility out of her voice.

"I'm sorry," he said.

"It's not your fault." She shrugged. "It comes with the job. You have to take the bad with the good."

"Is there good, too?" he asked softly.

"Yeah," she said thoughtfully. "If I didn't believe that, I couldn't do what I do. And the people I work with are like my family." She very much wanted to get back to work, despite the fear that rose inside her every time she thought of the inherent danger.

He seemed to accept her statement, and they sat in comfortable silence for a couple of minutes before he spoke again. "So what made you decide you want to be a homeowner?"

She looked out the window at the neatly trimmed hedge as a flood of childhood memories returned. "For my eighth birthday, my parents took me to the furniture store and let me pick out my first bedroom set." She smiled as she pictured the frilly white canopy. "They even let me choose the color I wanted the walls painted. Lavender." She glanced at Scott. "I loved that room. It was mine, and I always felt so safe and secure when I was in there, like nothing bad could ever happen." She fingered the locket at the base of her throat.

"A few months later, my mother was shot to death while walking from the parking lot into the grocery store. She happened to be in the escape path of a drug addict who'd just robbed the store." The sadness reflected in her words surprised her. Over the years, she'd learned to filter the emotion from her voice whenever she spoke of her mother's tragic death. Remembering her own pain made her think of the pain she'd inflicted on Brian's family when she'd killed him.

Scott sat quietly beside her. She could see he was moved by her story and the knowledge that she'd also faced the loss of a loved one. She didn't want pity and was grateful he offered none. "What happened after that?"

"Everything changed. We moved. My father remarried. He and his new wife had a family of their own." Though she'd lived in the same house, she remembered feeling separate and alone. "But I never forgot how it felt when I had my own room."

Shrugging off the memories, she glanced around at the blandness of her white-walled apartment and smiled. "I guess I still want to paint my walls lavender, so to speak, and have a dog or a cat if I choose." Laurel checked her watch, then reached for Scott's empty glass.

He caught her wrist as she started to get up. "You're full of surprises," he said, staring at her mouth.

She wondered if he felt her pulse skipping under his fingers. "We'd better be going."

As they walked to the car, Laurel noticed the rental car sticker on the rear bumper of the luxury sedan. The reminder of his temporary presence in her life caused a soft sigh to escape her lips.

"Sorry if you don't like the car. It's all they had left at one o'clock in the morning when I arrived." He opened her door.

"The car's fine." She ignored the misunderstanding. "How long before you have to return home?" *Very subtle, Laurel,* she thought, wishing she could retract the question.

Scott smiled and shut her door. He walked around the car and got in before he answered her question. "I don't know yet. I have some unfinished business here." A hint of laughter imbued his husky voice and a suggestive glint twinkled in his gaze.

Laurel let the words and implications fall silently between them.

A few blocks down the road, Scott picked up the conversation. "When I left four years ago, I sold everything I owned to scrape up enough money to go into partnership with Hershal Saxton, a friend of mine from college. His uncle was selling a small telecommunications company outside London, where Hershal had worked before college. We struggled through a couple of very lean years at the beginning when we wondered if we would make it."

"But what about your family?" Laurel couldn't hide the surprise in her voice. The Delanys were very wealthy, even by southern California standards.

"My father financed my education, though he was terribly disappointed I had no interest in pursuing a career in law like Brian." Laurel detected a distance in his voice. "He never approved of anything I tried to do. But I was determined to make something of myself in spite of him." Finally his expression softened. "Somehow the company survived, and we've been growing and branching out into other areas for the last couple of years. We're even considering moving our headquarters to the States."

Laurel's breath caught. She tried not to read anything personal into his statement, but couldn't deny the hope escalating inside her.

He smiled, and she saw a hint of pride behind his success story, but she also heard a note of sadness. He must have felt terribly alone.

"Do you have any regrets now?"

He turned his head from the traffic to meet her gaze for an instant. "Sure." He focused on the road again, and she thought he'd decided not to elaborate. Some moments later, he continued. "The way I took off after that last confrontation with my father and Brian really hurt my mother. I had vowed never to return again. I was angry at them and had good reason to be, but my mother deserved to be treated better than that."

He didn't say what his reason was, but she sensed that a powerful anger still lingered inside him after all these years.

At the restaurant, Scott pulled into the valet parking lot. Laurel stood on the curb and sucked in a deep breath of fresh salty air as Scott gave his keys to the parking attendant and retrieved his jacket from the back seat. Inside, the tiered dining area allowed every table a spectacular view of the ocean. After a brief wait, the maitre d' led them down a series of steps to a table beside the glass wall that looked out over the rolling breakers.

"This is perfect," she said, looking out the window as the sun faded into the ocean on the far side of the pier. In the other direction, lifeguard towers dotted the sandy white beach. She felt vital and alive as she watched the waves. "Someday, I'd love to have a house on the beach." She pulled her gaze from the view to look at Scott. She hadn't meant to say that. It was a foolish dream. "I know. It's not likely on a cop's salary. Besides, I'd be late for work half the time because I couldn't drag myself away from the view. It's mesmerizing.''

"You never know. I'd be the last person to shoot down someone else's dream.'' His voice was low and smooth.

She thought of the way he had made his own dream come true despite his father's lack of support. At first, she wondered why he would be so determined to reestablish such a painful relationship, but then she realized how the adversity he'd faced had made him the strong, self-confident man she was beginning to care so much about.

The intimate look he gave her caused a warmth to spread through her body. "With the right combination of determination and luck, anything is possible, Laurel.''

She might be able to match his determination, but luck had never been a part of her life.

The waiter arrived to take their orders. After listening to his entire spiel, they both opted for the broiled halibut. By the time their food arrived, she'd told Scott about her academy days and her last promotion.

"What's going to happen now with your job?''

Laurel swallowed the bits of halibut steak in her mouth and took a sip of wine. "It all depends on the grand jury findings,'' she said, fighting to keep her voice light and even. "If they believe me, and all they have right now is my word, the suspension will be lifted and I can get back to work.''

Scott put down his fork. She felt his watchful gaze penetrating her defenses. "And if they don't?''

Laurel didn't want to think about that now. So much depended on her being able to prove Brian was a criminal. She couldn't face Scott, so she looked down the beach to the first empty tower. "Maybe I could become a lifeguard.''

"Laurel." He reached across the table and took her hand. His fingers were warm as they brushed over hers. "There's got to be a way out of this."

For years Laurel had always taken care of herself. Until this mess occurred, she'd never had to ask anyone for anything. She told herself all she wanted from Scott was a way to find the truth, refusing to consider the possibility that it might be more, refusing to hope he would understand.

"What are you going to do about the documents?" she asked.

"I'll eventually have to turn them over to the D.A. Since I've inherited everything Brian owned, I have to make sure everything is legitimate."

"Eventually?"

"I want to do a little checking on my own first," he said.

"How long will that take?"

He looked at her levelly. "At least until next Wednesday."

Laurel swallowed. "I don't want you to get yourself into—"

"I know what I'm doing," he said, cutting her off. "If we find out anything definite before the hearing that will put an end to your suspension, I'll hand it over."

The documents they had so far could be used as effectively *against* her as they could in her defense. Laurel knew that turning them over to the D.A. would not be in her best interest. When Scott's father found out he'd held on to them, there would be a price to pay, she was sure. The fact that Scott had agreed to hold off even for a little while made her mind race. "Why are you doing this? Why are you risking so much to help me?"

His eyes darkened, and he stared at her for a long time before he answered. "Because I have to."

They finished eating in silence, and Scott paid the check. As they walked toward the door, she heard soft, slow music coming from the lounge and glanced in that direction.

"Do you like to dance?" he said.

She nodded and was about to say it had been ages since she'd gone dancing, but he was already propelling her into the dark room.

Scott led her to the crowded dance floor and pulled her into his arms, taking full advantage of the tight space available. Laurel fought the tingling sensation that spread out from where his hand rested on the small of her back. She ought to tell him to stop, to take her home or, better yet, call a cab to take her home.

He pulled her closer and bent down to whisper into her ear. "Relax, Laurel. You're perfectly safe. Just enjoy the music."

Safe was the last thing she felt while being held in his arms, though the tension brought on by their earlier conversation did start to fade. One song blended into another, and another. She swayed to the beat, her head pillowed against Scott's chest as though it was the most natural thing in the world for her to do. As the hour grew later, the music grew softer.

Laurel glanced at the young couple dancing beside them. They were locked in an intimate embrace, kissing deeply as the music ended. "I think it's time for you to take me home," she said quietly as she lifted her cheek from the soft material of Scott's jacket.

The sky was a clear indigo when they walked outside. The salty ocean breeze tickled the loose hairs around Laurel's neck. She turned her face to his. Slowly he moved closer and lowered his head until their lips were close enough for a kiss. Awareness rippled inside her. Lord, how she wanted that kiss.

"There you are, sir," the young attendant said as he held
the door open. Scott smiled and lifted his head, but he
whispered something to the young man as he handed him his
tip. When they got in the car, he turned the radio to an easy
listening station. The drive back to Laurel's apartment was
a quiet one.

She didn't want the evening to end, but she wasn't sure
exactly where she wanted it to go.

Scott held open the screen door as she turned the key in
the lock. She started to reach for the doorknob, but her
hand was shaking so badly she dropped it to her side and
looked up at him. He opened the door and ushered her inside, closing it behind him. "Are you all right?" A slight
frown tipped the corners of his mouth downward.

"I'm fine," she said, trying to ignore a feeling of apprehension she didn't understand.

"Good, because we started something in the parking lot
I'd very much like to finish." He reached for her hand and
pulled her into his arms.

As his mouth descended toward hers, her breath escaped
in short, deep pants, inspired not by arousal, but by an eerie,
irrational fear she couldn't explain.

An overwhelming sense of déjà vu pressed down on her,
suffocating her in its vividness. Realization struck swiftly,
causing her body to tense. She and Scott were standing in the
same spot where Brian had attacked her.

But this wasn't Brian. This was Scott, the man who'd held
her in his arms on three different occasions, stirring feelings of tenderness as well as longing, the man whose kiss
she'd wanted just a short time earlier.

When the anxiety began to ebb, Laurel realized Scott had
stopped kissing her. She opened her eyes to find him peer-
ing down at her, confused.

Scott kept one arm at her waist while he flipped the light switch by the door. "Laurel?"

The concern in his voice made her ashamed of that momentary flash of fear. Scott would never hurt her. She leaned her forehead against his chest.

He lifted her chin to face him in the dim light. "What happened just now?"

Laurel saw the tension in his face and wanted to soothe it. "I was thinking—" She shook her head. "Never mind. It was just a bad memory."

He stared into her eyes. "I'm not Brian."

"I know you aren't." She touched the smooth line of his jaw.

"Do you want me to leave?" he asked.

She shook her head. "It's gone now."

Scott led her to the sofa, where he guided her down beside him. He put his arm around her and brought her head to rest against his shoulder. After several minutes, he said, "It's not going to be easy for us, is it?"

Laurel lifted her head and tipped her face to his. Words her mother had used often came back to her. "Nothing good is ever easy."

She raised her hand from his chest to his face. Using the pads of her fingers, she traced the lines of his brow, the arch of his cheekbones, then the outline of his lips. She needed to reassure herself that what she'd said was true. He was different from Brian, different from any man she'd known.

As her fingers trailed down his neck, she felt his pulse and touched her lips to the spot. His chest rose sharply. She enjoyed the feeling of power, exploited it by flicking her tongue over the same spot.

He issued a low moan, then nibbled along her cheek until his mouth found hers. His tongue lightly touched her lips before slipping inside her mouth, bringing a wash of new sensations into play. With moist, parted lips, he spread kisses over the corners of her mouth, her chin, the side of her neck and down to the base of her throat. She tipped her head back, reveling in the delicious sensations. His warm breath made her skin tingle. As his mouth returned to hers, she felt a need building inside her. A need she hadn't indulged in a long, long time.

Laurel ran her hands under his jacket and over the smooth muscles of his back, learning the feel of his body. She brought her hands back around to explore the contour of his shoulders and chest. She wanted her fingers to memorize every inch of him. As she stroked and smoothed the hair on his chest, her fingers brushed across his nipple. She repeated the light touch until a hard peak formed beneath her fingers. His body trembled in response.

With a hungry groan, Scott pulled her onto his lap. The hand on her ribs moved up to the underside of her breast. With a slowness that threatened her sanity, he molded and shaped her breast in his hand, avoiding contact with her nipple. She arched against the pressure of his palm as her own need grew. As his fingers circled and finally tugged at the sensitive tip, she let out a low, satisfied moan.

He moved his attention to her other breast, inciting another moan of pleasure. When his hand slid down the front of her dress to rest low on her abdomen, her muscles tensed. She wanted him desperately, but she wasn't sure she was ready to take the next step.

Scott lifted his lips from hers. He rested his forehead against hers until his breathing calmed. Then, he whispered against her cheek, "I think you'd better kick me out now."

Laurel felt a tightness in her chest. Scott's ability to tune into her body language and understand her needs was something very special. She got up and walked him to the door. His body was still taut and unfulfilled like hers.

He reached his hand to her face, but dropped it before it made contact. He opened the door.

"Scott," she called out in a shaky voice.

He stepped out onto the porch and turned to look at her with dark, heavy-lidded eyes.

"Thank you," she whispered, unable to say more.

He reached out to her face again. This time he ran his thumb lightly over her lips as he stared into her eyes. She could see the desire still alive and struggling inside him. He bit down on his lower lip as he pulled his hand away and slipped it into his pocket. "Lock the door, Laurel."

Chapter 6

"Heard you're still lookin' for Coop," the young male voice said when Laurel picked up the phone the next morning.

Laurel's heart filled with expectation. She recognized the voice immediately. He worked at the surf shop down by the pier. Blond hair, early twenties. Mike or Mitch... That was it—Mitch Porter.

"That's right. Know where he is?" She held her breath, silently praying this was the break she desperately needed.

"Naw. Wish I did, though." Malice edged his laid-back tone. "He crashed at my place for like a week and then he snagged my rent money when he split."

Laurel's hopes started to deflate, but she persisted. "Have you heard anything?"

"That's why I called. I heard about this dude that may know somethin'."

"Who? Have you talked to him?" Laurel's hope returned.

"Hell, no. From what I hear, this guy is really bad news."

"What's his name?" She'd talk to the devil himself to find Donald Cooper.

"He's called Samson," the young man said. "Don't know if that's his real name."

"What's he look like?"

"You know that blond guy who played the Russian fighter in that *Rocky* movie? Imagine him with hair halfway down his back."

"Where does he surf?"

"Off Fifteenth Street—or anywhere he wants, from what I hear."

She jotted down everything he'd told her and thanked him.

"If you find Coop, get my money back," he said before hanging up.

At least she had a place to start. Glancing at the clock, she decided to slip into her running gear and head for the beach. Fifteenth Street. After the dinner she'd eaten last night, she knew she could use a run on the beach. Her thoughts shifted to the man with whom she'd shared that dinner and the heated kisses they'd shared back at her apartment.

The phone rang while she was changing clothes. Scott's voice came on the other end of the line as if she'd conjured him up from her thoughts.

"Hope you didn't sleep any better than I did," he whispered in a tone evocative of their intimacy the night before.

Laurel vividly recalled the feelings he'd stirred within her as his mouth and hands had moved over her. The intensity of those feelings scared her, just as the ambivalence of her feelings this morning worried her.

She had never been indecisive. If Scott was anyone else, she wouldn't hesitate to explore their relationship. But he wasn't anyone else, and all she had to do to remember that was to look at him. She wondered if the day would ever come when she could look at Scott and not see Brian. She also wondered if he would be in her life long enough for her to find out. If she was indicted, her only defense would be to prove his brother was a criminal. If it came to that, she worried about where Scott's loyalty would lie. He'd said he wanted the truth, but could he accept it if it meant more pain and anguish for his parents?

She remembered all the times she'd heard her stepmother say, "Blood is thicker than water." As a little girl, it had taken her awhile to fully grasp the meaning of the tired but truthful cliché. She didn't want to test its validity with Scott.

"I called to invite you to brunch," he said.

She sighed regretfully. "I wish I could, but I just got a tip on my informant. I've got to check it out." Despite her uncertainty, she couldn't deny the pleasure she received from his call and from the knowledge that he still wanted to see her.

"Have you found him?"

"No, but I've got a lead." She told him what the man from the surf shop had said.

"You're not going after this guy alone," Scott said.

"I'm a trained police officer—"

"I know that," he interrupted. "And I remember exactly how capable you are of taking care of yourself in a one-on-one situation. But you don't have a gun or a badge. And you have to admit, if you were on duty you wouldn't go in there without backup."

He was right. "The point is, I'm not on duty, and if I don't check this guy out, I may never be on duty again."

Scott cursed into the receiver. "All I'm asking is that you let me go with you."

"No." She responded automatically, thinking of Scott's safety even as the doubts surfaced in her mind. Why did he want to be there? Didn't he trust her?

After a long pause, Scott's voice hardened with determination. "Damn it, Laurel, you owe me this one."

She'd hoped he wouldn't bring it up, but he *had* let her into Brian's house and shared his findings with her. Grudgingly, she agreed to wait for him, but she made it clear she wanted him to stay back and out of the way. "If I get into trouble, I'll need you in a position to call for assistance."

Scott grunted dubiously in reply.

While she waited for him to arrive, she went over everything that had happened the night of the shooting, for what seemed like the billionth time. Finally, she told the whole story into a small tape recorder, then played it back to herself, hoping that in hearing it in this way, she might remember some small detail she'd forgotten.

The exercise revealed only one thing—she had a very weak case. She should have called into the station for backup the minute Donald Cooper had contacted her, but hindsight had no place here. She had made a judgment call on the spot, letting her experience and instinct guide her. Unfortunately, her judgment had proved faulty.

Laurel stood and paced in front of the window as she recalled how the inaccuracy of Coop's information had left her with egg on her face several times in the past. Her fellow officers had teased her mercilessly about the reliability of her informant. But Coop had also given her information that had led to arrests on two separate occasions. Therefore, she couldn't afford to ignore what he told her that night. By the time he'd gotten the information to her, she didn't have time to arrange surveillance. And besides, the very vagueness of his information and the last-minute timing wouldn't have gotten her very far with the watch commander.

Although Laurel and Gary had agreed the tip would most likely be another wild-goose chase, they had to check it out. If there was even the most remote possibility they had a lead on the person supplying drugs to the local students, she had to follow it through. She figured that since they were only a couple of blocks away, the most she had to lose was a little time.

She couldn't have been more wrong.

Coop had been right this time. Almost. If the exchange had taken place in the building he'd indicated, it had concluded before Laurel arrived. Brian had been talking to someone in the alley, she was sure. If Coop knew Brian was going to be there, he probably knew Brian's contact, as well. She had to find Donald Cooper.

Several small stores and refreshment stands fronted the boardwalk near Fifteenth Street. The corner tavern served a mixed clientele, including both the local surfers and a seedier lot, as well. Laurel strolled into the bar. To give her eyes a moment to adjust from the bright sunlight to the dim tavern lighting, she paused inside the door and made a small production of removing her headphones and turning off her portable radio.

She hoped Scott would stay put at his spot on the beach in front of the bar. The added pressure of his presence was like having a civilian beside her on a "ride-along," only worse. Having to worry about a civilian passenger's safety in those first critical seconds when a situation exploded could give the bad guys that tiny advantage that could cost a life. And in this case, her concern for Scott's safety exceeded anything she'd ever experienced. It was a frightening realization.

Laurel chose a small table at the end of the narrow room, the only seat where she could place her back to the wall and observe both exits. As she made her way to the corner, she stole a glance at the other patrons.

A group of six or eight men were gathered at the front end of the bar. She spotted two large guys with blond hair pulled into ponytails at their napes. She could feel the adrenaline urging her heart to beat faster. Years of training and experience helped her to control her breathing so no outward signs of her nervousness would be obvious.

The bartender drew the beer she requested and brought it to the table. As she paid her tab, she noticed that the conversation at the front of the room had ceased. She took a swig and glanced toward the window, which framed the blue Pacific beyond.

The larger of the two blond men sat with one leg thrown carelessly over the arm of his chair. He was staring straight at Laurel. It wasn't a flirtatious stare so much as a defiant one. Hair prickled along the back of her neck.

He whispered something and the men closest to him laughed. One of them stood and strolled toward her. Unlike the others, this guy looked more like a biker than a surfer. He wore a black leather vest and worn jeans. The chain fastened through his belt loop rattled when he moved. From behind his heavily bearded face, he smiled down at her. "You lookin' for somebody special, sweetheart?"

The men behind him chuckled.

She wanted to gag. "Could be."

"He got a name? Maybe Jackknife?" He placed both hands on the table between them and leered at her.

The men chuckled louder.

"Goes by the name of Samson," she said evenly, watching his eyes. "You know where I can find him?"

"Maybe." He straightened up. "Who wants to know?"

"Delilah," she returned sarcastically.

The biker looked blank.

The large blonde behind him laughed loudly. "What do you want, Sergeant?" he asked with a cocky smile. "Or is it meter maid now?"

The men burst out laughing.

Damn, she was irritated at herself for underestimating them—or at least one of them. Her picture had been in the papers, but she'd assumed these guys hadn't seen it, much less read the article. "Just a few words in private, if you wouldn't mind."

He lifted his eyebrows in mock disbelief. "Old Jackknife here might get jealous. I think he's sweet on you."

Again the men roared. Jackknife moved around the table and started to place a proprietary arm around her shoulder.

It was a bad idea. Laurel reacted so fast, the biker never had a clue what hit him. She caught his thumb and twisted it around until he was on his knees with his arm bent behind his back.

Scott appeared, as if by magic, between her and the agitated group of men. "Don't even think about it," he warned the first man who got to his feet. His menacing tone sent them back to their chairs.

In the calmest voice she could manage, she told the biker, "Don't move or I'll break it."

"I'm Samson. What do you want?" The blonde stood up slowly and stepped away from the others, his gaze shifting back and forth from her to Scott.

Laurel raised the biker to his feet, then gave him a shove toward the others, who sat watching the foam in their beers.

Scott stood with his feet apart and his arms folded across his chest, keeping an eye on the other men while she spoke to Samson.

"I'm looking for Donald Cooper." She studied Samson's face, but found no trace of recognition. "He goes by Coop. I heard you were in touch with him."

"Sorry, ma'am. I don't know no one by that name," he said, his poker face firm.

She gave him a description, anyway.

"What do you want this guy for, anyhow?" His expression remained as innocent as a newborn's.

"He skipped out on a friend of mine without paying his part of the rent." She kept the rest to herself.

A slow smile touched the corners of Samson's mouth, but darkness filled his eyes. "Well, if I were you, I'd tell that friend to start looking for a new roommate."

He turned his back on her and headed for his chair. She heard a few muffled snickers of agreement behind her, then Samson's tersely whispered command, "Shut up, you idiots."

She stepped toward the exit, confident of Scott's ability to protect her flank. Silence followed her out the door as she and Scott made a hasty retreat down the boardwalk to the next street over, where she had parked her car.

As soon as they slipped inside, Scott pulled her into his arms in the tightest embrace the console between them would permit. His hand found her chin and brought her mouth to his for the longest, deepest kiss they'd shared yet. His lips moved over hers, demanding her response. She gave it willingly. She needed the connection, needed to feel the warmth of his touch.

All too soon, he lifted his mouth from hers. The sound he made, husky with relief, came from deep in his chest.

Slowly, her head cleared. As she thought of what had happened back at the bar, she pushed him away. "What if they'd recognized you? I told you to wait outside!"

"While that sleaze pawed you?" he scoffed. "Fat chance."

"He didn't paw me. And, as you could see for yourself, I had the situation under control." Laurel watched his gaze narrow on her before he turned away.

She thought of the previous relationships she'd had with men who couldn't let go of their egos—or whatever outdated idea made them believe they had to be the dominant person in the relationship at all times and at all costs. Even those who professed to be "liberated" men had discovered that letting go of tradition wasn't as easily done as said.

Scott turned back to face her, his expression still troubled. "I didn't want you to get hurt."

His eyes convinced her he was telling the truth, but she sensed he'd left something important unspoken. The suspicious nature she'd acquired with her experience in law enforcement suddenly kicked in, despite her attempt to hold it at bay. She wanted to believe Scott really cared for her. Yet she couldn't help wondering if he had other reasons for wanting to keep her safe.

Chapter 7

At Captain Larson's urging, Laurel kept her appointment with the department psychologist Monday afternoon, though she feared it would be a big mistake. She found it nearly impossible to think of anything but the grand jury hearing scheduled for the following day.

The session with Dr. Perry went well, until he started probing into her relationship with Brian. "How well did you get to know Mr. Delany while working on the project?"

Laurel became nervous and agitated. Rather than tell an out-and-out lie about the extent of their relationship, she released the fragile hold on her temper. "Really, Dr. Perry, this is a tremendous waste of time and taxpayer money." She stood, preparing to leave.

"Sergeant, I don't think you've fully acknowledged the real source of your anger—Brian Delany." He spoke so softly, she could barely hear him. "As I've said, it's not uncommon for police officers to feel anger toward the person they shot. From what you told me, it sounds as if Mr.

Delany put you into a position where you had to do something you didn't want to do. You have a right to be angry at him for that.''

Laurel started to speak, but a tightness clasped at her throat. He was right. She wanted Brian to be alive so she could pound out her frustration on his chest and scream at him for the pain he'd caused his family and everyone left behind. She couldn't begin to explain the reasons for her pain or the depth of her anger, so she turned and left the office without another word.

Scott called when she got home. "How did it go today?"

She groaned. "I really blew it. He started asking me questions about—" She cut herself off abruptly when she realized what she'd been about to say.

"About Brian?" Scott finished.

After a short pause, she said, "Yes."

Scott remained quiet for a moment. She wondered what he was thinking and feeling during that moment, but she couldn't bring herself to ask.

"I'm coming over," he said before she heard the click of the line disconnecting.

She should have been angry, but she felt too much relief to worry about it. He got there in record time. Seconds after he stepped through the door, she was in his arms. It was becoming a habit, one she could get used to in a hurry. He pressed her closer. His fingers threaded through her hair as he held her head for a long, delicious kiss. "I needed to make sure you were all right," he whispered as he pulled back enough to see her eyes.

"And what did you find out?" she replied breathlessly.

"You're better than all right." He smiled. "Much better."

She returned his smile as she stepped back out of his arms. They walked to the kitchen, where she poured them each a glass of ice tea. She needed the drink to cool the fever Scott created with the simplest touch.

"Do you have plans for the evening?" he asked. The invitation burned in his eyes, though the words he spoke sounded harmless enough.

She wished she could say no; she almost did, anyway, despite her better judgment. "I need to go over some notes and make a few more."

"I should let you get to work then," he said. "I guess it would only complicate things if I went with you tomorrow."

She nodded. "But thanks for offering."

"I'm sure you'll do fine," he said. "I'll call you afterward."

"Thanks." It seemed so inadequate, but it was all she could manage. She appreciated his concern and support, but knew she had to do this part alone. He brushed his lips softly across hers, then left without another word.

She had a fitful night's rest.

On Tuesday morning, she took extra care with her appearance. She selected a tailored beige suit that looked crisp and professional. Her matching heels clicked on the polished marble floor as she walked into the grand jury courtroom on shaky legs. She hoped she looked a lot more confident than she felt.

The courtroom, normally a familiar arena for her, held an ominous presence today. Although she'd testified as a witness for many cases, none had ever been so important to her.

Laurel took her seat at the marred wooden table facing the jurors, who sat in a horseshoe-shaped panel before her. The district attorney was seated at the table with the court officers.

The fear gnawing at her stomach differed from what she'd felt in the alley that night. She'd had an even chance against

Brian Delany. She didn't feel that now. Going up against the D.A. himself put her at an immediate disadvantage.

He began the questioning in a routine manner, verifying information in her written report.

She testified to the events leading up to the incident.

"Sergeant Tanner, can you tell us why you decided not to call in for backup when your source indicated the scope of involvement you've stated in your report?" He remained perfectly still, waiting for her answer.

Laurel's mouth went dry. She took a few seconds to consider her reply before she started speaking. "The information I was given lacked the details to convince me of its validity at the time. The informant said he was certain about the location and repeated the address. He emphasized the necessity of a prompt response. Since my partner and I were only a few blocks away, and based partially on the reliability rate of this particular informant in the past, I decided to proceed to the location and make a preliminary check before calling for backup."

"Are you saying this informant's information has proven to be unreliable?"

"I've made two good arrests as a result of his information."

"And how many times has his information been inaccurate?"

Laurel swallowed, feeling the weight of the jurors' eyes upon her. "Several times, as I recall."

The questions continued for hours. She answered as directly and succinctly as she could. An indictment could be handed down only if twelve of the nineteen thought there was sufficient evidence to warrant a trial. She had to convince at least eight of the jurors she was telling the truth.

"You say that you heard more than one voice in the alley coming from the direction where you saw Mr. Delany emerge. Is that correct, Sergeant?"

"Yes, sir."

"Were you able to identify either voice at that time, before you actually saw anyone step out of the fog?"

"No, sir."

"So it's possible that there could have been more than two people in that alley?"

"Yes, sir."

"And would you say it was also possible that neither of the voices you heard belonged to Deputy District Attorney Brian Delany?"

"It's possible, but he would have had to have heard the voices also. He was closer than I was." Her pulse accelerated.

"Did you consider that he may have been there on the same tip you received?"

"No."

"And if he was acting on that same tip, and had heard these same voices, would you say it would be within reason to suspect he would arm himself?"

"If that was the case, yes. But he raised the gun and shot me *after* I identified myself and instructed him to drop his weapon. He even called me by name first." Laurel slowly sat back in her chair, finally aware of where he was going and that she'd helped him get there.

"He called you Sergeant Tanner before he shot you?"

Laurel hesitated. Perspiration trickled down between her breasts. "Not exactly."

He locked his challenging gaze on her. "Can you tell us exactly what he said to you? You may refer to your field notes if you wish."

She knew that was exactly what he wanted. If she'd brought her notebook into court, it would be subject to subpoena. "He said, 'Laurel. Let me explain.'"

"Laurel. That's your first name?"

"Yes."

"And did you let him explain?"

"I told him to lower his gun to the ground first."

"And did he do so?"

"He started to." She swallowed as the memory intruded. "Then he lifted the barrel, aimed and pulled the trigger."

"Did he say anything else while this was happening?"

Pressure crushed at her chest.

She heard him ask if he should repeat the question.

She said, "No, I remember. He looked me in the eyes and said, 'Okay, honey. You win—again.'"

The district attorney remained silent for an uncomfortably long moment, slowly nodding. "Can you explain why he would have addressed you in this manner, Sergeant Tanner?"

Laurel took in a breath as she gathered her courage. Lifting her chin slightly, she kept the rest of her body as motionless as possible and spoke in a calm, even tone. "I have no way of knowing what Mr. Delany was thinking. I can only testify as to what happened."

The struggle to contain her frustration exhausted her. She knew exactly what she'd seen and heard in the alley that night, but listening to the D.A.'s probing questions caused her hope to fade.

If the suspect had been someone with a record of criminal activity, or even if he'd just been an ordinary citizen, the courts would usually accept the sworn testimony of a police officer. But when the suspect was a respected member of the court, with the district attorney himself serving as prosecutor, the likelihood of a jury taking her word at face value was practically nil.

Though her hope had dwindled, Laurel tried to keep up the facade of confidence as long as she could. When the last question had been asked and answered, she was dismissed. Her legs felt boneless. She prayed they would carry her as far as the other side of the door the bailiff held open. Mercifully, they did.

Laurel dreaded the waiting more than she'd dreaded anything in her life. There was nothing left to do but sit at home until the final report was issued.

Shortly after she'd reached her apartment and changed her clothes, someone knocked on the door.

"Scott! What are you doing here?" she asked as he stepped past her.

"How did it go?" His face was lined with tension as he took both her hands in his.

"I'm not sure. As well as could be expected, I guess. I told them everything I could. Now they have to decide if they believe me or not." Laurel felt a little of her anxiety ebb as Scott rubbed his hands up and down her arms.

"How long?" he said.

"I should know within the next forty-eight hours."

"You need to stay here, don't you?"

She nodded.

"I can't let you wait here alone." Scott stood less than a foot away, looking into her eyes with profound conviction.

Relief poured over her like a summer shower. Until that moment, she hadn't realized how much she'd needed his company and his support. She stepped toward him at the same moment he moved to her. He hugged her close. Not the intimate embrace of a lover, more like the warm, comforting hug of a longtime friend. When they pulled apart, Laurel felt something had changed inside her.

They sat together on the sofa for a while. Scott held her close without asking for conversation. After a time, they tried to watch a movie, but it didn't keep her mind off the impending verdict. Scott's efforts to divert her attention made her more nervous and edgy.

He put together sandwiches and fruit and coaxed her to eat. While she nibbled at her food, she told him about the upcoming volleyball game and how much she missed playing with the team. Scott commiserated, but it didn't help. When they finished eating and washing the dishes, they watched another movie, and Scott tried to interest her in a game of cards to distract her.

"Ever play strip poker?" He grinned mischievously as he shuffled the cards.

Laurel laughed, but the temptation was greater than she let on. "You've been too kind already. I couldn't accept such a generous, unselfish offer." She could probably beat the pants off him, but not tonight.

It was late when Scott said he had to go.

"I'm really glad you came over." She took her time gazing into his eyes.

He cupped her face with both hands as he lowered his mouth to hers. Her body swayed into his contours.

She was the first to pull back this time and say goodnight. She wanted to ask him to stay, but she knew she couldn't. The time wasn't right for them yet. Depending on the outcome of the grand jury report, it might never be right.

Scott had a hundred things he needed to do today, a half dozen places he needed to be, but he couldn't get Laurel out of his thoughts. He placed the take-out order of Chinese food on the passenger seat and turned the car toward Laurel's apartment.

He'd talked to his father again last night, but with no greater result than before. The man had grown more stubborn with age. That Scott had told him so was more of an act of frustration than a lapse in judgment.

Scott hated the waiting and could only imagine how much worse it had to be for Laurel. When he'd first arrived back in the States, he'd gone directly to his father. The tenuous agreement they'd reached that day again hung in jeopardy as the wheels his father had set in motion slowly ground away at Laurel Tanner.

It wasn't until Scott had spent several hours staring at the ceiling last night that he fully grasped the meaning of a grand jury indictment. The thought of her spending even a single day in a jail cell made his insides ache and his temper flare.

Scott parked the car and carried the take-out bag to the door. He rang the bell and waited. He started to ring again when the door opened. Laurel's face was a little pale. The fear in her eyes tore at his heart. He wanted to kick himself for not calling first. She exhaled a huge breath, obviously relieved when she saw it was him and not an officer with an arrest warrant.

He forced a smile. "My mother taught me to always bring food when I invite myself to a meal at a beautiful woman's house."

She looked at the ground between them and slowly shook her head before she stepped back and let him enter.

He watched her carefully as he set the bag down and unpacked the small white containers. She set plates and forks on the table, but her thoughts were obviously elsewhere.

"Hope you weren't kidding when you said you loved Chinese food." He'd picked up enough for a small army.

She gave him a halfhearted smile. She ate a bite or two, but mostly she just pushed the vegetables around. He found that he, too, was unable to eat. They made a few attempts at light conversation, but failed miserably.

Finally he dealt one hand of cards, but neither had the concentration to stick with it. When she rose to stand before the living room window, he followed and wrapped his arms around her.

It was what he had wanted to do since he'd walked in. As her fingers moved slowly over the muscles in his back, it took all his self-control not to crush her to him. He wanted to take their minds off their problems and the impending decision. He wanted to give her a short reprieve from worry. Hell, he wanted Laurel Tanner, period.

Her soft curves pressed against him. He saw the surrender in her eyes and knew that all he had to do was make the first move and she would be his. Her lips were so close, so achingly close... But he didn't want that kind of surrender, not in defeat. When she gave herself to him, he wanted to be able to revel in the sweetness of victory, a victory he fully intended to share.

"I...I think I'd better leave," he said, letting his thumbs trace the sides of her face.

Her chest rose sharply and she blinked a few times before nodding in agreement. The desire expressed on her face made his breath catch. He had to turn away before he made a mistake they would both regret.

At the door he turned to face her again. "Do you want me to be here tomorrow?"

"I don't think that would be wise. But thanks for offering," she said in a voice as tremulous as her smile. "I'll be fine."

Scott didn't like leaving her alone. "How will you...find out?"

"The captain promised he'd...let me know...as soon as he could. If he calls, it's good news...."

Scott held her gaze for several moments, unable to break away. But neither one said anything more about it. They both knew what would happen if she was indicted.

Laurel cleared the table and put their dishes in the dishwasher. The good feeling Scott had brought with him didn't last very long. Her problems intruded and she found no escape in the memory of his embrace, only anguish at what could have been and what might never be.

She slept little that night.

The next morning, she took her shower and got dressed with all the enthusiasm of a funeral procession. At a little past ten, Detective Sergeant Polk appeared at her door, his expression as somber as the outdated gray suit he wore. "Sgt. Laurel Tanner, I have a warrant for your arrest."

Devastated by his words, she couldn't find her breath to speak.

"You have the right to remain silent," he continued. "Anything you say can be used against you in a court of law."

She couldn't believe it. How many times in her career had she quoted those words? Yet never once had she heard their ominous ring. Nothing had ever felt as lonely as being on the receiving end of the Miranda warning.

"You have the right to have a lawyer present while you are questioned."

She hadn't even considered counsel.

"If you cannot afford a lawyer, the court will appoint one for you at your request without any expense to you."

She recognized the two uniformed officers who stood behind Detective Sergeant Polk with their eyes cast downward. The officers were new to the department and thus received the worst assignments.

"Do you understand your rights as I've explained them to you?" Detective Sergeant Polk asked, meeting her gaze.

"Yes." She nodded as the word stuck in her throat.

He pulled out a pair of stainless steel handcuffs exactly like those she carried. The humiliation of what she was about to endure struck her with the force of a shotgun blast. She bit down hard on her lower lip, determined not to let a single tear escape.

Chapter 8

Laurel entered the station through the sally port as she'd done hundreds of times before. The electronically locked doors seemed to buzz louder from her new perspective. She walked into the station with her head erect and shoulders squared. The silence that fell over the central processing area as she entered added to her humiliation. Across the room, Alice Johnson escorted a hooker to the fingerprint desk. Alice met her gaze with pity, and Laurel had to look away. Two rookies shot scornful glances her way, as if she'd betrayed them personally. No one spoke to her.

Despite the natural cynicism that came with years on the force, down deep inside, she still wanted to believe in the ideals that had led her into law enforcement. But it was damned hard to believe in anything at the moment.

Nothing looked the same as she remembered. She wondered if it would ever look the same again. Slowly, she lowered her gaze to her hands. The ink-stained pads of her fingers branded her like a scarlet letter. She drew in a deep breath and fought the ridiculous but nonetheless powerful urge to shout out the words *I'm innocent!* How many times had she heard them herself and thought, *Yeah, right!*

After what seemed like an eternity, she finally had some time alone with her attorney, Jeffrey Hays. She'd requested him for counsel because she liked and respected him. His youthful exuberance buoyed her spirits somewhat.

"I want you to tell me exactly what happened on the night in question." He put his pen down and leaned forward in his chair, watching her and listening carefully to everything she said.

She told him her account of the shooting, sure that he, like everyone else in the county, had already seen the skewed version in the paper.

His gaze came to rest steadily on hers. He spoke with quiet serenity. "Sergeant Tanner, I believe you."

She closed her eyes and let out a long, slow sigh. She hadn't realized how desperately she needed to hear someone say those words out loud. She only wished it had been Scott saying them.

"There's got to be a way of proving Mr. Delany's involvement. Drug profits are too lucrative to hide. We'll just have to look deeper into his finances and I'm sure something will turn up. In the meantime, I'm going to get you out of here." He wrote something on a yellow pad. "Give me a list of all your assets and available cash."

Laurel groaned.

Finally she had her arraignment. She entered a plea of not guilty and the judge set a trial date. To her great relief, Jeffrey Hays managed to get her released on her own recognizance.

It was nearly midnight when Laurel slipped inside her apartment and made her way to the kitchen in the darkness. The telephone rang and out of habit she reached to pick it up. "Hello."

"Sergeant Tanner, this is Mark Ross with the Orange County *Chronicle*."

"I have no comment, Mr. Ross." Laurel replaced the receiver and it immediately started ringing again. As soon as it stopped, she turned off the answering machine and took the phone off the hook for the night. For once, she just wanted to be left alone.

Scott put the phone down for the last time. The operator confirmed that Laurel's phone was off the hook, which meant she'd at least made it home. He had little confidence in that young attorney representing her. He wanted Laurel to have the best attorney money could buy.

Reluctantly, he had to admit that Jeffrey Hays had effectively kept anyone, including himself, from getting to her today. The kid had also gotten her out on her own recognizance, which Scott had learned when he called his own attorney to arrange for her bail. Realizing she was undoubtedly exhausted, he fought his own desire to see her tonight in favor of letting her rest.

The next morning, Scott went to his parents' home in response to a request his father had left on his answering machine. He knew better than to hope that the judge had had a change of heart concerning Laurel. He found his father waiting for him in the study.

The judge didn't waste time with a greeting. "Did you have money wired from London to post that woman's bail?"

Scott clenched his teeth to keep a vulgar retort from slipping off his tongue at his father's audacity. Losing his temper wouldn't help either of them. But he wasn't surprised by the bank's disclosure—the bank manager was a longtime friend and supporter of his father. "The charges against her are absurd."

His father scowled at him. "The accusations she's made against Brian are ludicrous."

"Well, you've just forced her to prove them in open court, haven't you?" Scott challenged.

"I didn't make that decision—a grand jury did. But of course, you've never been interested enough in the law to find out how it works," his father accused.

"I know how it works for some people," Scott said. He blew out a long breath, then continued in a more civil tone. "Laurel has no choice but to prove Brian was in some way connected to that drug deal. She won't give up—she can't afford to. She'll keep digging until she finds something."

"She won't find anything, because there is nothing to find," his father said with absolute authority.

"Are you so certain of that?" Scott fought the urge to tell him about the documents in Brian's safe. "Forgetting your own career for a moment, do you know what a scandal like that will do to Mother?" He took a few steps toward his father and looked him squarely in the eye, wanting to make him understand. "Damn it, Father, Brian is dead. Don't let that blind spot you have for him destroy Mother...or Laurel."

His father's eyes narrowed, piercing in their intensity as they studied him. Scott's skin prickled and once again he knew he'd said too much. As his father continued to stare at him in an intense silence, Scott had the feeling someone else would have to pay for his mistake. From the distant, thoughtful look that settled over his father, he surmised that person would be Laurel.

Scott stopped by the kitchen, where his mother was having her morning coffee. He greeted her warmly, hiding the anger his father had stirred inside him. He struggled to keep his mind on their conversation as they shared poppy-seed muffins and coffee. After a few minutes, Scott looked at his watch. "I have to run. I have to make a call to New York."

"You can use the phone in the study, dear," his mother offered.

It was tempting, but as angry as he was at his father, he didn't want him to have a stroke. Scott smiled as he bent to kiss her cheek. "Thanks, but I didn't bring the documents I need with me."

The following day, Laurel reported to Jeff's office, as requested. She knew she was going to have to start from scratch and retell every detail. She sat down in a comfortable chair as the door shut behind her.

Jeff dropped his legal pad on the desk and sat down heavily in his chair. "Exactly what is your relationship with Scott Delany?"

Startled by the question, it took her a couple of seconds to respond. "What do you mean?" she asked cautiously, noting the scowl on his face.

"I found out this morning that a pricey lawyer from L.A. has been inquiring about your case. He was prepared to post your bail." Jeff's gaze didn't flinch. "I must say it took no small effort on my part to find out that Scott Delany had put him up to it."

"He did?" As the meaning behind Scott's gesture clarified, a warmth infused her and she felt moisture gather in her eyes.

"Yes, he did. If you want this guy to represent you—"

"No," she said. "I want you."

"Don't be hasty. Think about it. He's one of the best. He has—"

"No," she repeated. "I don't have to think about it."

Jeff hesitated, taking her measure. "Okay. First, I have to advise you against getting involved with any of the Delanys until the charges against you are dropped or you're acquitted."

"I understand," she said without agreeing.

He picked up his pen and put it to paper. "I've got to know everything or I can't help you, Laurel. I can assure you the prosecution will know."

She told him how she and Scott had met and about the trip to Brian's house, where they'd discovered the papers in the hidden safe. Jeff scribbled notes on his yellow pad while she spoke. She mentioned her hunch about Scott knowing something more about Brian that might help her case.

He stopped writing and stared at her. "I'll have my investigator talk to Scott Delany."

"Scott is really caught in the middle. He wants to do what's right, but he doesn't want to hurt his parents. And neither do I."

Jeff put down his pen and sat back in his chair with his hands steepled in front of him. "Someone always gets hurt in a trial, Laurel."

She looked away, not wanting him to see her own doubt.

"Sergeant, I must caution you to be careful." He picked up the pen. "Okay, I'm going to bring in my investigator now and we'll start at the beginning."

Jeff introduced her to his private investigator, Phil Macky. Standing beside her young attorney, the investigator looked as if he ought to be in high school. Jeff caught her look and explained that Phil's youthful appearance was one of the reasons he'd been chosen for this particular job. He could infiltrate groups like the one at the tavern a lot more effectively.

She spent several long, tedious hours going over and over the details of the shooting with Jeff and Phil. Jeff also asked her to recall everything she could about Stanley Murdock and the documents in the safe.

Phil asked her questions about her past relationship with Brian Delany. She told him everything except what had happened that night in her apartment. That part, she'd decided, was best kept to herself.

After Phil left, Jeff ran her through a long, tiring session of questions designed to help prepare her for the trial. Finally he said she'd had enough. "Why don't you go home and get some rest? You look like you haven't slept in days."

"Sleep won't make my troubles go away." She ran a hand wearily through her hair.

"No, but there's nothing else for you to do right now. Take the weekend off. Try to put this out of your mind for a few days. Give me a chance to see what I can come up with." He was asking for something she didn't give easily—her trust.

Laurel stood and extended her hand. "I'll call you next week." She thanked him and left the office.

She hadn't seen Scott since before the indictment, but not for any lack of trying on his part. He had left several messages on her answering machine. The sound of his voice on the tape had her yearning to see him again, longing for the comfort she knew she could find in his arms. She'd been giving Jeff's advice careful consideration. Experience had taught her to go with her gut feeling—only in this case, she wasn't sure if it was her gut speaking or her heart.

Late Friday evening, Scott called again. It was good to hear his voice. "You need a break, Laurel." He paused. "And I want to see you."

Her pulse picked up speed. She wanted to see him, too, but she hesitated.

"My family has a cabin in the mountains near Big Bear. It belonged to my grandfather." He sounded a little nervous. "After the way the last few days have gone, I know you could use some relaxation."

"That's what my lawyer said. You guys make it sound so easy." Jeff had asked her to give him a little time to work on her case. Both he and Scott were right about her present physical and emotional state. She was exhausted; perhaps she'd be more clearheaded if she allowed herself this short respite.

"I don't know." She stalled for time to think about where the weekend might lead on a more personal level. She cared for Scott deeply and she was certainly attracted to him physically. He had a powerful effect on her, she couldn't deny it. But she wasn't ready to make a commitment on the spot.

"It's peaceful and quiet up there. There are lots of trails to walk and the cabin is big and comfortable. Three bedrooms . . . with doors that lock."

"Are you reading my mind?" She laughed.

"I'm afraid to." He laughed, too, and the tension eased somewhat. "Seriously, though, I know this sounds like a line, but I'm not trying to push you into anything you're not ready for. I just want us to be able to spend some time together—"

"Away from here." She finished for him.

"Yes," he admitted. "You—that is, we—need to put this aside for a while."

"All right," she said, forcing Jeff's warning out of her mind. She told herself that the butterflies in her stomach were just anticipation of some time alone with Scott.

Early the next morning, Scott placed her suitcase beside his in the trunk of his car. They left the coast and headed inland for San Bernardino and the mountains beyond. Three hours later, they passed through the bustling city and began to climb out of the smoggy urban valley. Scott cursed and hit the brakes when someone cut in front of him without signaling.

"There's no better way to get to know a person than watching him drive through bumper-to-bumper traffic," Laurel said. Scott looked chagrined, and she laughed. She already felt better just getting out of the familiar territory of her city. The more she thought about it, the more she looked forward to the time away, the time with Scott.

Rugged pines dotted the winding mountain road as they continued toward Big Bear. Eventually, they stopped at a market in the little mountain community of Running Springs and bought groceries. What had always been a tedious chore in the past now had Laurel in stitches, as Scott picked up items and recited lines from commercials, adding a decidedly British twist to each. Suddenly, he stopped in the frozen food aisle. "Butter brickle," he exclaimed as he reached for the carton of ice cream. "I haven't had this since I was a kid."

She groaned. "Do you know how much fat there is in that?"

"No problem." He led her to another aisle. "We'll clean out our arteries with a little wine." He picked up two bottles.

Laurel was still shaking her head when they got back into the car. Shortly they arrived at an isolated cabin nestled in the pines. It wasn't anything like she'd expected. Though large, as Scott had said, it was old and rustic and totally charming. From what little she knew of the Delanys, she realized she'd expected something more pretentious.

"Like I said, it was my grandfather's place." He handed her the lighter bag of groceries and lifted the other one for himself.

It was Laurel's turn to be chagrined. She didn't usually fall prey to preconceived ideas about people or places. It embarrassed her that she had now and that Scott had seen it in her expression.

Original log walls formed the exterior of the house. The red metal roof had been a recent addition, no doubt because of the fire danger in the hot, dry summer months. From the front porch, she looked around outside. The rugged terrain concealed any neighbors they might have.

Inside, they went straight to the kitchen, which was actually one corner of a huge open room. She placed her sack on a long table that sat across from the kitchen. The living area held tradition, both in design and decoration, from the massive stone fireplace to the crocheted afghan on the rocker by the picture window. The homeyness filled her with wonder. It also reminded her of something out of her reach.

"Sorry there's no air-conditioning." He leaned over the sink to open a window, then turned on a ceiling fan. When the groceries had been put away, he went to retrieve their baggage. "Come on, I'll give you the tour." He placed her bag in the first bedroom, which was between the bathroom and another bedroom at the north end of the house. Scott took the room beside hers, then showed her the third bedroom, at the other end of the house. It was much bigger than his.

The light, cheerful atmosphere they'd shared all morning elevated her spirits. She couldn't help but smile as they stood in the big bedroom so far from hers, watching each other carefully. "Wouldn't you be more comfortable in this big room?" she asked.

He smiled. "But it would be so far for you to walk if you got lonely in the middle of the night."

She laughed. "You did say all the bedroom doors had locks, didn't you?"

"Every one of 'em," he said with a grin.

"Good." In a rush of bravado, she let her shoulder brush against his chest as she walked past him to the door. "You might need a lock on your door before the weekend is over."

She was all the way to the kitchen before the house filled with the deep rumble of Scott's laughter.

Chapter 9

After settling in, they took a long walk in the forest behind the cabin. Holding her hand as they walked, Scott talked a lot about his grandfather. He'd spent many happy days here as a boy before the elder Delany died. In all his reminiscing, Laurel noticed that he didn't mention Brian or his father. She wouldn't be surprised if he was avoiding the topic out of consideration for her feelings, and to some extent she was sure that was the case, but she detected something else. From what little he had told her of his father and Brian, she wondered if he truly had no fond memories from his youth to call on for comfort in these trying times.

At the top of a small ridge, he turned his back to the valley and leaned against a large boulder, pulling her to stand between his thighs.

She rested her hands on his shoulders as she looked at the beautiful expanse of ponderosa pines beyond the rim. The warmth of his hands seeped through her thin top to her waist. A gentle breeze stirred the treetops and carried a fragrant pine scent to their private vista.

He pulled her closer.

She looked into his eyes as her pulse found a new pace. "You're missing the view."

He chuckled. "Don't bet on it." His mouth met hers halfway. There was nothing hurried about the kiss. Their lips came together lightly, moved one way, then another. At the same moment they pulled back, eyes seeking eyes. She didn't know what she expected to see—perhaps lust? To some degree that was there, but she saw much more. She saw need and understanding, passion and compassion. Certainly she couldn't be imagining all that.

He tipped his lips up ever so slightly, just enough to be an offering. She accepted and delighted in it. He kissed her cheek, her chin, her throat. His lips moved along her collarbone, then he pulled her into a tighter embrace and buried his face against her neck. He held her like that for a long time.

Amidst the soft whistle of the breeze, the two of them grew quiet.

"What are you thinking about?" she asked, combing his hair with her fingers.

He sighed against her throat. "We can't really get away from it completely, can we?"

She pulled back to see his face. "Maybe we shouldn't try."

"Maybe."

Laurel brought his head to her chest. Hugging him close, she rested her chin on his hair and closed her eyes. If only things could be different....

Her thoughts and feelings for Scott were so twisted into what was happening around them it was hard to separate the two, but she wanted to know everything about him. She didn't want him to have to edit every story about his relationship with his family because of her.

"Tell me what it was like growing up in your family and being an identical twin."

Scott tensed beneath her embrace. Slowly he lifted his head. He wore a frown of forewarning.

She gave him a reassuring smile. "I want to know everything about you."

He told her about his relationship with Brian. "It was great when we were little. I always had someone there for me, a companion and a confidant. Mother usually dressed us alike, so we drew a lot of attention. We thought alike, too. It was kind of weird sometimes." The lift of his brow questioned her receptiveness.

"How so?" she encouraged.

"For example, one of us would start a sentence and the other would finish it, word for word. Sometimes we would just look at each other and know things. As we got older, we began to resent the intrusion into our private thoughts. If one of us had a crush on a particular girl, the other always knew." The corners of Scott's mouth slanted downward.

She thought briefly about her date with Brian.

He started speaking again and the frown vanished. "We got into more than our share of mischief, too. Brian came up with some pretty crazy schemes."

Laurel wondered what had caused that momentary frown. Was it a memory from his childhood or something more recent? She didn't intrude.

"Brian was more than an extrovert. Ever since we were kids he had this—" he paused and shrugged his shoulders "—this presence. I know it sounds crazy, but my dad knew it and so did Brian. He could get people—grown-ups and kids alike—to stop and listen to him, to do whatever he said.

It was a magnetism like some popular religious or political figures have. John Wayne had it, too."

"So did Charles Manson and Jim Jones," Laurel said without thinking.

Scott dropped his hands to his thighs.

"I'm sorry. That was a thoughtless thing to say." Laurel sighed and rubbed her temples.

Scott let out a long, slow breath. "No, you're right." He reached for her hands. "I think I knew it a long time ago, I just didn't want to admit it. The bond we had went beyond that of normal siblings. It's funny, but admitting to Brian's faults is like admitting to my own." He lowered his gaze to their entwined fingers. "I can remember all the times I covered for Brian, knowing I shouldn't, but feeling somehow responsible for him."

A distant tone invaded his voice. "Brian always knew what buttons to push, and I let him push them, over and over, until it became a habit for both of us." Years of regret shone in his eyes.

She placed her hands on his shoulders and kneaded the tight muscles beneath her fingers, listening to each word, though it hurt to hear.

"Before we were born, my father used to tell my mother how much he wanted a son," he went on somewhat wistfully. "My grandfather was an attorney. He did what he could to pave the way for my father's career. Father, in turn, wanted to do the same for his son. From a very early age I rebelled against the idea. But Brian took to it right from the start. I'll never forget the day he told Father he'd been accepted at law school. Father had tears in his eyes when he hugged Brian. Part of me was jealous and part of me was proud."

Laurel watched the expressions play across Scott's face, and her heart ached for him because of all the hurts he'd silently endured. Scott lived with guilt he didn't deserve, guilt that would remain unresolved because of Brian's untimely death. She bit down on her lower lip as her own sense of guilt prevailed.

Though she had tried to hide it, she was having trouble dealing with the shooting. To extinguish a human life would bother anyone, regardless of who was to blame. But she hadn't killed an unknown assailant, and the fact that the man she'd killed was Scott's brother, his identical twin brother, made it all the harder for her. Every time she saw that face, her chest tightened before her mind made the correction.

Scott cursed softly and stood up, pulling her into his arms. "I'm sorry. I wasn't thinking." He hugged her close. "I shouldn't talk about Brian like that."

"It's okay," she said. "We knew this was going to be complicated."

"But I shouldn't have said—"

"Yes, you should have." She blinked away the stinging in her eyes. "Brian and his death are standing between us. If we're going to have any kind of relationship, we've got to be able to talk openly to each other, even if it is sometimes painful to hear."

Scott swallowed.

She could see his hesitation in the fine lines creasing his brow. She lifted her hand to his cheek.

Covering her hand with his own, Scott turned his head to place a kiss on her palm. The warm breath of his sigh tickled her skin.

"It must have been very hard for you growing up watching your father develop such a close relationship with Brian." She kept her hand on his cheek after he released it.

"I had my own way of handling it." He finally grinned, easing the tension a little. "I played the rebel. Oh, I didn't get into any real trouble. I simply spoke my mind at the most inappropriate times. Once I nearly caused my poor mother to have a heart attack during a bridge club meeting." His smile became melancholy. "She was an innocent caught up in all our troubles. If I had it to do over again . . ."

"Life doesn't work that way, Scott." She wanted to convince him to let it go. "We have to learn to live with the decisions we make and pray we don't repeat the bad ones." She placed both her hands on his chest and felt the steady rhythm of his heart beneath her fingers.

"That was one of my intentions when I left for London four years ago. Brian had gotten himself into some serious trouble. He'd always been a thrill seeker. He liked living on the edge. High-stakes gambling provided that thrill. Of course, illegal gambling didn't sit well with his chosen profession. Brian never thought he'd get caught, but just in case, he had set up the perfect alibi. Me."

Laurel's heart pounded, but she didn't interrupt.

"Brian had used my identity when he gambled. He'd dressed like me. He even had my ID duplicated. God, I was furious at him." Scott shook his head in dismay.

Though he didn't say so, Laurel suspected he'd also been very hurt by the way Brian had used him.

"Anyway, something went wrong with his ruse. Someone had found out the truth. Brian was in way over his head. He said if I didn't help him get enough money for a payoff, this guy would expose him, and his career would be ruined. He didn't have to say how that would affect our parents. We both knew."

"So what happened?" she asked.

Sadness filled his eyes. "I'd never seen him that desperate. Brian needed more money than I could scrape together. He begged for my help, begged me to ask our father. For the sake of the family, I agreed and told him I needed the money to start my business in London. My father saw through the lie and assumed I was the one in trouble. I never understood how he could be so quick to judge and condemn me and be so fair with everyone else. He said I was irresponsible and he wasn't about to bail me out.

"When he lashed out at me that last time, telling me all the things I should have told Brian, I knew the cycle was over, and so did Brian. I wanted to get as far away from them as I could. I finally realized I'd been wrong—about myself and about Brian. His drive was fueled as much by a weakness in his character as it was by a need to fulfill our father's expectations." Scott sat quietly for a few seconds, the expression on his face a banner of remorse.

"I kept perpetuating that weakness every time I bailed him out of trouble instead of letting him take his lumps like everyone else. Maybe if he'd learned at an earlier age—"

Laurel framed his jaw with her fingers. "What you did, you did out of love. You can't go around second-guessing yourself or using hindsight to judge your actions."

"That's easy for you to say. If you had it to do over again, you'd do the same thing. Laurel, I can't say that."

"That's true, but I'm a cop, and to me, Brian was just another suspect. He was your *brother*. When you love someone, you don't always behave rationally."

His chest rose sharply. "God, don't I know it."

Their eyes met, and her heart began to beat faster. *Love*. Was that what she felt for Scott? She could see him puzzling over the same question. Whatever it was between them, they had both resisted it as long as they could. As he lowered his mouth to hers, rational thought left her. She returned his kiss with a bold hunger of her own. The low groan he released sent a wave of fire rippling through her. Her body felt formless as she melted against his firm contours, pulling him closer.

The breeze caught her hair, reminding her they were on a public trail. Slowly, she ended the kiss, but in her heart she knew it was only a matter of time. The electricity building between them grew stronger and more difficult to contain with each kiss. The more time she spent with him, the more her reasons for restraint dissolved. "We should be getting back. You're bound to be hungry by now."

Scott smiled, but made no comment as he held her waist until they were both steady on their feet. Lacing their fingers together, they headed back the way they'd come, strolling along the path in companionable silence.

Halfway to the cabin he stopped and gave her a serious look. "There's something I should have asked you before."

She held her breath.

"Can you cook?"

Her eyes widened in surprise and embarrassment, then they both broke into laughter.

Throughout lunch they talked and laughed, frequently touching as they sat side by side at the table. They kept the meal simple: cold sandwiches, fruit and diet sodas. Her troubles slipped farther away as Scott peeled an orange and fed her juicy slices with his fingers. It was nearly two o'clock when they finished eating. Laurel stood and took her plate to the sink. Scott followed close behind. He reached around her to set his plate in the sink as she turned. He didn't back away. She smelled the tangy scent of the orange they'd shared.

All she had to do was lift her hand to his chest and give a gentle push. She couldn't do it, didn't *want* to do it. Her heart pounded with excitement. She tipped her head back slightly to look into his eyes. Their darkness captivated her as they moved from her eyes down to her mouth and back.

"I want you," he said in a low, husky tone free of all pretense. His hands rested on the counter on either side of her, but he held his body away from her. The decision would be hers alone, not made under duress or under the hypnotic spell he could weave with his touch.

Laurel reached up to pull him closer, but he resisted. She wasn't surprised to find he needed to hear the words. "I want you, too."

Slowly he narrowed the distance between them, keeping his eyes steadily fixed on hers. He enclosed her in the circle of his arms, moving his hands down her back, creating a fire under the soft cotton of her T-shirt.

She wrapped her arms around his neck, pulling him tighter with a spell of her own.

He lowered his head until his lips touched hers, the lightness of the touch at once erotic and maddening. She stretched upward to deepen the kiss. His hands stroked up and down her sides, his thumbs lightly skimming over the sides of her breasts. She ached to know the feel of his bare skin against hers. When she strained against him, he let out a slow moan, then moved his hands to cup her buttocks.

Lifting her off the floor, he sat her on the edge of the countertop, rotating his hips into the space between her legs. Her breath grew short. He pulled his mouth from hers and trailed moist, butterfly-soft kisses down her neck to her collarbone. The light caresses left her wanting more.

"So sweet . . ." he whispered against her throat.

She wanted a lot more. "Wait," she breathed heavily.

As he lifted his mouth from her skin and gazed into her eyes, she reached for the hem of her T-shirt and pulled it over her head.

Slowly, he let his gaze drift downward. She felt a moment of anxiety as she remembered the unfeminine scars of the bullet wound. Scott slid the strap of her bra down her shoulder, then lowered his mouth to the entrance scar, kissing the still-puffy pink flesh with tenderness. He ran his fingers lightly over the larger scar on her back. "Do I need to be careful of these?" He looked into her eyes.

She shook her head.

He cocked his head to one side, unconvinced.

"They aren't too sore anymore," she said, knowing he'd be careful, anyway.

He held her gaze for a long moment. "You are so beautiful." He traced a path with the pads of his fingers, starting at her eyebrows and working his way down the bridge of her nose. As he traced her lips, she captured his finger with her tongue. He sucked in a deep breath and she released him. He drew a moist line down the lacy edge of her bra. When his tongue followed his finger, Laurel gasped for breath.

He pushed the fabric aside and circled her nipple with his tongue again and again before he began to suckle. He repeated the caresses on her other breast.

She forgot everything but Scott. He made her feel. He made her want. As he satisfied one need, he created another.

"Laurel," he said in a husky whisper. When he lifted his face to hers, his eyes held a fire to match her own. His lips were warm and moist. She couldn't resist a quick taste. "Are you sure?" He kissed her again in a frenzied haste, then spoke in a raspy voice. "I want you, but you have to be ready."

She smiled against his lips. "I couldn't be more ready."

"That's not what I meant, and you know it."

She slid her mouth gently over his, nibbling and teasing until he moaned.

"Laurel?"

His blue eyes bored into her with such intensity she could hardly breathe. She'd never felt like this before. Need consumed her. "Scott...Delany..." Her breathy whisper grew from a plea to a demand. "I want to make love with you. In your bed. Now."

He kissed her again, then scooped her off the counter and carried her to his room. As he lowered her feet to the floor, her bravado slipped away.

He pulled his T-shirt over his head. She pushed her fingers through the dark curly hairs sprinkled over his broad chest. Her open palms explored the hard muscles of his shoulders, his back, the plane of his abdomen.

She reached for the waistband of her shorts.

His hands covered hers. "Let me." His fingers caressed her skin as he slowly worked the elastic band over her hips. His mouth found hers again. He kissed her chin, her neck, her chest, before he dropped to his knees. She quivered with excitement as his mouth moved down her abdomen. Through the smooth nylon of her panties, he gave her a kiss that promised more intimacies to come.

Scott reined in his self-control as he stood and slipped out of his jeans. He couldn't remember ever wanting anyone so badly, but he also wanted their first time to be as special for her as it already was for him. He reached for a condom and set it on the nightstand before lifting her into his arms again. He placed her on the bed and laid down beside her, content for a moment to simply look at her.

She didn't stay put for long. Instead, to his delight, she pushed him to his back, leaned over his chest and began a foray with her tongue that was sure to elevate more than his blood pressure.

At her slightest touch, his skin tingled with pleasure. She stirred within him feelings both new and familiar. As her tongue skipped from one of his nipples to the other, her hand skimmed over his hips and thighs, bringing a moan to his lips.

"You don't play fair," he said with a ragged breath.

"Who says I'm playing?" Laurel's eyes flashed a challenge he couldn't resist.

Grasping both her hands in one of his and holding them above her head, he rolled her to her back. He leaned over her, his mouth millimeters from her inviting lips.

Then he remembered her proficiency at self-defense. He pulled back and, while resting on his elbow, glanced at her knees. "You're not going to hurt me again, are you?" he said.

"Don't you trust me?" She stared up at him with warm, sparkling eyes.

When he let go of her hands, she rolled onto her side, facing him. Slowly she brought her knee up between his legs until he felt the front of her thigh pressing intimately against his briefs. When her hand slid slowly down his chest and abdomen, he took in a deep breath and held it, awaiting her touch.

"This time," she said as she ran her open palm over the straining cotton, "if I hurt you, I promise I'll kiss it and make it better."

Scott knew he'd reached his limit of teasing. He wanted her too much, needed her too badly. When he captured her mouth with his, he knew there would be no stopping either one of them from then on. He unfastened the clasp of her bra and slid it from her shoulders. He lowered his head to suckle at her breasts. Her soft gasps and sweet sighs inflamed him. He slid her panties down and off. Her hands were as quick and demanding as his own as they worked together to remove his briefs. He returned to her mouth, kissing her long and deeply. He caressed the curve of her waist and the gentle flare of her hips. As his hand moved lightly down her abdomen and over the mound of tight feminine curls, he felt her shiver in anticipation.

It took more control than he realized he possessed to make his exploration of her slow and gentle. But he wanted to give her pleasure, wanted that very much. He dipped one finger inside her, then began the slow gentle massage that made her moan and melt beneath him. When he felt her body tense and tighten, he held still and let her control the pressure of the contact through her climax.

When her breathing slowed, he began again. Only this time he would be with her. When she was ready once again, he slipped on the condom and spread her legs just enough to slip between them. He supported himself on his elbows, not because it was the gentlemanly thing to do, but because he wanted to see her face, look into her eyes when he possessed her. He could feel her heat now as he paused, waiting. "Laurel."

She opened her eyes.

Slowly, he sheathed himself in her warmth. As her body adjusted to accommodate him, he began to move. "You feel so good."

Her fingers threaded through his hair, pulling his head down for a kiss. It was long and slow, mimicking the motions of their bodies. He withdrew from her, teasing her with only the smallest portion of what he had to offer. She lifted her hips to him, demanding more. Their rhythm built to a frantic pace. He couldn't last much longer. She whispered his name in a plea filled with desperation. Her body went rigid, and he felt her quiver. The last thing he heard as he met his own end was the sound of her voice calling his name, binding his heart to hers as tightly as she'd bonded with his body.

He collapsed against her for a moment, totally spent, yet full beyond measure. Pondering the strange sensation, he turned to his back, pulling her close. For the first time since Brian's death, Scott felt like a whole person again. He'd found something precious in the woman beside him, something that made him feel complete. And that completeness scared him.

The invisible bond between him and Brian had been broken forever. For so much of his life he'd been half of a whole. His identity had been defined not only by who he was, but who Brian was, as well. But was his identity now dependent on Laurel? Was he substituting one kind of a bond for another?

Laurel snuggled up closer and threaded her fingers between his, squeezing the questions from his mind.

Chapter 10

Laurel fell into a deep, trouble-free sleep after making love with Scott. When she awoke a few hours later, the space beside her was empty and Scott's clothes no longer littered the floor. She dressed and stepped silently into the living room. Scott stood across the room, his hand braced against the window casing as he stared out into the woods, a frown spoiling the perfect lines of his face. All of a sudden, she felt vulnerable and unsure of herself. With all the problems between them, it was probably silly to think his expression might have something to do with their lovemaking. But that didn't stop her from worrying as she walked across the room to stand beside him.

As he reached for her hand, the smile on his lips and in his eyes laid her fears to rest. He wrapped his arms around her in a loose embrace. "There's one more place I'd like to show you if you think you're up to another walk."

Looking up into a pair of sharp blue eyes, she realized she had some things she needed to tell Scott. But she didn't want to do it here. "Are you insinuating there's something wrong with my body?" She gave him an intimate smile.

He pulled her close and whispered in a low, seductive voice, "There's not a thing wrong with your body...not the way it looks—" he slid his gaze appreciatively over her "—or the way it feels—" his hands wandered down her spine "—or the way it moves when—"

"Okay. That's enough." She slipped out of his grasp. "Or we won't make it out the door."

This time when they left the cabin, they followed a small winding path down through the woods. Scott's arm stayed across her shoulders and she held him close at the waist. She wondered why she wasn't having any second thoughts about making love with him. By all rights, she should be concerned about her future and how it would look at the trial if anyone found out about her relationship with the identical twin of the man she shot. But none of those things seemed to matter when he held her in his arms and stared deeply into her eyes. They strolled at a leisurely pace, stopping from time to time to admire a squirrel at play or to share a kiss.

"When we talked earlier, we agreed that we needed to feel free to be open with each other about our past." She searched his eyes.

The arm around her shoulder tensed slightly. "That's right."

"You also said once that you wanted to hear the truth, even if it wasn't pleasant." She paused for a moment. "Do you still feel that way?"

Scott turned and placed his hands on her shoulders. Caring and concern shone in his eyes. His voice was whisper-soft. "I want to hear anything you feel you need to talk about."

Though she was encouraged by his sincerity, she stumbled over the words. "I'd like to tell you about Brian and me...before the shooting. I...I want you to understand."

His eyes narrowed, causing tiny creases at their corners. "I want to understand, too," he said with a hint of caution.

She took his hand and started walking slowly down the path, hoping her nervousness wouldn't show. "It's kind of ironic, but Brian and I worked together on a special drug-free-youth program about two years ago." Her step faltered for a second as it occurred to her that Brian might have been involved with drugs at that time. If so, he'd had the perfect opportunity to infiltrate the high schools and junior highs. She tried to recall if there were any particular kids he'd been close to or to whom he had given special attention.

"How long did you work with him?" Scott interrupted her thoughts.

"About three months. We met with various groups of students and with parents. Once the program was set up and in place, he was pretty much out of the picture. The department continued on its own.

"The day his portion was finished, he asked me out to dinner. The invitation hit me out of the blue. He'd been polite and professional the whole time we'd been together, but he'd never shown any personal interest in me." She stopped and turned to face Scott. "He was attractive, and I hadn't been seeing anyone for some time. It's not easy to meet people or start relationships when you're a cop. It's even harder when you're a female cop."

A muscle quivered in Scott's jaw as he waited for her to continue. She knew this was going to be hard for him to hear. Lifting her hand to stroke his cheek, she said, "It takes more than a little attention or a pretty face to get to me."

She brought her hand down to the center of his chest. "It's what's in here that counts. After several hours alone with Brian, I realized I hadn't learned anything about him. I mean . . . I didn't know him any better than I had before we spent the evening together." She paused, remembering how he'd talked about himself during dinner as though he was a political candidate seeking reelection.

"Anyway, he apparently thought we were getting along better than I did." She shivered slightly as the memory intruded. "He kind of fast-talked his way in the front door when he took me home. He said he wanted to give me a good-night kiss, but there was nothing good about it."

Scott stood perfectly still. No emotion showed on his face. She wasn't sure if she should continue, but now that she'd started, she had to get it all out.

"He didn't listen when I tried to tell him I didn't feel the same way. When he ignored my demand to stop, I panicked and froze for a few seconds. He tore my blouse." She was no longer on a trail in the mountains, but back in her apartment. Her body began to tremble, but she couldn't stop the words. "I couldn't believe it was happening to me. Then all of a sudden I realized it was up to me to stop him. I used my knee to get away, then I pulled my gun out of my purse and held it on him."

Scott's hands moved slowly up and down her arms until her trembling stopped. The warmth of his touch stilled the chilling memory. "I should have busted him right on the spot." She shook her head. "He said the bad press would destroy all the good we'd accomplished with the program. He was right, so I gave him a strong warning, told him he couldn't have everything in this world just because he wanted it, and let him go." She searched Scott's eyes. "Don't you see? I did the same thing you were kicking yourself about. I didn't make him accept the responsibility for his actions, either.''

Scott stood there in a thoughtful silence for a few moments, then spoke with a slow realization. "That's what you were remembering that night when we'd been out to dinner and I took you home, back to the exact spot, and kissed you?''

Laurel licked her lips and nodded. For a second, she saw Brian's face before her.

"Damn. I wish I'd known.''

"It wasn't the same, if that's what you're thinking. I felt I knew you and could trust you long before we got back to my apartment that night. Without knowing I needed proof, you gave it to me, anyway.''

"Yeah. And I kicked myself all the way home.'' He shrugged off her praise in a way that was so typically Scott. "I wanted you so badly I didn't get to sleep until dawn.''

Laurel smiled. "I was fighting what I was feeling for you.'' She framed his face with her hands. "Guess I'll have to make it up to you, won't I?''

She snuggled closer, needing the reassurance of his arms around her. Her breasts pressed against his chest. Her nipples tightened, craving his touch.

A noise sounded in the bushes off to one side. She reacted instinctively, focusing her attention immediately on the source. A young doe crossed the path several yards in front of them. Laurel sighed, releasing the tension with her breath.

"There's a small stream up ahead,'' Scott explained. "We used to play there when we were kids.''

They made the short walk, and Laurel couldn't resist wading in the cool water. Though the conversation had lightened since the doe first appeared, a niggling sense of uneasiness tugged at her mind. It began when she had started wondering if Brian had been involved with drugs two years ago, but it was more than curiosity about the past. She sensed that something important was eluding her, some vital piece of information that lay within her grasp, yet remained undefined.

Dinner consisted of steaks grilled outside on the barbecue, a tossed salad and baked potatoes. Afterward, they sat out on the deck until the mosquitoes chased them inside.

It was too warm for a fire, but they moved to the sofa that faced the empty hearth and finished the bottle of wine they'd started with dinner.

Their time together was growing short. Laurel knew she would soon be back in the city, spending every free moment trying to prove her innocence.

"I have a business meeting with my partner in Los Angeles next week," Scott said. "It's about the telecommunications company we're trying to purchase. If you need me to be there..."

She laced her fingers in his. "Thank you, but I'll be fine."

He told her that the negotiations were progressing as expected and that everything looked hopeful. If circumstances had been different, she'd be thrilled by the prospect, but she couldn't allow herself to hope. Laurel had known too much disappointment in the past. She couldn't think that far ahead just then, when her own future was so uncertain. All she could count on was what she had right now.

"I think I'd like to take a bath." She stroked his thumb lazily with her own.

The smoldering look came back into his eyes. "Do you want some company?"

He turned her hand over and nibbled at her palm. Her breath caught. All she could do was nod.

"Go ahead. I'll put things away here and join you," he said, releasing her hand.

As Laurel went into the bathroom and started running water into the old claw-foot tub, she heard Scott closing the windows and locking the front door. She knew there would be no interruptions in what might be their first and last night together.

She piled her hair on top of her head, then peeled off her clothes and lowered herself into the tub of warm water. She heard sounds coming from the bedroom as she closed her eyes and leaned her head against the rim of the tub.

"That can't be very comfortable on your neck," Scott said from the doorway.

Laurel opened her eyes but didn't move. "You have a better suggestion?"

"As a matter of fact..." Scott slipped his bathrobe off to reveal his lean, sinewy body.

She let her gaze linger over the mat of dark curly hair that tapered toward his waist. His legs were sprinkled with the same dark hair. His skin had an even, bronze tone except for a narrow patch across his hips, which drew her immediate attention.

He stepped closer.

She raised herself up straight, pulling a much-needed gulp of air into her lungs as she did so.

Scott slipped in behind her, his legs straddling her hips. "Now, try this." Holding her shoulders to his chest, he leaned back against the back of the tub. "Better?"

"Much." Laurel closed her eyes as Scott's arms wrapped around her, one high on her chest, the other at her waist. She sighed with delight as she placed her hands on his forearms and rested her head comfortably on his chest. She wanted the serenity to last forever.

He leaned his cheek against the side of her head and issued a sigh that echoed her own contentment. They stayed
like that for some time, not speaking or moving, enjoying
the simple pleasure of their closeness as they lay in the warm
water.

Slowly Laurel let her fingers explore the hair-roughened
texture of Scott's forearm. She opened her eyes as his hand
scooped up the warm water and dribbled it down first one
breast, then the other. His fingers followed the droplets,
trailing lightly down her chest, then skimming over her nipple. She delighted in every sensation.

He took the bar of soap and began to languidly cover her
skin. Each cleansed spot felt vigorously alive as he raised her
up to a sitting position. With soapy hands he rubbed her
shoulders and back. The sensual massage relaxed some
muscles while tightening others. He rinsed off the soap, then
turned her around to face him.

Laurel was surprised by her own lack of modesty as he
lifted her legs one at a time and placed them on top of his so
her bent knees gently touched his sides. The soap slipped
from his hands and fell between them.

"I'll get it," she said a little too quickly, causing Scott to
smile.

"That's not the soap," he gasped, closing his eyes.

Laurel had a heady feeling of power as she turned the ta-
bles on him. She ran her soapy hands over his arms, his
shoulders and his chest. As the slick pads of her fingers
traced concentric circles around his nipples, their centers
rose to tiny hardened peaks and a small tremor shook his
body.

"Is the water getting too cold?" she asked coyly.

The look he gave her alone could have raised the temperature ten degrees. He reached for the back of her neck,
drawing her forward, and kissed her hard on the mouth. "I

think my body's had about all the bathing it can take for now.''

They quickly finished their bath and stepped out of the tub. She let him take her towel and dry her off as slowly and as thoroughly as he wanted, knowing she'd get her chance at him, too. As he bent to dry her legs, he placed a soft kiss low on her belly.

When it was her turn, she took her time, enjoying the solid feel of his body as she worked. His shoulders were broad and strong as she moved over them with the soft cloth. She molded her hands to the firm curve of his buttocks, then down the back of his legs. She dried his feet and the front of his legs. As she slid her cloth-covered hand up the inside of his thigh, she heard his sharp intake of breath. Slowly and carefully, with painstaking detail, she patted every masculine inch of him dry.

Still kneeling before him, Laurel found his growing arousal impossible to resist for both her fingers and her lips. She dropped the towel and caressed him gently with her hands. She flicked her tongue over the tight pink skin, then brought her lips down over the same spot.

"Laurel, honey..." he whispered with a note of caution, but continued to move his hips with gentle pressure. After a feeble plea to his deity, Scott lifted her to her feet and kissed her deeply, possessively, holding her body close to his with that gentle strength she was fast coming to love.

He lifted his mouth from hers, but didn't back away. Instead he studied her face, seeming to memorize each feature as his gaze drifted. Scott was everything she'd ever wanted in a man. He loosened the clip on her hair and it tumbled around her shoulders. He combed a few straggling hairs away from her face. "I guess you know how much I want you," he said with a lightness that belied the intensity of his gaze.

She smiled and wrapped her arms around his neck. "Do you think you could want me in the bedroom? It's getting a little chilly in here."

Laughing, he lifted her into his arms. Instead of returning to his room, he surprised her by taking her into hers. The covers on the big bed were neatly turned down and the nightstand held a handful of condoms. He placed her in the center of the bed.

She eyed the foil packets, then sent him what she hoped was a challenging glance.

Scott stretched out beside her, supporting his weight on one elbow. He traced a line down her nose, then touched her chin. He wet his lips and touched them briefly to hers before glancing back to the nightstand. "I hope you don't mind missing out on a little sleep tonight."

"I think I'll survive," she replied, but in her heart she wasn't all that sure it was true. She was beginning to care more deeply for Scott than she'd ever cared for anyone. In fact, she realized as his lips moved over her body in ways that deprived her of lucid thought, she was in love with him.

He turned her on her side, her stomach, again to her back, murmuring nonsensical words and phrases of delight as he tasted her in ways no other man had dared. His tongue teased and probed her with an intimacy he claimed like a birthright.

It felt so good. In that dreamy, starry-eyed way, she knew she couldn't last much longer, just as she knew she needed something more.

"Scott." His name came urgently from her mouth. "I need..."

"Tell me what you need, baby," he urged in a voice hoarse with the promise she could have anything she asked for.

"You, Scott..." she moaned, feeling as though she were melting into the sheets. "I need you. Inside me. Now."

A moment later, he was prepared and slipping between her legs. She clung to him, urging him to complete their union.

"I need you too, Laurel," he whispered.

The welcomed pressure gradually filled her until the empty ache inside her vanished.

He held still as he spread kisses over her eyes, her cheek, her mouth. When she felt him begin to move, she looked up to find him watching her. He continued to watch her as each thrust built in intensity. She absorbed his impact, then returned it with a building need of her own. The need grew stronger, more demanding.

Scott met her demand and challenged it. She couldn't breathe fast enough, then she couldn't breathe at all. Her body was paralyzed with convulsing spasms of pleasure so intense she couldn't even think.

Scott made a low guttural sound as he strained against her, thrust hard, then strained again.

Though sated, Laurel held him tightly, silently telling him she didn't want him to leave her. He returned her embrace. Their bodies were slick with sweat, but Laurel didn't care. Scott was in her arms and inside her body. Nothing could be better than that.

She began to imagine what it would be like to have Scott like this every night, to know this sheer peace and contentment every single day. She saw herself pregnant with his child, his lips on her swollen belly, his love shining in his eyes. But it was a foolish, idealist's dream. She blinked away the moisture she found claiming her eyes.

"I hope those are happy tears," Scott said softly as he looked down at her, his body still intimate with hers.

"*Happy* doesn't begin to describe it." She put her hand to his sweat-dampened face, wondering how she'd ever survive without him in her life.

He glanced at the half dozen or so condoms left on the nightstand. "There is something to be said for quality over quantity, I guess."

She laughed, and he laughed with her. That felt good, too.

Two more packets disappeared off the nightstand before morning. He'd taken her on her side the next time, gently waking her with the movement of his lips on her shoulder and the side of her neck. She'd snuggled her back against his hairy chest, and he'd reached around to massage first her breasts, then lower, down her abdomen. When his finger slipped inside her she was more than ready. He rolled on the condom, then entered her quickly, simultaneously stroking her with his fingers to match the cadence of his thrusts until they climaxed together again with loud, ragged cries of delight.

The third time, she awakened before dawn hungry for him again. A new and powerful feeling possessed her. She began by softly stroking his chest until he began to stir. Her fingers became bolder in their explorations. She slid one hand intimately between his thighs. Slowly stroking and caressing him, she felt him begin to grow hard as she held him in her palm. The smile she felt on his lips when she kissed him, and the lazy, satisfied moans that escaped from his throat, told her she was doing fine. This time, she controlled their lovemaking, from the opening of the foil packet to the moment she collapsed astride him in completion.

He laughed and hugged her tightly to his chest. A few minutes later, as they cuddled together before drifting off to sleep, Scott whispered in her ear. "The last one up makes breakfast."

* * *

Laurel tried unsuccessfully to contain her laughter as she watched Scott twist his mouth into different contortions, as though one particular pose might help to get the eggs turned without breaking the yolks.

"Do you think you can do any better, Ms. Up-at-the-crack-of-dawn Tanner?" He scowled.

Laurel laughed all the harder. She'd been getting up early for years. Just as she scooted her chair back and told him to relinquish his apron to the superior cook, a firm knock sounded at the door.

Scott shot her a questioning look. Laurel shrugged. She certainly wasn't expecting anyone. She'd only given Jeffrey Hays the address out of necessity when she told him she was spending the weekend with "a friend."

Her finely tuned instinct warned her of trouble. She glanced around the room as if seeing it for the first time, while quickly assessing possible weapons, cover and escape routes. She stepped back into the kitchen, where she wouldn't be seen right away, and peeked out the window. She could see nothing.

Scott crossed the room and opened the door. "Father," he said in surprise. "What are you doing here?"

There was a long pause. Laurel could almost see the judge scanning the room. "We have to talk, son."

Scott's eyes narrowed. "You haven't called me that in over twenty years. What is it?"

"It's about that woman."

"If you're talking about Laurel—" Scott had his fist clenched at his side when she stepped out from behind them and into the living area. Both men turned to stare at her.

"What the hell do you think you're doing? Are all your brains in your pants?" Raymond Delany muttered disgustedly.

Rage and indignation erupted inside her. "How dare—"

"Stay out of this, Laurel," Scott said in a deceptively calm tone. Then he addressed his father. "You're right, we do need to talk."

Raymond laughed, ignoring Scott's comment. "You don't get it, do you? She's using you like she used Brian."

Shocked by his words, Laurel fought to control her temper and find her voice. "What's that supposed to mean?"

"It's nonsense," Scott replied.

"Is it?" Raymond turned and smiled at her, a smile that reminded her very much of Brian. "Did you think you could shoot my son, then accuse him of being a drug dealer without my having *you* investigated? Surely you're not that naive, Sergeant. How long did you think you could hide the fact that you had an affair with Brian, or that he rejected you?" The judge glanced smugly at Scott before continuing. "I see killing Brian wasn't enough to get even. You had to seduce the only son I have left."

Laurel couldn't believe the man's cruel tone. Her mouth was open, but no sound came out. Her lungs felt as if they were filled with cement. She was furious at his accusation, but even more so at the demeaning way in which he referred to Scott.

"Watch it," Scott said, taking a step toward his father. "You're way out of line here."

The judge took a half step backward.

Laurel finally found her voice. "I know you've suffered a lot of grief, but that's no excuse to make ridiculous accusations." Scott placed his arm across her shoulders. His presence beside her helped her tremendously.

The judge raised both hands, palms open and facing forward. When he spoke, his voice was calm and controlled, possessing the same air of omnipotence he used in the courtroom. "I have no intention of standing here in a yelling match with you two like rival street gangs." He lifted his nose a half inch higher. "You are indeed naive, Sergeant Tanner, if you think I would make an accusation without corroborative evidence to back it up."

Laurel realized the truth of what he was saying. Though all of his accusations were false, she didn't doubt that he had somehow misconstrued, twisted or manufactured some kind of evidence against her. "What do you want, Judge?"

He smiled.

She hated the arrogance of his smile.

"Wise of you to ask." He paused theatrically. "I'm willing to give you one week to retract your testimony."

"That's out—"

He held up his hand. "I'm not asking you to say that you lied, only admit that you could have made a mistake. After all, it was a foggy night, it happened so fast and *someone* had shot you."

"But I know what I saw!" she insisted.

Scott raised his hand this time to stop his father's reply. "And what will you do at the end of the week if she doesn't go along with this?"

Judge Delany stepped so close to Laurel's face she could feel his breath as he spoke. "Please understand. The last thing I want is a scandal, but if you don't put a stop to these ridiculous rumors about Brian, I'll provide the district attorney with enough evidence of motive for him to get the charges against you changed from involuntary manslaughter to murder."

A wave of shock rolled over Laurel. "What evidence? That's impossible!"

"One week." Confidently, Judge Delany turned and walked out the door.

"Murder!" Laurel cried out in disbelief. The outrageous charge infuriated her. She had a powerful urge to run after the judge and demand he withdraw his threat, but her feet wouldn't move. "He can't be serious."

Scott placed his arm around her shoulders. "I'm afraid my father doesn't joke—about anything."

She lifted her face to his. The worry in his expression frightened her more than his father's words. "He doesn't strike me as the type to make idle threats, either." She hated the vulnerability she heard in her voice.

Scott pulled her into his embrace. "I don't know what to say," he said with a sigh against her hair. "He's always been . . . unpredictable when it comes to Brian." He rubbed his hands up and down her arms. "When I was a kid, I used to get mad as hell when my father's rules held firm for me, but always seemed to bend when Brian tried them." Scott expelled a long, resounding breath. "I'm sorry, Laurel. I wish I could tell you he'd change his mind in a few days, but I think he's got justice and vengeance all mixed up in his head. I do know that he means what he said."

"But it's not true." She stopped her protest. She'd been in law enforcement long enough to know that being right wasn't always enough.

"I know," he sympathized.

She disliked throwing Scott into the middle of the conflict between her and his father. The fact that he'd stood by her when his father had made his threats and accusations caused a lump to form in her throat.

"Come on. I need some help in the kitchen." Scott grasped her hand and propelled her forward. "Why don't you start over with the eggs while I work on the toast."

She recognized his transparent tactics. "It'll take more than food to get my mind off your father's threat." Laurel turned and caught a speculative look in his eyes. "But thanks for trying."

"We'll have breakfast. Then, if you want to go home, we'll leave. How's that?"

She nodded, not surprised that he'd anticipated her thoughts. He'd done quite a bit of anticipating the night before, she recalled with both warmth and sadness. "I don't think I can afford to give Jeff the time he asked for." She looked over at Scott. "I'm going to have to check out the information we found in the safe myself. I have to see Brian's financial statements and tax returns."

"The detective took those, too," he said. "I already checked."

Laurel turned. His attempt to help uncover the truth touched her. She knew what it cost him, what it would continue to cost him when they found the proof of Brian's guilt. He'd said that before he'd left London, he'd reconciled himself to the task of patching up his relationship with his father and reuniting his family, no matter what it took. She alone stood between him and the successful completion of his goal.

Scott put two slices of bread in the toaster. "I don't know what the detective did with Brian's files."

"They'll be locked up in evidence. I've got to figure out a way to get in and have a look at them," she mumbled, more to herself than to him.

"Could your partner do it?" he asked.

"I don't want to get Gary into any trouble." She thought about it for a moment. "But maybe..."

Her mind started racing. It would depend on who was working at the evidence desk. "If Gary could get the file pulled..." Her heart raced to keep pace. "Just because I'm on suspension, there's no reason I can't go by the station to visit." Her voice rose as the possibilities unfolded. "If I could arrange a diversion that would take Gary away from the desk . . .''

She tapped her fingers on the table. "It would only take me a few minutes . . .''

Chapter 11

By the time Laurel finished washing the dishes, a dark foreboding had replaced the initial shock of the judge's threat. An uncomfortable silence grew between her and Scott. She resented the fact that his own father had forced him to choose sides. New lines of worry creased his forehead. She understood how much he wanted to maintain his ties with his family, and she couldn't help but wonder where he'd stand when the week was over.

Anxious to be home and working on her case, she gathered her belongings, then paced in front of the living room window.

Scott placed their bags in the car and made a final check of the cabin. At the front door he halted and turned to Laurel. "Okay. Bags are in the car and the motor's running. Do you think it's safe to kiss me now?"

Laurel ignored the warmth stinging her face as Scott pulled her into his arms. True, she had avoided kissing or even touching him since she'd made the decision to start home right away. She had been unsure about how he was feeling after he'd had some time to think about what his father said. But now, in the safe haven of his arms, she knew it would take little coaxing and they'd be back in bed, making love and blocking out the problems that needed to be solved. "I thought I'd kissed you quite thoroughly already this morning."

Their eyes met, reflecting the memory of their shared intimacy. "You certainly did." He brought his lips down to hers, punctuating his tender kisses with words as heat flooded her face. "Very...thoroughly."

They drove all the way down the mountain and through San Bernardino, stopping only once for gas on the journey back to Crystal Cove. Laurel worried over her problem. She tried to figure out what evidence the judge could have against her, but it was impossible. Her best defense—if not her only one—was a stronger offense. She had to find proof Brian had both motive and opportunity to shoot her. She had to find his briefcase and his gun, but she also needed to find whoever was in that alley with them to tie the evidence to Brian.

Brian.

She wondered if he knew how much pain and misery he would continue to cause after his death, for her and for his brother.

Laurel took in a long, slow breath as her gaze shifted to Scott. The similarities between him and Brian were obvious, but the differences ran deeper and were harder to discern. She watched Scott's hands on the wheel as he maneuvered through the heavy Sunday traffic. A fine sprinkling of dark hair stretched down his forearms to his wrists. His fingers were long and slim. The memory of their skillful touch brought a new warmth to her cheeks. Though he held the wheel loosely in his grip, power and strength were there if he needed it. It was his nature, she'd learned through hours of loving, to hold that strength in check as long as possible.

Her gaze traveled upward to his neck and face. As he concentrated on his driving, she took the opportunity to study his profile. She saw strength there, too. He moistened his lips with the tip of his tongue. She remembered the feel of that tongue on her own lips, her throat, the back of her neck.

"If you don't stop staring at me, I'm going to have to pull over and take you right here." He glanced her way with one eyebrow arched.

"There's no shoulder on the road and no parking along here," she informed him, appreciating the momentary distraction.

He let out a short grunt of acknowledgment. "They may save lives, but right now I'd like to strangle the person who invented seat belts."

She followed his gaze to the harness that held her firmly out of his reach and understood immediately. She'd like nothing more than to scoot over beside him, feel his body close to hers, and maybe...

"What if—" He eyed the release button speculatively.

"Seat belts are more than just a good idea." She quoted the old safety jingle, lowering her voice to match the mood of the words. "It's the law."

"Would you arrest me?" he asked.

She felt a moment of tension as she thought about her suspension. She looked his way and their gazes met.

"You know, we are still out of your jurisdiction." His tone was light, as though he'd belatedly realized the implications of his words.

"It's not just the law. It's also a good idea," she said.

"Touché," he replied, returning his attention to the road.

She smiled, but there was no doubt about her sincerity. It forced a small distance between them she thought might be wise after all.

Unfortunately, that thought made her wonder if letting their relationship get this far was a good idea. She wasn't sure she'd recognize a good idea just now if it bit her on the nose.

Their relationship was so new and tenuous, she wondered if it could survive what lay before them. That she was a cop didn't seem to bother Scott as it had the men in her past. But she and Scott had had so many other things on their minds, and she'd been on suspension the entire time she'd known him.... How could she be sure it didn't bother him? Other than when she'd initially admitted to shooting his brother, he'd made no disparaging remarks or insinuations. And so far he'd accepted the inherent dangers of her work, even if he didn't like them. She rubbed at her temples, trying to erase some of the confusion complicating her life.

Her gaze focused on the highway before her while her thoughts drifted back in time. Things had been a lot different with Dan Reeves, the last man she'd become seriously involved with. She had thought Dan had accepted and supported her career in the months they had dated. When he'd proposed marriage, she'd joyfully accepted, only to find out later that he'd assumed she would quit working once they were married. In trying to reason with him, she'd made another discovery.

"Dan, we've never talked about my giving up my career," she had said. "You know how much it means to me." Underneath her anger, an ache began to build inside her.

"I told my mother about our engagement when she called last night," he had replied. "She felt it would be improper for you to continue working once we begin our family."

He had continued to speak, but Laurel didn't need to hear more. If Dan had one noticeable fault, it was that he let his widowed mother hold too much influence over his life. Laurel didn't begrudge their love or closeness, but she didn't want to spend her life subjugated by that relationship, either. Marriage vows meant a lot to Laurel. They were a commitment to someone as well as an acceptance of who that someone was.

She knew it took a special person to marry a cop. When that cop was a woman, it took someone even more special and supportive. In a society where men were traditionally the ones to go to war or make the country safe, it would take a man with modern philosophies and ideas to accept, respect and love a woman who took on that goal and responsibility for herself. Such a man would have to be strong and confident about himself before he could accept a woman on those terms.

Her disappointment with Dan—and with herself for not realizing sooner what he was really like—hurt her deeply. Dan had not been the first to display that attitude, but he'd hurt her the most. Hurts like that healed with time, but they always left scars.

Laurel looked over at Scott again and sighed, knowing the pain of losing him would be greater than anything she could imagine. *Does he have what it takes to hang on during the long haul?* she wondered. She hoped there would be enough time for them to find out.

They continued the drive in silence. Laurel's apprehension grew as they neared Crystal Cove. The time constraint placed on her by Judge Delany nudged away all thoughts of her past mistakes.

"What are you going to do when we get home?" Scott asked suddenly.

She wasn't surprised he'd been thinking along the same lines. "First I'll call Gary and see what I can set up. It's going to be tough convincing him to go along without telling him what we've got, but I can't let him risk suspension, too."

"Can I help?"

Laurel appreciated his offer. "I don't want you to get in trouble, either."

He grinned. "I can be a great distraction."

Her pulse fluttered. She knew that was true.

Stepping into the squad room was like coming home. Laurel never would have thought the cluttered desks and dirty coffee cups left over from the day shift could evoke such a warm, nostalgic feeling.

Evenings at the station, Sundays in particular, could seem deceptively calm. Tonight, everything looked quiet. Laurel knew all the members of the skeleton crew manning the station. She stopped to speak with each, explaining her presence with a whiff of Italian spices from the white take-out bag she carried. She knew sharing a dinner break with her partner would arouse no alarm or suspicion in her co-workers.

"Boyd was back in one of the interrogation rooms, but if you can't find him, I'd be happy to take his place," Martin Malone offered, rubbing his slightly protruding belly and raising an eyebrow.

"You're too easy, Malone," Laurel tossed back at the older man.

She proceeded to the hall at the back of the station. The door to the left led to the evidence room. Off to the right was the row of interrogation rooms, all but one dark. Through the open miniblinds, Laurel saw Gary poring over a file in the first room.

His eyes locked with hers as she stepped through the door. There was no smile or greeting. He shut the file and pushed it to the other end of the table.

Laurel swallowed when she read Brian's name on the file.

She set the bag down and pulled out a large covered plate for each of them. The aroma of piping hot mozzarella and spicy Italian sausage filled the room.

To say Gary had been less than enthusiastic about her idea would have been a gross understatement. They both knew having him examine the evidence taken from Brian's home could result in a strong reprimand. Obviously, he was still a little miffed at her because she wouldn't confide the whole story to him, though he said he'd take responsibility if necessary.

"I have no idea what I'm supposed to be looking for," he muttered, sounding a lot like a student who didn't see any possible reason for memorizing a math theorem he would never use outside the classroom. He cut into the thick slab of lasagna with the plastic fork she'd brought along. She'd ordered his favorite dish from his favorite restaurant and prayed it would help him forgive her for what she had to do.

As they ate, they nodded or waved to the people who passed through the squad room. Sometimes they exchanged insults good-naturedly, as if nothing had changed, reminding her of how much she missed the people as well as the job.

"Hey, Sarge," Malone said from the door. "You coming to the volleyball playoffs game?"

"Wouldn't miss it," Laurel replied. She forced herself to choke down a few bites of lasagna, but didn't touch her coffee.

Finishing his last bite, Gary gave a satisfied sigh. "At least the whole evening hasn't been a wash."

Laurel bit back a moan. She really hated this, but she had no choice. She brought her coffee to her lips and tested the temperature. It had cooled considerably. She turned and looked Gary in the eyes. "I'm sorry," she said, then dumped her coffee down the front of his shirt.

Gary got up so fast that his chair tipped over. "Jeez, Laurel!" Then he looked into her eyes and understood. "Hope you know what the hell you're doing."

He stepped out in the hall, muttering curses and dabbing at the dripping mess on his shirt with a wad of paper napkins. It would take him at least ten minutes to get to the locker room and change into the clean uniform she knew he kept there.

Laurel felt horrible, but she knew she had to work fast. She pulled out the file and scanned through the financial statements and tax returns. There was no mention of the holding company or the building. Nor could she find where he had declared another source of income other than from his position as a deputy D.A. She completed her search and closed the file just as Gary returned.

"I'm really sorry about your uniform. I'll pay for the cleaning." She didn't meet his eyes as she edged by him, heading for the door.

"You can't afford to pay for the cleaning, Laurel," he reminded her.

His words reflected not only the truth of her financial situation, but a deeper meaning, as well. She had to be careful.

Scott waited for Laurel to turn off the engine and get out of the car. When she didn't move, he worried something had gone terribly wrong. Thanks to his father, *terribly wrong* was fast becoming the norm. He walked up to her car and opened the passenger door. His heart wrenched when he saw the agonized expression on her face.

"What happened?" He slid in and shut the door. "Didn't you get to look at the files?"

Forlornly, she took in a breath and let it out. "I looked at the files."

He couldn't understand what had upset her. "Did you get Gary into trouble?"

She moaned and leaned her head against the steering wheel.

"Laurel, what happened? How did you get him to leave you alone with the files?"

She turned her face toward him. "I poured a cup of coffee down the front of his shirt so he'd have to go downstairs to change into a clean uniform."

Scott couldn't help it. He laughed so hard he thought he'd pulled something.

"It's not funny. You should have seen his face."

He knew she was serious, but it reminded him of some of the crazy stunts he and Brian used to pull. Besides, the relief of laughter felt too good. After a moment, she joined him. The sound of her laughter stirred a warmth within him. The cost of cleaning a uniform was a small price to pay for the happiness he felt at that moment. "Don't worry, I'll take care of the cleaning bill."

The laughter faded and her somber mood returned. "I didn't find the building or the holding company listed among any of his assets."

He took a moment to think about what she'd said. He didn't need to have it spelled out for him. Brian had to have been using the holding company and probably the building itself for illegal purposes. He hated to admit it, but he'd suspected as much ever since Stanley Murdock's name appeared in Brian's safe. His real concern was what would happen when he had to tell his father the truth.

"I'm sorry." She leaned her head back.

"I know. Me, too. Only I'm not really surprised." He felt it was time to tell her what else he'd done. "I hired an investigator to check out Brian's friend in New York."

Her head jerked around. "When? Why didn't you say anything?"

"I didn't want to stir up more trouble or give you false hope if everything checked out. I thought now you needed to know." Scott continued to struggle with the battle between his heart and his conscience. He'd done everything he could think of to bring this to a peaceable end. He didn't want Laurel hurt further, nor did he want to do anything that would completely cut his ties with his father. It reminded him of the horrible position in which Brian had always placed him. He hated being caught in the middle, and he hated being used.

Laurel opened the door and got out. She unlocked her front door, then held it open. He knew he should go home and try to talk to his father, but he couldn't find the strength to turn away.

She plopped her purse down heavily on the entry table. "I'm going to take a shower and go to bed."

After slipping out of her shoes, she left a trail of clothes behind her. She went straight to the bathroom and turned on the shower before she caught his stare. A flash of uncertainty entered her eyes, and he found it endearing. They'd been afraid of having their relationship made public, but now that his father knew, it didn't matter anymore. When she finally spoke, it was the honesty in her voice that got to him.

"I want you to stay," she said.

A voice inside his head warned him to think about what he was doing. But he had the meeting in Los Angeles coming up, and there were so many unknowns. What if he didn't get another chance to be with her? He simply couldn't deny himself this night.

They finished undressing without talking and stepped into the shower, where they quickly washed themselves. There was something decidedly erotic about watching the delicate movements of her hands as she spread the lather down her neck and over her breasts. He ached to reach out and help her, but discovered excitement in the restraint.

She passed him the bar of soap. He caught the hunger in her eyes as she watched him perform the same cleansing ritual. He endured the torture of not touching her, and it added a new depth to what they shared.

When they were finished, she flipped off the light and reached for his hand, leading him to her bed. She slipped under the covers, then raised them for him to join her. He turned on a small bedside lamp before doing so. She was so beautiful. He wanted to look at her, see her response as he loved her. Trailing his finger slowly from her chin to her abdomen caused a sharp rise in her chest.

"You're so lovely," he whispered, running the pads of his fingers along her collarbone, then down to the swell of one breast. He circled her nipple until it peaked beneath his touch. His control slipped as he lowered his head and flicked his tongue over the soft mound.

Laurel moaned and arched her back. He saw her knees press inward. Need hit him like a fiery jolt. He wanted to draw out their lovemaking, to give her more pleasure than she could stand, but her hands moved over him in ways that denied him his free will. She rubbed her legs against his. He kissed her long and deep, exploring, claiming. Breathless, he pulled away long enough to protect her, then was kissing her again.

She was pulling him closer, enticing him with her tongue and the gentle thrust of her hips.

"You're driving me wild," he whispered against her lips.

"Let's be wild together," she replied, spreading her thighs. "Come to me."

He sheathed himself within her, forcing himself to go slowly, which brought a flood of pleasure far too great for silence. He let the raw sounds pass freely from his lips, expressing his need as well as the satisfaction of their intimate contact.

Laurel lifted her legs higher, locking her calves behind his back. He drove into her with a madness that possessed his entire being. She called his name. He tried to hold the steady rhythmic pace as long as he could, allowing her to draw out her own pleasure, but he soon slipped beyond control, beyond reason. Her knees dug into his sides as her embrace tightened. His own release came at the same moment. Hard. And full. And glorious. With a ragged breath, he called her name. In his heart the word shouted.

Again he felt the dizzying sensation of completeness that could not be totally explained by the physical satisfaction he was feeling. This time it was not the sensation that frightened him, but the fragility of it. He held Laurel close and mentally acknowledged that he wanted this feeling to last forever. But he knew his father well enough to realize the full potential of his threat to Laurel and to both their futures.

They held each other through the night, and in the morning he made love to her again. Slowly, thoroughly, as he'd meant to do the night before, strangely fearing it might be their last time.

* * *

"Being an early riser has its advantages," Laurel said with a satisfied smile, as she and Scott made breakfast. She tried to shake the niggling sense of uneasiness that had tugged at her mind since she'd come fully awake. She still had the feeling that something important was eluding her. She felt she'd been close to figuring it out when Scott reminded her he was going to have to leave soon for a meeting in Los Angeles. They also talked about the upcoming police volleyball tournament and made plans to attend, but Laurel was distracted.

Whatever it was, it had something to do with the shooting. She went over everything in her mind as she stood at the counter. Every time she got to the alley, something stopped her.

Scott appeared behind her, his lips on the curve of her neck, his arms around her waist. "Okay, what's the matter?" He rubbed his hands over her abdomen. "You may be standing here in my arms, but your brain is miles away."

As she was about to succumb to the sweet temptation of his kisses now at the hairline of her temple, her thoughts began to congeal. She turned quickly in his arms and gave in to a brief sigh of regret as she looked into his eyes. "I know this is lousy timing, Scott, but do you remember those two boys in the alley the day I saw you there?"

Scott rubbed his hands along the column of her spine. "I don't remember seeing anybody except you."

She pushed aside the small bit of flattery and described their physical characteristics as though she'd seen them only yesterday. "The taller boy wore a purple bandanna and black gloves."

She paused, remembering something odd. "They were driving gloves, not the fingerless ones the kids wear. And the boys behaved strangely, too. It was broad daylight, but they seemed spooked. I was hurrying down the alley to see what frightened them, when I saw you. Seeing you and going back to the place where I was shot must have been a lot harder for me than I realized because I forgot all about the boys."

Scott released her and took the pitcher of orange juice to the table.

"What's the matter? Do you remember something?" she asked.

"No." He sighed. "But I can pretty well imagine the strange look you described. Growing up as an identical twin, you see all kinds of curious reactions."

She heard a hint of bitterness in his voice and remembered from her own childhood how tactlessly cruel children could be. Suddenly she snapped her fingers. "You think they were frightened because...they thought they were seeing *Brian!*"

They looked at each other. Hope rose inside her. It was a small lead, but it was better than no lead at all. Then she saw Scott's expression turn glum.

"What is it?" she said.

"Your description of those boys made me remember something about Brian." The sadness in his voice clutched at her heart. "He always wore driving gloves, too, but I didn't see any mention of them in the list of his personal effects."

"That's right," she affirmed. "He must have left them at home that night."

"I guess that's possible. Four years is a long time. Habits can be broken, but ever since our sixteenth birthday, he always wore them when he drove."

She put a hand on his arm and listened as he relived the story in his mind.

168 					Hard Evidence

"Without the other one knowing, we had gone out and bought the exact same pair of black leather driving gloves for each other. Brian never drove without them. It was almost an obsession."

Laurel tried hard to recall if Brian had worn gloves that night in the alley. The darkness and the patchy fog could have hidden that detail. Her attention had been clearly focused on more important elements at the time, like the semiautomatic pointed at her heart.

"That birthday was the last really special time we had together," Scott said softly. "From then on, things didn't go smoothly. Brian used the gloves as an example of that creepy bond between us. That's why he always wore them. Whenever he asked me to bail him out of trouble, he had on those gloves. It was like he knew what I would be thinking when I saw them, and he was right. I couldn't help it."

Laurel's heart tugged in two different directions. She wanted to comfort him and erase the tortured look in his eyes, but she also wanted answers to the puzzles of that night. Only with the truth did they have any hope for a future together. After only a second, she stepped in front of him and reached up to touch his cheek. For a moment, the uncertainty left his eyes as he allowed her a glimpse inside. The hope she saw touched her deeply.

But time was running out. With a long sigh, she pulled her hand away and forced herself to put her personal feelings aside and let her mind go back to the kids in the alley. "If whoever took Brian's gun and briefcase also took his gloves, that would explain why there were no powder tracings on his hands. I bet those kids in the alley had something to do with it."

"Laurel, Brian wasn't the only person who wore that type of glove," he said softly.

"I know, but when you consider the way those kids looked, it makes sense." The idea inspired her. It felt right. "If it was you who frightened them, if they thought you were Brian like I did..." She turned the possibilities over in her mind. "I've got to find out who they are. I have to talk to them."

"You don't have much to go on," he reminded her.

Then she remembered the car. Excited, she turned to Scott. "I remember I watched them run down the alley. There was a bright yellow Camaro parked at the end of the street. It shouldn't be too hard to find."

"There must be hundreds of them," he protested.

She shook her head and smiled. "But this one wasn't stock."

Chapter 12

Laurel grabbed her purse and keys and opened the front door, anxious to begin her search for the boys from the alley.

Scott caught her arms and pulled her back to him for one last kiss. Her lips felt sweetly tender from the night before.

A strange muffled sound on the porch captured her attention. The second sob was louder. Sitting on the concrete, with her ankles crossed and her head tucked down to her knees, was Laurel's fourteen-year-old neighbor. Laurel stepped outside and bent down beside the girl. "Heather, honey, what's the matter?"

"I wish I was dead. My mother hates me. She lets Carrie and Zach do whatever they—" Heather's head came up as she spoke, and she saw Scott standing there. Obviously embarrassed, she quickly got to her feet, tucked in her chin, and started to leave. "I'm sorry, I—"

"Wait, Heather. It's okay," Laurel said. "This is my friend, Mr. Delany." She watched Heather give him a caulous nod. "Why don't you go inside and wash your face and have something to eat. I'll be right in." She looked at Scott. "I'm sorry."

"That's okay," Scott said. He smiled down at Laurel and something melted within her.

Heather went on inside.

"She's had a rough time. Her parents are divorced. Her mother is trying to raise three teenagers all by herself." Laurel saw the frown wrinkle Scott's brow.

"You take care of Heather and I'll call you later." He leaned down and kissed her quickly on the lips.

Laurel went to the kitchen, poured two glasses of orange juice and sat at the table. Nothing worked faster to take her mind off her own problems than to listen to those of a teenager.

Heather took a long drink, then waited no more than a second before she spoke. Her voice rose steadily as she told her story. "Now Tiffany is going to be stuck in San Diego all by herself with nothing to do all day long while her dad's working for two weeks! There is no reason I shouldn't be able to go. It wouldn't cost me anything, and her dad already said it was okay with him."

Laurel had met Heather's friend Tiffany. She was a nice girl, if a little overindulged. "Did your mother tell you why she didn't want you to go?"

"No, but I know it's because she hates me. Well, I hate her, too." Heather started crying again.

Before Heather could build up too much steam, Laurel said, "So what options do you have now?"

Heather sniffled. "I could go live with my dad."

Laurel knew Heather's father had a drinking problem and a foul temper. "Would that be better?"

Heather pouted.

"What other options do you have?"

Heather frowned as she stared at the table. "I guess I could wait until Mom's next day off, when she's not so tired, and I could ask her again."

"That sounds reasonable to me," Laurel replied. "Your mother works hard. She may not be able to spend as much time with you as you'd like, but I know she loves you very much. Give her a little time."

"At the rate she's making me lose friends, I don't have a lot of time." Heather wiped her eyes.

"Oh, come on. You have plenty of friends. You belonged to several clubs at school last year," Laurel countered.

"Yeah, and the people I got to autograph my yearbook didn't even fill one page." Her voice rose, but the tears were gone. "Carrie had to buy two yearbooks just to hold all the signatures."

Laurel froze, her glass halfway to her mouth. In the back of her mind she could hear Heather asking her what was wrong, but her brain was too busy to answer. It was a slim chance. "Heather, I think you may have helped me with a big problem of my own. Could I borrow your yearbook?" Laurel hesitated, thinking. "And Carrie's, too? For a couple of years back?"

"Sure, but why?" Heather asked, her voice suddenly infected with Laurel's enthusiasm.

"For a case I'm working on. I need to identify a couple of boys, but they may not even be local," Laurel said.

"But I thought you weren't a cop anymore. Mom said—" Heather stopped suddenly and looked up at Laurel.

Laurel tried to hide the hurt. "I'm still a cop. The suspension is temporary." She wanted very much for those words to be true. She made them sound so. "Will you help me?"

Laurel could have gone to the school for the yearbooks, but Heather seemed thrilled that she'd been asked to help. Agreeing easily, she ran home to get the books requested. Laurel watched her dash off. She really was a sweet girl, in spite of her insecurity.

Twenty minutes later, Heather returned with four yearbooks. Laurel sat on the sofa, looking slowly and carefully through the first one. Heather sat beside her, fidgeting.

"Police work isn't always as exciting as they make it look on TV," Laurel said. They agreed there was nothing else Heather could do to help, and Heather said she was going to go home and call Tiffany. Laurel thanked her and promised to return the yearbooks when she finished.

Laurel studied the photos of each male, looking for either of the teenagers she'd seen in the alley the morning she'd run into Scott. Unfortunately, it was *that* very male presence that kept distracting her from her task. Special moments from the recent memories she'd shared with Scott drifted through her mind. Looking at the high school yearbook had her thinking and feeling like a teenager. They'd been apart only a short time, yet she found herself thinking about him and wondering when she would see him again. She longed to be with him. Laurel put down the yearbook, folding her arms across her chest, and closed her eyes.

Basking in the warmth of her visions, Laurel napped. A short time later she opened her eyes. Needing to get up and move about for a while, she did the dishes and a few other chores. Then the phone rang.

Scott's deep voice greeted her. "I wanted to make sure you and Heather were all right."

She assured him they were both fine. "There's nothing like a crying teenager to bring you back to the real world."

"Laurel," he said, "last night may have seemed heavenly, but as far as I'm concerned it was very real."

A wave of heat pushed upward from her chest. "We were good together, weren't we?"

"No. We *are* good together," he corrected. "And not just in bed, although there isn't any doubt about that."

She couldn't deny the truth of his statement. She wanted so much to believe they had a future together, but there were so many obstacles between them.

"I got an idea from Heather this morning," she said. "I borrowed some of her high school yearbooks to look for the kids in the alley. She found out how boring watching me look at pictures is."

"I don't think watching you do anything could ever be boring, but I'm sorry I can't be there all the same." They talked for a few more minutes, then Scott promised he'd call her as soon as he got home from Los Angeles, if it wasn't too late.

Laurel hung up the phone and went back to the yearbooks. Feeling a weary kind of nostalgia, she chose the one from two years ago—the year she'd been at the school with Brian, campaigning for a drug-free campus.

She waded through the pictures of football games and cheerleaders, photos which often included Carrie. Her breath caught as, near the back of the book, she found a picture taken at one of the antidrug program's first school appearances.

The picture showed a small group of somewhat nerdy-looking students gathered to ask questions after Brian's speech. The photographer had captured a spontaneous debate in which Brian and one boy were each holding up their index fingers to make a point, looking as if they were sword-fighting with their fingers. The caption read Just Say No.

Laurel took a closer look at the boy. Her pulse stepped up its beat. She turned back through the pages to look for a better shot of him. She found one of him in the chess club and one on the debate team. Then she found his class picture. The dark eyes staring back at her looked older than his years and very much like the dark eyes of the taller boy in the alley. She read the name aloud. "Jon Dever." Then she got up to get the other yearbooks. In the book from last year, she saw him again. He was a senior. She looked at the club pictures. He was still there, still active, still clean-cut, but the intelligence in his expression hinted at something more, something almost calculating. It didn't make sense.

She needed to know what had happened to the boy since high school. Her first thought was of Gary Boyd. Her second was of the fiasco she'd put him through the night before. She spent an hour wrestling with her conscience before she picked up the phone to ask for his help.

Scott fought to keep his mind on the negotiations as he listened to his partner, Hershal Blane Saxton III, who sat beside him at the table in the conference room of Douglas, Britton & Whitney. The acquisition of Remshaw Industries had been Hershal's project from the start. Scott had only recently shown enthusiasm for the purchase. The company would double their net worth, but, more important, it would give Scott a reason to move back home to California. Not that he didn't have a perfectly good reason already.

Laurel Tanner was more than a reason to relocate. She made him feel things he hadn't felt in years, think thoughts he had long ago cast aside as unrealistic. Laurel Tanner was reason enough for—

A sudden, sharp pain shot through his right ankle. Scott looked at Hershal, who had just kicked him under the table.

Behind the polite smile lurked a scowl. "Do you mind if I step outside and have a word with my partner?" Hershal asked the group as he rose from his seat.

Hershal ushered Scott into a small office next to the conference room. "Look, Scott, I know your brother's death has upset you. Losing someone before you've had a chance to settle your differences is a tough break. If you're not up to this meeting, let's hold off for a while."

"What do you mean? I'm fine. I want this move more than ever now." After he'd first talked to his parents, the idea of moving back had started to appeal to him. He especially wanted to be near his mother after all he'd put her through in the last four years. Though he and his father had started speaking again, their recent words had all been exchanged in anger. The dispute with Laurel had erected new barriers between him and his father. His unresolved conflicts with Brian made him more determined than ever to make sure the same thing didn't happen with his father, but after last weekend, Scott worried about his ability to ever patch things up with his dad.

Hershal placed a hand on Scott's shoulder. "You didn't say anything when their accountant suggested allocating the purchase price by paying the owner a consultant fee for the next five years." His irritation was edged with concern.

Scott looked at his partner in disbelief. The fees would provide a tax deduction for the purchaser while deferring part of the taxable gain to the seller. Though the details could be worked out legally, the tactic skimmed the edge on the ethics side. Could he really have missed something that important? He and Hershal had a polished negotiation tactic Hershal often likened to the old "good cop/bad cop" routine. It didn't work worth a damn as a solo act.

"I'm sorry, Hershal." Scott wiped his hand down his face. Now, with Laurel a part of his life, he couldn't wait to acquire Remshaw Industries and start making plans for the future.

Of course, his father still stood in his way. He hadn't had a chance to talk to him about Laurel. He kept going over in his mind what he would say; he planned to have that talk as soon as they wrapped up the negotiations here. But his preoccupation with Laurel and the pending confrontation with his father was counterproductive to his immediate goal.

Hershal was still staring at him.

"It won't happen again," Scott promised. He couldn't *afford* to let it happen again. He had to concentrate on every word exchanged at the bargaining table. The end result was too important.

"Okay, mate, but don't forget you're the one who has to bring up the due diligence study." Hershal put his hand on Scott's shoulder.

"Right. Let's do it." As Scott started toward the door, he silently reaffirmed his vow not to let his concentration slip again. That wouldn't be too hard now. His ankle hurt like hell.

Unfortunately, even with both Scott and Hershal giving matters their full concentration, the negotiations carried on late into the evening and they still weren't finished. Scott was going to have to spend the night so they could get an early start again in the morning.

Laurel decided she'd wait until eleven o'clock for Scott. If he hadn't called by then, he probably wouldn't. At a quarter to, the phone rang.

The sound of his voice filled her with an inner tranquillity.

"I'm still in Los Angeles. I'm afraid we didn't get finished today. I'm going to try to get this wrapped up in the morning. How did you do today?"

"I found the boy's picture in one of Heather's yearbooks. So far all I have is a name, but that's a good start."

She didn't tell him she'd called Gary Boyd and asked him to access the department computers for priors on Jon Dever. Until Gary got back to her with an answer, there wasn't much use in bringing it up.

"That's great," Scott said. "What did Jeffrey Hays think about it?"

"I haven't told him yet. I don't have enough information." She sighed, frustrated that Gary hadn't gotten back to her today. She'd promised she wouldn't do anything rash, but she hadn't expected it to take him so long. Of course, Gary had no way of knowing about the time constraint she was working under. And he'd made a point of telling her how much time he'd spent taking his uniform to the cleaners. She'd tried to stress the urgency, but as much as she wanted to, she couldn't tell him about Judge Delany's threat.

"I assume you know what you're doing, but please promise me one thing." A note of worry tightened Scott's voice.

"What's that?"

"Promise me you'll be careful, darling, and that, like the good cop that you are, you won't take any unnecessary risks."

The tenderness with which he used the endearment stirred a warmth inside her. "That's two things." She tried to hide her true emotions in the lightness of her teasing.

"Laurel," Scott warned.

"I promise," she agreed.

As Scott said good-night and wished her sweet dreams, Laurel hoped she would be able to keep that promise. Time was running out.

Scott suppressed his own need to see Laurel when he got home Tuesday evening in favor of seeing his father on her behalf. The struggle between his loyalty to his family and his loyalty to Laurel was tearing him apart. Maybe if he sat down calmly with his father, they could straighten things out.

Surprised to see his mother still up, he walked into the family room and kissed her cheek. As he sat down beside her on the sofa, he noticed that she looked extremely tired. "It's late. Why aren't you in bed?"

"Your father said you were coming by, and I wanted to know how your meetings went. I've been praying for your success," she said quietly.

He knew she wanted him back in the States and back in her life. He couldn't take Brian's place, but he could be there for her. "It took longer than we expected, but it looks promising. Our attorneys are drawing up the papers for signatures."

"That's wonderful, dear." Her smile brought a sparkle of light to her eyes. "It's going to be so good to have you home again."

Scott lifted her small, fragile hand and placed it carefully in his own. He thought of the countless times when he was a small child that she'd held his hand in hers. He remembered the strength he'd found there and the confidence her strength had given him.

He was about to tell her he'd always be there for her, always be a part of her life now, even if the acquisition fell through. He wanted to say he was sorry for the pain he'd caused her, but his father's presence in the doorway made him hold back.

"Scott." His father's voice had that familiar regal tone that inspired respect from so many. "I'd like a word with you in my study."

"Yes, sir," Scott replied automatically to his father's request, as he had so often in the past. He turned back to his

mother. Worry tightened the lines around her eyes. He gave
her hand a little squeeze. It felt slightly cool and clammy.
"Good night, Mother." He leaned over and kissed her cheek
before he headed for his father's study and the confrontation it promised.

His father sat behind his huge mahogany desk. In front
of the desk were two burgundy leather wing-back chairs. He
and Brian had spent hours in those chairs when they were
kids, waiting for their father to dole out punishment for
their childish offenses.

His father gestured to the chair on the right. "Sit down."

Scott wondered if anyone had ever found the spots underneath the seats where he and Brian had carved their ini-
tials. Out of habit, he sat in the one on the left.

"Still the rebel," his father muttered resignedly under his
breath.

Then, to Scott's surprise, the elder Delany asked about
the acquisition and his company's legal representation. The
questions reminded him of the kind of normal questions a
concerned father might ask his son, the kind of questions he
wished his father had asked him four years ago.

After they'd been talking for some time about his work,
his father changed the subject with startling abruptness.
"I'm worried about your mother."

Scott heard the sincerity in his father's words.

"She's not as strong as she used to be. Not physically or
emotionally. This last month has really been hard on her,"
his father said softly, as though he were delivering a solemn
judgment. "It's never easy for a parent to bury a child, no
matter how old they may be."

His mother and father had been married nearly forty
years. She had always had a quiet inner strength that enabled her to hold her own against the overwhelming personality of her husband.

His father cleared his throat. After a brief silence, his melancholy gave way to a stronger emotion. "Now that that woman has stirred up all these lies and accusations about Brian—"

"Father." Scott tensed with anger at his father's reference to Laurel. He had to force himself to speak calmly. "First of all, Laurel isn't lying. And at this point, I no longer believe she's mistaken." When his father's chest expanded with outrage, Scott held up both hands as if to stay the explosion. "There were a lot of things about Brian that you never knew."

"There are things about that woman that you don't know, either," his father countered. "Brian had her pegged right. I warned you. She's trying to get the charges dropped and she's using you."

"Well, she damn sure wouldn't be the first." Scott clenched his fist, thinking again about Brian.

His father ignored what he'd said and leaned forward with a satisfied smile on his face. "I have witnesses that will testify they saw them go out together. The next morning, when two of those men asked Brian about his date with the sergeant, he told them, 'You have to watch out for the easy ones, the social climbers. They'll use you like yesterday's newspaper, then throw you away.' Both men remembered the quote as if it was only yesterday. And that's just the beginning."

Scott slammed his hand down on the desk. "Damn him."

"I think maybe your anger is misdirected," his father said smugly.

"No!" Scott's temper finally got the best of him. "No, it's not. I know exactly why he said what he did, and it makes me sick. I'd hoped you'd never have to find out this part of the truth, but I guess it's too late for that now. It's true Laurel and Brian once dated." Scott felt the words sticking in his throat. "As it turned out, Brian wanted more from Laurel than she wanted to give him."

Scott watched his father frown. He wanted to rid his father once and for all of that horrible blind spot he had for Brian. "Damn it, Father, Brian tried to rape Laurel when he took her home. He would have succeeded, too, only he'd spent the whole time they were together talking about himself and hadn't bothered to find out she's a fourth-degree black belt." Scott let that sink in. "He swore he'd get even for the injury she inflicted upon him."

"That's outrageous! She's lying," the judge shouted. "Besides, she could never prove it in court."

"Are you willing to bet on it? Do you want this battle to be played out in the media across the country?"

His father's face reddened with rage.

"Listen, Father, the further we get into this, the dirtier Brian looks. We've got to stop it. I've already found a connection between him and Stanley Murdock."

"Murdock?" His father scowled with distaste. "That's preposterous. You don't expect me to believe Brian would have risked his reputation by associating with someone like that, do you? *He* had more sense."

Scott stared at his father. It was as though he was staring at a total stranger. The man would never change his opinion of Brian, no matter what proof he was handed. Nor was it likely he'd change his opinion of Scott. They were never going to resolve the problems between them. He'd been foolish to even try.

Scott knew it was useless—nothing he did would ever please his father. "Your mind is so closed, I don't know why I bothered trying to talk to you."

"Scott, tell her to recant her story. She'll listen to you."

"I'm afraid not, Father. You'll have to do your own dirty work."

"I'm not without influence in the community," his father said with a confidence born of years on the bench and assurance of his political power.

Scott scoffed at him. "I never should have left London."

"You know what this will do to your mother."

Scott knew, and he hated the prospect of causing her any more pain, but she was stronger than his father gave her credit for. "I can't help that. I didn't start this, but I intend to see it through." He placed both his hands on the desk and leaned closer toward his father. "If you try to have Laurel charged with murder, I'll fight you every step of the way. I'll use every resource I have for her defense. You can consider me dead, too."

A small squeak sounded from the direction of the door. They both turned toward the noise. His mother stood in the doorway clutching the doorknob with one hand, a pale, frightened look on her face. Her other hand pulled at the neckline of her silk blouse, causing the top button to pop off and roll across the hardwood floor.

"Mother!" Scott leapt toward her as her eyes rolled backward. Before he reached her, she collapsed to the floor. His father remained frozen with panic.

"Call 911!" Scott had to repeat it twice to get his father to move. "She's having a heart attack. Call 'em now!" he yelled. Then he lowered his cheek to just above his mother's mouth and tried to see if she was breathing. His own heart and lungs were working so fast he was shaky. It had been years since he'd taken a CPR class. He prayed that he could remember the right things to do and that the ambulance would get there soon.

He tipped her head back and gave her two quick breaths. He felt for a pulse, trying to hold his fingers still over the artery in her neck. Damn. Where was the ambulance?

He began chest compressions, counting to fifteen out loud, then giving her two more quick breaths. He didn't know how many cycles he'd completed when he felt something give under his hand and heard the popping sound of bone. "Oh, God!" he cried. Her ribs.

He felt light-headed and sick to his stomach. Then all of a sudden help was there. Another man took his place. "I think I broke her rib," he confessed to the paramedic. The man said something about that happening before and about saving her life, but Scott was so distraught he didn't hear it all.

The next few minutes passed in a blur as the paramedics attached needles and wires to the pale, lifeless woman on the floor. She looked nothing like his mother. One man communicated with a doctor over a cellular phone. At the doctor's direction, he placed two paddles on her chest and delivered a countershock that jolted through her body, but had no effect on her heart. Scott gritted his teeth as two more countershocks were quickly delivered. The third finally restored her normal heart rhythm.

Scott wiped a hand down his face and expelled a huge breath he hadn't realized he'd been holding.

The two men in white placed her on a stretcher and took her by ambulance to the hospital. His father rode along with them.

Scott prayed she would make it.

Hundreds of questions fluttered through his mind as he quickly locked up the house. Had he really broken her rib? If so, it could puncture her lung. He'd been so busy arguing with his father, he hadn't even seen her standing in the doorway. How much had she heard? He wondered if the heart attack had been brought on by their conversation. He tried to remember what he'd been saying. As Scott followed the ambulance in his rental car, the words he'd told his father came back to haunt him. *You can consider me dead, too.*

He slammed his fist against the steering wheel, wanting to cut out his tongue.

In the long hours of waiting while the doctors did tests and prepared her for surgery on her damaged heart, Scott longed to call Laurel. He needed the comfort and support that he knew was only a phone call away. Yet he couldn't make that call. She would come and wait with him, but to see her here with him now would be more than his father could take.

The more Scott thought about it, the more certain he became that his conversation with his father had triggered his mother's condition. Had she heard about Brian's rape attempt? Guilt welled up inside him, and he faced the dawn alone.

Two doctors finally came out and told them she was in recovery and doing fine. Scott sighed with relief and ran a hand down his face. "Thank God."

His father said nothing, but wept openly with relief.

"You can see her for a couple of minutes." The older doctor spoke with an authority that reminded Scott of his father. "It's important that she not be upset," the doctor cautioned.

Scott watched his father wipe his eyes with a handkerchief, then turn to face him.

"I don't want you to see her, Scott. She's not strong enough to deal with you. Not now. Maybe not ever. You come in and out of her life at your choosing, and she's devastated each time you leave...or threaten to leave."

Scott felt as though he'd been slapped. "What? You can't believe I'd say anything to upset her."

"Perhaps it would be best if you went home and got some rest," the doctor said, then turned and escorted his father through doors marked No Admittance.

Despair filled Scott's heart as he stared at the closed doors. His mother was still in critical condition. He just wanted to look in on her, to tell her he loved her, even if she couldn't hear him. He would never say anything to hurt her. Then he thought again of the conversation she'd over-heard, and the pain stabbed at him. Had his careless words really brought all this on?

He charged out of the hospital in a fury directed mostly at himself. He got into his car and started driving, anxious to get away. *Damn.* Why was it always his mother who got hurt when he and his father fought?

Scott cursed vehemently at a driver who cut him off. He felt like hell—worse than when he'd learned of Brian's death. He remembered his mother's ashen face as she'd been carried out on the stretcher. Now his father openly blamed him for her condition, and he couldn't help but feel the ac-cusation was justified.

He raked his hand through his hair in frustration. Ev-erything had gone wrong, and he was the cause. Laurel's troubles had escalated the day he had first questioned his father about the shooting. If he'd have kept quiet, perhaps she would have served her suspension and been back on the job by now. She sure as hell wouldn't have had anyone threatening her with a murder charge.

"Damn," he shouted, tightening his hands on the steer-ing wheel. He wished again that he'd never left London.

Scott focused his thoughts on Laurel as he drove through the now familiar streets. Their relationship was more than complicated—it was impossible. There was no way out. He had to end it before it got any worse.

Chapter 13

"Okay, Laurel, I'll go out on a limb and meet you at a coffee shop, but no tricks this time," Gary Boyd told her. "It's my choice to help you with this, so I'll take whatever responsibility comes with it."

She appreciated his help and was glad he made no further mention of Scott Delany. She'd deflected his earlier concerns about involving Brian's brother in this, though she was sure he suspected there was more to it than she admitted.

"Meet me at the coffee shop on Seventeenth in thirty minutes, and I'll bring what I have on the kid so far," Gary said. "And don't be late. The captain has me swamped with special projects. I won't have any other free time until the end of the week."

"I won't be late. I promise," she said.

Gary hesitated. "I have to warn you, it looks like we're skimming the surface of something big."

Her curiosity erupted. "Why is that?"

"Your young Mr. Dever has been accepted at three major universities."

"So?" she said impatiently. "We knew he was bright."

"But we didn't know his chosen field of interest."

"Gary!"

"When he entered high school, he professed a strong academic interest in mathematics. A year and a half ago that interest shifted unexpectedly. Now his major is . . . chemical engineering."

The implications immediately formed in her mind. "Designer drugs?" she wondered aloud. "If he got in, learned the ropes and made the right connections through Brian Delany, he could use that knowledge for his own benefit at some future date."

"Exactly. And he must have had good reason to think that Delany's supplier was large and well connected."

"Thanks, Gary. I can't tell you how much I appreciate this." Laurel's heart pounded with excitement. It looked as if she was finally making some progress.

"Yeah, well, keep it under your hat. Someone is really turning the screws at HQ. We're not even supposed to talk about the case, much less start investigating leads on our own."

"I will," she agreed.

"The boys from internal investigations have been asking a lot of questions, too."

Laurel shuddered. She didn't want to think about I.I. or the shooting review board. She hated the idea of her ability and integrity being questioned and doubted by her own people. But Judge Delany's threat to have her charged with murder clearly outweighed the other consequences. She had to prove Brian's guilt to prove her own innocence and stay out of prison.

Prison. The word brought horrible images to her mind. Cops didn't fare well among the inmates.

"Thirty minutes, Laurel. Don't be late," Gary said, interrupting her gloomy thoughts. "I mean it," he added before hanging up.

Laurel raced to shower and dress. She chose light blue slacks and a cotton floral-print blouse. Her hair was still damp, but she'd used up twenty minutes and the drive would take at least ten. She'd promised Gary she wouldn't be late and she had to keep that promise. The time constraint Judge Delany had placed on her made every minute precious.

Quickly, she grabbed her keys and her purse. She swung the front door open and nearly collided with Scott. A startled breath caught in her throat. For the first time, she realized how rattled she was. "Scott, you scared me."

He was leaning against the doorframe, looking tired and disheveled. She'd never seen him so depleted, not even after a night of ardent lovemaking.

"You're leaving," he said, is words clipped.

Sure she'd misread him, Laurel said, "I have to meet Gary. I figured out who the kids in the alley were, and he's done some background checking for me. It sounds like he may have something important." She couldn't keep the excitement out of her voice. The possibility of discovering the first significant lead for her defense had her heart pounding.

Deep frown lines creased his brow. He ran his fingers through his hair and down the back of his neck. "I have to talk to you."

On closer inspection, she noticed the wrinkled clothes he wore. His shirt looked as if he'd slept in it, or perhaps on top of it. And his jaw bore a night's growth of whiskers. Under other circumstances, she might have thought his rough appearance sexy. But the distant look in his eyes this morning made her suspicious.

"What's wrong, Scott? Are you all right?" she asked, painfully torn between worry over Scott and her need for haste. She glanced at her watch, nervously aware of the seconds slipping away and the fact that Gary would not be able to wait for her. Her heart pounded more erratically as Scott took his time before attempting to answer her.

"I'm fine. It's not me I'm concerned about." He ran his hand down his face. When his fingers passed over his jaw, she heard the familiar raspy sound it produced.

She wondered for a moment if his business venture had folded and wished she had time to ask. "Why don't you go inside and get some rest. When I come back, we can talk."

He grabbed her arm. "I don't want you to go." The hardness in his voice startled her. "We've got to talk *now.*"

This was a side of him she hadn't seen before. A side she didn't like at all.

"Scott? What's wrong with you?" She looked down at the spot where his fingers gripped her arm. "I won't be gone long. We can talk when I get back. I promise. But I have to talk to Gary, and it has to be now. I need that information."

"Damn it, Laurel. Does everything always have to be done your way? You're the bossiest woman I've ever met."

Laurel got a sick feeling in her stomach. "What's going on here? What are you saying?"

"I'm saying I won't be here when you get back," Scott shouted down at her. He dropped her arm, his eyes filled with contempt. "You're so concerned with yourself and clearing your name that nothing else matters to you. Maybe my father was right. Maybe you were just using me to find out more about Brian."

Shock rippled through her at his accusation. Laurel couldn't believe what she was hearing. She stood frozen to the spot, unable to form the words running through her mind. His words stabbed at her like a knife. Finally she said, "You can't believe that."

"Oh, I can't? Why don't you stick around and explain it to me?" he challenged.

The sick feeling and the disbelief slowly grew into anger. "This is important to me. Thanks to your father, it's not just my *job* anymore."

She thought quickly of Dan and the other men who'd misled her into believing they'd accepted who she was and what she did. Could she have been wrong about Scott, too? Questions and doubts flooded her mind. She glanced again at her watch, then reached behind her and slammed the door to her apartment. Time had run out. She battled the confusion and the pain caused by this sudden and unexpected change in Scott. How could he do this to her?

Rage pushed away the hurt, at least for the moment. She knew how much restoring his relationship with his family meant to him. Now that she had the first solid lead to clear herself and implicate Brian, Scott had turned on her. Had this been his intent all along? "I've got to go. There are some problems you can't just walk away from."

"Laurel. I don't want it to end like this between us. I want to explain. All I'm asking for is a few minutes of your precious time." Scott reached out to stop her. "Be reasonable."

"Reasonable?" She yanked her arm from his grasp. "You want me to be reasonable! Brian is dead and you're still covering for him."

"I'm trying to protect the people I care about," Scott returned, his voice angry.

"No one needs that kind of protection—least of all me."
She shoved past him, took a few steps, then turned back. "I
guess I don't know you as well as I thought I did. You damn
sure don't know me."

Her anger kept her moving all the way to the car. She
turned the key and stepped on the gas, not looking behind
her. A car horn tooted at her, and she swerved to the right.
When the car had passed, she took in a deep breath, fastened her seat belt, then cautiously moved into the traffic.

Laurel's hands trembled on the wheel as the pain of betrayal lodged once again in her chest. Biting back tears, she
sped toward the coffee shop where she was to meet Gary.
She wished she'd had more time. Scott's sudden change of
heart had devastated her. She knew she couldn't conceal her
feelings from Gary. She only hoped she could keep the hurt
from leaking down her face like a drippy faucet.

It was stupid. Jeffrey Hays was absolutely right. She
never should have gotten personally involved with a Delany. *Personally involved.* She snorted at the clinically ed-
ited term. What she'd done was fall head-over-heels in love
with Scott Delany. She'd given him her heart long before
she'd given him her body—when she shouldn't have given
him the time of day. Fighting the pain strengthened her resolve.

Laurel sped through an intersection on the tail of a yellow light. She directed her rage primarily at herself for not
being wiser—she'd convinced herself the situation was different this time around. When she'd been betrayed by Dan,
she'd been young and naive. That wasn't the case now. Fully
cognizant of the potential heartache, she'd taken the risk,
and it was time to own up to her misjudgment.

Laurel pulled into an empty space at the curb and turned
off the ignition. She started to remove her sunglasses, then

reconsidered. After a quick check in the mirror to make sure she didn't look too wretched, she went inside.

Gary sat alone at one of the booths in the rear. He glanced down at his watch.

She slid in across from him. "What have you got?"

He frowned. "Hello to you, too."

"I'm sorry." Laurel sighed and tried to drive all thoughts of Scott Delany from her mind. "It's good to see you."

Gary looked down at his coffee cup. "No surprises?"

She forced a smile. "I am sorry for what I did to you." She stumbled through the words, but couldn't dismiss the pain it caused to admit how out of control things had gotten on so many levels in her life.

"I can't tell you how much this means to me," she said. "The judge isn't going to let up on me until I get some hard evidence that Brian Delany was in that alley for the purpose of selling drugs." But the judge wasn't the Delany on her mind at the moment. Try as she might to forget about Scott, she couldn't quite chase his image from her thoughts. His disheveled appearance hinted that he'd at least had to wrestle with his conscience for a while before coming over. But that didn't change anything. He'd still betrayed her.

"I don't know how much good it will do you to know this stuff. I wish you'd let me check this kid out a little more thoroughly." Gary placed the manila folder on the table. "I did track down one of his teachers from last year. She said Dever has a great mind—and an attitude."

Laurel thought about that for a moment. The kid she remembered from her appearance at the high school with Brian had shown intelligence as well as confidence in himself.

She looked at the address on the paper in front of her.

Gary caught the surprise in her expression and smiled.

Jon Dever lived in the most exclusive neighborhood in Crystal Cove. "So what do you think the story is? Spoiled rich kid? Product of a dysfunctional family? If he really is intelligent, maybe he's bored?"

"I don't know," Gary said.

She glanced at the next page which included data on Dever's parents, Albert and Eloise.

"I found out Albert Dever owned several pieces of property in the area. The one that caught my attention was a warehouse located less than a block from where the shooting went down." A worried look came into his eyes.

"You think there's a connection?" she asked.

"I don't know. That's why I wish you'd give me a little more time to check this out. And Jeff Hays hasn't exactly been sitting on his thumbs," Gary pointed out.

"I know, I'm just so damn frustrated." *And angry,* she added silently. Each minute that slipped by put her closer to a murder charge and a prison cell.

"Well, be careful. Don't do anything dumb. Remember, you don't have any backup out there." They both knew that anytime an officer needlessly risked his or her life it was stupid, not courageous. But she couldn't explain to Gary the reasons driving her to action.

He looked at his watch. "I've got to get going." He pushed his cup and saucer away nervously, but didn't get up. "Laurel, is there something else you want to tell me?"

She shook her head.

"Are you sure? If Delany has—"

"He hasn't." She didn't give him the chance to finish. She knew she had to push aside her personal feelings about Scott and his father to concentrate on solving her case. There had to be a way to connect Brian with Jon Dever.

Unfortunately, she couldn't tell Gary about Judge Delany's threat without bringing out the whole horrible ordeal that had occurred between her and Brian two years ago.

She thanked Gary again, and he started to leave.

"See you at the game tomorrow night." He waited for confirmation.

Temporarily drawing a blank, she stared at him.

"The volleyball tournament." He looked at her strangely, his eyebrows drawing together. "We're in the championship playoffs. Final game's tomorrow night against Huntington Beach." His concern was justified. It wasn't like her to forget about the annual tournament.

"Oh, yeah," she said without enthusiasm. She'd been on the team for two years and knew the Huntington Beach team was their major rival. Everyone at the station rallied behind the team with support matching that of the high school booster club. She might not be able to play while on suspension, but nothing could keep her from cheering on her teammates. Besides, showing up at the game would reiterate her confidence in her innocence. "I promise I'll be there."

Gary nodded, apparently satisfied by her word.

Laurel remained seated for a few minutes after he left. The manila folder lay on the table beside her water glass. A short time ago she'd been so anxious to get her hands on the information contained within the file. Now, the deep ache in her chest made her wonder if she was making a mistake putting her ideals before her heart.

But it was more than her ideals. The high school drug problem would probably continue, anyway. But she would never be able to live with herself if one single student died from the sale of those drugs. Why couldn't Scott understand that? And why had she let herself fall in love with

him? As she picked up the file, to take it home and examine it in private, she realized she'd never had a choice.

At home, Laurel carefully pored over the contents of the
file. Finding nothing particularly incriminating in the data,
she decided to check out for herself the places mentioned.
Besides, she had to get out of the house, away from the reminders of the night of lovemaking she'd shared with Scott,
reminders of what had been and could never be again.

She slipped on jeans and a dark blue T-shirt. She chose an
old pair of running shoes and knotted the laces so they
wouldn't come undone at a time that might prove dangerous.

The residential address Gary had provided spanned a
greater distance from her one-bedroom apartment than
mere miles; the people who lived in that neighborhood were
in a different stratosphere. The huge, rambling, oriental-
style home stood on one of the most choice lots in the small,
terraced development overlooking the Pacific Ocean. The
manicured grounds boasted expensive ornamental shrubs
and trees. There wasn't an oleander or eucalyptus in sight.
She also noticed the house and grounds were void of any
signs of people. The drapes and gates were all closed.

She left the development and headed for the area of town
zoned for light industry. She had to pass her own neighborhood, which served as a buffer between the homes of the
elite and the factories they owned. As she neared the warehouse, she decided not to park right away, but made a quick
reconnaissance of the surrounding blocks to get her bear-
ings. The building owned by Albert Dever stood one block
west of the one owned by Brian Delany, but backed up to the
same alley where she'd been shot.

Jon was in the alley the day she saw Scott. He could have
been there the night of the shooting, as well. Sometimes
kids—especially teenagers—liked to hang out at their par-

ents' place of business. Playing the role of the boss's son could give Jon a sense of power and authority he could not otherwise enjoy.

Down the street she found a parking space from which she could observe the building. The front of the structure contained two large doors marked for shipping and receiving and a standard entry door beside them. She saw the logo of a familiar computer company stenciled on the door. That explained Albert Dever's financial situation. Whether he owned the computer company or simply supplied the parts from this warehouse, he had to be making a fortune.

She watched the building for some time without seeing any sign of occupancy. The small parking lot to the side of the building was empty. She waited. Waiting was the hardest part. Despite her efforts to concentrate on her case and bring this agony to an end, Scott kept creeping back into her thoughts.

After another hour she got an idea. Picking up her cellular phone, she got Albert Dever's office number and dialed it.

"I'm sorry, but Mr. Dever is out of the country on business," the secretary said. "He won't be back for another month. Perhaps I can direct your call to one of his assistants?"

Laurel had to think fast. "Actually, I'm a Realtor and I have a client interested in a piece of property Mr. Dever owns." She gave the secretary the address. "Perhaps you could tell me. Is he still utilizing the warehouse for storage or is it vacant at this time?"

The secretary hesitated. "I'm not certain. If you would give me your name and phone number, I could have Mr. Dever get back to you."

"That's all right. I'll wait until he comes back. Thank you very much." She hung up quickly.

Laurel continued to watch the building past normal work hours. The possibility of Jon Dever suddenly driving up to the door was a long shot at best, but one she felt she needed to gamble on. Ascertaining no change from her vantage point down the block, she cautiously slipped from her car and crossed over to the same side of the street. As she approached the building, she noticed a small unmarked door at the rear of the structure, on the side near the parking lot.

Casually, she walked to the door at the front of the building and tried the knob as though she had business there. When the knob remained stationary in her grasp, she walked to the back of the building and similarly gave that knob a gentle turn. To her surprise the knob responded. She held her breath, trying to listen for sounds from the other side. She heard none.

After a moment, she quietly opened the door and stepped inside. The total darkness temporarily blinded her after all the time she'd spent in the bright sunlight. In the brief time the open door had illuminated the interior, Laurel had seen that she was in a long, empty hall. She stood against the wall for a couple of minutes, waiting for her eyes to adjust. After a while, she noticed a faint light at the far end to her right. It appeared to be coming from behind a partially closed door. Opposite the door was the entrance to the main storage area.

Laurel proceeded cautiously, walking with a stealth that would make her *sensei* proud. At the end, she paused again to listen. After a few moments of uninterrupted silence, she stepped past the door to glance into the large room on the left. Except for one long row of boxes bearing the computer logo, the tall shelves were all empty. Satisfied there was no one in the darkened warehouse, she stepped back to the room from which the light shone.

From the doorway she'd seen no sign of anyone working inside. The large file cabinet to the left of the door carried a heavy coat of dust on top. She prayed she wouldn't sneeze at an inopportune moment and give away her position. Slowly she edged her head farther into the opening. A large wooden desk filled most of the remaining office space. Luckily, she found no one lurking behind the door or inside. She stepped in and crossed the room to explore the small bathroom off the far wall. She wrinkled her nose at the musty smell. Rather than reassuring her, the empty bathroom caused her greater uneasiness.

Laurel walked back to the desk. Behind it, she noticed a smaller file cabinet and a credenza. They, too, were covered in a layer of dust. She looked down at the waste basket beside the desk. It was empty.

Something wasn't quite right. Surely someone could have left the light on by accident, but the door had been unlocked, as well. She had the feeling of being on the verge of discovering something important when she turned back to look at the desk. She stepped closer. With the index finger of her left hand, she made a swipe across the desk. Even in the dim light she could tell there was no dust adhering to her finger. Someone had used the desk fairly recently. She put her hand lightly to the metal shade on the lamp. It was hot.

She moved around behind the desk and reached for the middle drawer. The outer door of the building suddenly swung open and light filled the hallway for a few seconds.

Laurel heard voices coming in her direction and looked around the room for a place to hide. There was no time to make it to the bathroom; she scrunched down under the desk.

Laurel could discern at least two distinct voices. Male. Probably young. Something heavy landed on the desk above her head. She heard the sound of rustling paper, then the aroma of greasy french fries filtered down to her hiding place. Laurel wished she'd taken the time to eat when her stomach began to growl.

The next thing she heard was the distinct sound of metal sliding on metal as the first round slipped into the chamber of an automatic weapon.

Chapter 14

"**D**amn her!" Scott pounded his fist on the steering wheel as he drove away from Laurel's apartment. If she'd just given him a few precious moments of her time, he could have ended this peaceably, but no. Nothing was ever that simple. She was being unreasonable, but he was really angry at himself. How could he have been such a fool?

He was so tired, he couldn't think straight. Pushing his fingers through his hair, he released a long yawn. His eyes burned and his muscles ached from sitting on his butt for so much of the last forty-eight hours. The negotiations had been exhausting, but nothing could compare to the toll the last ten hours had taken on him. He'd come so close to losing his mother his chest hurt to think about it. He didn't know what he would have done if she had died after overhearing his conversation with his father and he never had a chance to explain. Every time he thought of Brian dying, with all the harsh words and unresolved problems between them, a sharp pang of guilt stabbed at him. Never again

would he lose someone he loved under those circumstances.

He drove straight to Brian's, anxious to get out of his
dirty clothes and rest his tired eyes. Between yawns, as he
made his way to the guest bedroom, he decided he didn't
want to think about the pigheaded woman who'd caused
him so much joy and sorrow. Why couldn't she see he was
doing what was best for her? Their relationship was a thorn
in his father's side. He knew his father wouldn't let up on
Laurel until he stepped out of the picture. How had things
gotten so screwed up?

He dragged a hand over his face and sat on the edge of the
bed to rest for a moment, too exhausted to get undressed.

It was dark outside when a bad dream awakened him.
Having forgotten to set the alarm, he uttered a pithy epi-
thet he'd picked up from Hershal and rubbed his eyes. He
stretched and yawned. A glance at the bedside clock confirmed it was too late to go to the hospital. Instead, he
picked up the phone and checked with the nurse on duty.

"She's sleeping comfortably now," the woman said.

He also learned the doctor had not yet rescinded the order which kept Scott from seeing her. "Please leave word for
the doctor to call me when he makes rounds in the morning. Tell him to ask my mother if she wants to see me. I'll
respect *her* wishes."

As soon as he'd replaced the receiver, his thoughts went
back to Laurel. He groaned. Now that he'd had a little sleep,
he could view their argument more clearly. He'd really
blown it. Showing up on her doorstep looking like a refu-
gee from a flea market was probably his first mistake. He
realized with increasing dismay that he hadn't told her about
the fight he'd had with his father or how it had nearly cost
his mother her life. In fact, he hadn't told her much of anything that had happened in the last forty-eight hours. All

he'd done was show up and make demands. He'd been a first-class jerk.

Scott picked up the phone again and punched out Laurel's number. He rubbed the heavy stubble on his jaw as he listened to the fourth ring before the answering machine came on.

"Laurel, if you're there, pick up. I need to talk to you."

Nothing. After a moment the line disconnected.

An uneasiness grew inside him. He tried to think of all the reasons that she might not answer her phone. Their fight had upset her. She probably didn't want to talk to him, and under the circumstances he could understand that.

After he'd showered and shaved, Scott felt much better. He tried Laurel's number once more, just in case. She still didn't answer. He wandered to the kitchen and pulled a barbecued chicken dinner from the freezer. He heated it in the microwave and poured a tall glass of milk.

While the chicken warmed, he thought about the accusations his father had made the night before. Scott realized now that they weren't fair and they weren't accurate. But, even more important, he realized that it no longer mattered to him *what* his father thought of him—or of Brian. The only opinion about himself that counted was his own.

He recalled Laurel's accusation about his still protecting Brian, even after his death. She'd been right on target with that little zinger. His father had pushed the right buttons, and he had automatically fallen back into his old ways. No more.

He owed Laurel an apology. Hell, he owed her several.

Because it was so late, Scott decided not to go directly to Laurel's, to try to make amends. After a good night's sleep she might be more easily persuaded to forgive him. He finished eating and went back to bed. Sleep eluded him at first.

He used the time to think about Laurel, and he wondered if it was already too late.

Laurel held her breath as a pair of denim-clad legs stepped behind the desk.

"Don't move," a trembly voice commanded. Jon Dever squatted down. He held a .38 semiautomatic with an unsteady hand.

Laurel froze, remembering the last time a gun had been pointed at her. She knew she couldn't let her fear debilitate her. First and foremost, she had to defuse the situation.

"Okay, take it easy," she said in a disarming tone, slowly raising her hands to where they could be clearly seen.

Another kid stood beside Jon. Laurel had no idea what his name was, but she was certain she had seen the face before. Perhaps he had been the boy with Jon that day in the alley.

He tugged at Jon's arm, the one with which Jon held the gun. "That's the cop from—"

"Shut up!" Jon shoved the boy away.

"But, Jon," he continued in a panic.

"I said shut up a minute, Mike!" This time, Jon spoke with an authority the other boy didn't question. He turned his attention back to her. "What are you doing here?"

"It's kind of cramped in here. Mind if I stand up?" Laurel's eyes fixed on the gun as her mind raced to come up with an idea.

The boys backed up, but Jon Dever held his gun pointed at her chest. Memories of the shooting rushed back to Laurel, but she forced them aside.

"I wanted to talk to you and Mike before the narcotics detectives got to you," she said with surprising calm, though sweat dampened her palms.

"I don't know what you're talking about." Jon spoke just as calmly. The boy beside him shuffled nervously at the mention of his name.

She forced out a harsh laugh and shook her head from side to side, never letting the gun out of her vision. "I wanted to talk about the contents of Brian Delany's brief-case—" she saw Mike glance quickly at the credenza behind the desk "—and about a pile of trouble so deep you can't even imagine what you've gotten yourselves into."

Mike started fidgeting like a junkie in need of a fix. Jon shot his companion an irritated glance before responding to Laurel. "I still don't know what you're talking about."

She lowered her eyes again to the .38 automatic in his hand. Could it be the same gun Brian had fired at her? "For starters you're holding a dead man's gun." She saw Jon's eyes widen and knew she'd guessed correctly. "A gun that ballistics will prove was used to shoot a police officer." She paused. "Police officers don't like it when someone shoots one of their own. It's like family, only worse." She made a clucking sound and slowly moved her head from side to side again. "I sure wouldn't want to be found in possession of that gun."

Laurel could see Jon begin to squirm. The boy was more nervous and unsure of himself than he let on. She cautiously increased the pressure.

"When this goes down, you don't want to get caught in the middle. As it stands, you could get off pretty easily if you cooperate. We're not after the kids who get the drugs, we're after the suppliers." She watched for a sign of weakness.

Jon continued to play dumb, but sweat beaded on his forehead in the air-conditioned room.

"Of course, if it comes down to kids or no one, the district attorney will nail the kids. By the way, Mr. Dever, when was your eighteenth birthday?'' Laurel saw the slight flaring of Jon Dever's nostrils. She'd scored a direct hit. He realized he would be tried as an adult.

"Get something from the other room to tie her up with," Jon ordered.

"Why not just shoot her where she is? We could say we were here to check on your dad's warehouse while he's in Europe and we caught her going through the drawers. We thought she was a burglar." Mike seemed to see no flaws in his plan.

"And have the police and the newspapers crawling all over the place before—" Jon stopped abruptly. "Before we're ready for them? I don't think so." She could tell he immediately regretted his outburst. Though he spoke to Mike, Jon stared coldly into Laurel's eyes as he said the words. "Tie her up."

Mike came back with several lengths of the flat plastic band used to strap boxes for shipping.

Laurel thought about trying to jump them before they could tie her up, but the possibility of taking another bullet made her hesitate, and Jon was holding the gun at a distance that guaranteed a hit. Besides, he never let Mike come between her and his gun.

They bound her hands and feet, then for good measure sat her down beside the heavy desk and ran a length of the plastic strap under the desk leg and around her hips. The thin strip cut into her wrists and ankles.

Jon appeared to possess not only the intellect the teacher had spoken of, but also a sharpness of mind that enabled him to think on his feet. That made him more dangerous, but it also meant she had a chance to reason with him, to convince him he had a choice to make and explain how he could make the right one.

"Should we stick something in her mouth to keep her from yelling?" Mike asked.

"Let her yell if she wants. No one will hear her through these concrete walls, especially with all the noise the air conditioner makes." There was a cockiness to his intelligence Laurel didn't like at all.

"What are we going to do with her?" Mike asked.

"Shut up and wait for me out there," Jon said to Mike. Then to Laurel he added, "Don't try anything stupid. You've presented us with a little problem, but we'll come up with a solution. I'm real good at solutions."

"Think real hard, Jon. Your whole future is riding on your decision," she said.

Jon stepped to the door. As he flipped off the light, plunging her into darkness, he said, "So's yours."

The next morning, Scott called Laurel again. There was still no answer, so he tried the hospital. The doctor had left word that Scott could see his mother if she was awake.

He drove straight to the hospital. The nurse allowed him only a brief visit while his mother was in the cardiac recovery unit. She needed her rest, but he didn't see how anyone could rest amidst the foul odors of disinfectant and alcohol permeating the corridors.

Scott paused at the door as he got his first glimpse of the frail woman lying in the hospital bed. Despite the doctor's bright prognosis, he thought she still looked very close to death.

Her eyes flickered open and focused on him. Slowly her lips formed a faint smile. Her smile brought her face back to life. "Scott," she breathed.

He smiled back. "Good morning, Mother. You're looking beautiful today." He meant those words more deeply than he could convey. "How do you feel?"

"Better," she said softly. "Thanks to you."

He puzzled over the reference as he gently lifted her hand and placed it in his own. "Mother, I want to tell you how much I love you and how sorry I am for causing you so much pain. If I'd had any idea my argument with Father would have brought on—"

"Scott," she interrupted, "that had nothing to do with my problem. I've been having symptoms for months. I thought they'd go away on their own."

The admission stunned him. "Why didn't you tell anyone?"

"You know how your father overreacts. I didn't want him to make a fuss." She squeezed his hand.

"Some things are worth making a fuss over." He looked down at her with affection in his heart.

The nurse came by to tell him he had to go.

He kissed his mother on the cheek. "I'll come back later."

She tugged at his hand as he started to turn away. "Your father told me what you did. Thank you for saving my life."

The shock stayed with him after he left her room. Had his father really told her he'd saved her life? His inept attempt at CPR had broken her rib and caused her additional pain. He knew his father held him responsible for her heart attack. It didn't make sense.

Scott started to call Laurel from a pay phone at the hospital, then reconsidered. If she was home, she still wouldn't answer. Anyway, he needed to apologize in person for the cruel words he'd said.

As he pulled up to the curb where Laurel usually parked her car, an unsettling feeling crept over him. Her car was nowhere in sight. She could have a reserved space in the back somewhere that she used at night, he reasoned.

He strode up the walk and knocked on the door. When she didn't answer, he knocked louder. After a moment he called out. "Laurel? Laurel, it's Scott. Please open the door."

No response.

The apartment remained dark and quiet inside. He walked around the side of the building and looked for her car in one of the carports.

The red sports car was not there, either. Disquiet settled over him. He tried to convince himself that she was fine, that she'd probably gotten an early start on her investigating. And he knew she could take care of herself. But he still worried.

After yesterday, maybe she just wanted to get away by herself and rethink all of this.

Scott went home to do some rethinking of his own. They had made plans to go to the volleyball game tonight. He knew she wouldn't miss the playoff game for anything. If her pending trial and his father's threat had not kept her away, their fight certainly wouldn't. Laurel Tanner had more strength and character than any woman he'd ever known.

He thought back to what she'd said the day before about there being some problems you couldn't run away from. Though her own problem looked unsolvable, she continued to try. She was probably out now, tracking down a lead.

Between trips to the hospital and trips to Laurel's apartment, Scott received a call from the investigator he'd hired to check out Stanley Murdock, Brian's friend in New York.

"The DEA is very close to an arrest," the investigator said. "They're waiting for a move from some Colombian dealer named Raul Ortiz. He's the one they're really after. But your friend Murdock is making quite a name for himself, as well. He defended Ortiz a few years ago and got him off on a technicality. They've been tight ever since. And it seems Murdock has been well compensated for his services. He's throwing around a lot of cash."

A dreadful idea occurred to Scott. Murdock had acquired his windfall before Scott had left for London. When Brian had failed to get the money he needed through Scott and his father, could he have turned to Murdock?

As the conversation drew to a close, Scott's uneasiness increased. Laurel had hinted that she was on to something important. He hoped it wasn't Murdock. He had faith in her ability to take care of herself, but she hadn't the time to slowly phase back into police work the way she said officers normally did after a shooting. If she tried to go after someone like Murdock on her own, she'd be in great danger. He knew her service revolver had been taken from her; he wondered if she had another.

Scott decided to make one last trip to the hospital to see his mother. She seemed to be doing great, and the doctor said she was making excellent progress on her recovery.

"You've got something on your mind," his mother stated.

"I have plans for the evening, so I won't be able to visit again." He reached for her outstretched hand.

"You don't have to protect me, Scott. The doctor says I'm doing fine. Tell me what's bothering you." She smiled the smile he remembered so well.

"I'm going to the police volleyball game tonight," he said.

"You're seeing this sergeant who shot Brian?" she asked.

"Yes," he answered, unable to discern her feelings. He took her hand between both of his. "Father is wrong about her." He searched his mother's face for a shimmer of understanding. "Brian didn't give her a choice. There's a lot you didn't know about him."

He waited for a response. When she gave none, he continued. "I know this must be hard for you to accept—it certainly was for me. I may have blown it already, but I intend to try and make things right. I want you to know that I love you and that will never change. No matter what happens, I'll never close any doors between us again."

"I love you, Scott," she said as the nurse stepped into the room to tell him his time was up.

For the time being, that was all he needed to hear.

Scott drove directly to Laurel's from the hospital. Her car was still gone, but he tried the door, anyway.

"Hello, Mr. Delany," a small voice called from behind him.

He whirled at the sound, but he knew even before he turned it was not Laurel's voice calling to him. "Hello." He mentally hunted for the girl's name. "How are you, Heather?"

"Fine," she said, beaming. "Are you looking for Sergeant Tanner?"

"Yes, I am. Have you seen her?" He held his breath as he waited for the girl to answer. His hope was quickly dashed when she shook her head.

"I don't think she came home last night. I thought—" Bright pink flooded Heather's cheeks. "I was kind of worried."

He understood exactly what she thought, and he wished with all his heart it was so, but it wasn't. "I haven't seen her since early yesterday morning." He started to say he was worried, too, but he didn't want to alarm Heather. "If you see Laurel—Sergeant Tanner—please tell her I'd like to speak with her. It's very important."

Worry nearly drove Scott mad. Though he had no appetite, he decided to stop by a fast-food restaurant on his way to the game and get something to halt the grinding in his gut.

His stomach was so tied in knots, what he ate didn't matter. He got halfway through his greasy meal when he changed his mind and tossed it in the trash.

He called once more before he left for the high school gym where the game was being held. The whole way there he kept telling himself she would show up. The possibility that she might not scared him to death.

He parked the car and went inside. A boisterous crowd already filled half the stands. Scott stood at the gym door where he could scan the bleachers for her. After a few minutes, he determined she had not arrived.

He recognized her partner from a picture in her living room. Gary was on the court warming up with the team. He, too, scanned the growing crowd. Their gazes clashed. For a time neither man let his eyes falter. Scott saw challenge and accusation in the younger man's eyes. The contact broke as someone called out to the officer and tossed him the ball.

The game started and still Laurel had not arrived. Scott's apprehension grew. He went to a pay phone in the hall adjacent to the gym and dialed her number. She didn't answer. He waited five minutes, looked through the gym, then dialed the number again. Still no answer.

She wouldn't miss the game. No matter what was going on in her personal life, Laurel needed that connection with her friends and co-workers. She treasured them as much as he treasured his family.

Scott looked out over the gym and felt the wrongness as if it were a living, breathing thing. He could think of only one thing that would keep Laurel away tonight.

Quickly, he called the police station and asked to speak to Laurel's captain. By the time Captain Larson got on the line, Scott's respirations had doubled.

"Something is very wrong," Scott said. "I think Sergeant Tanner is in serious danger."

Chapter 15

Laurel's legs cramped and her back felt as though it had been fused into a permanent C-curve. She tried to ignore the empty pangs in her stomach, but the lingering aroma of French fries made it impossible. Jon and Mike had been gone for hours. She'd struggled against the plastic restraints until her chafed wrists bled.

Late in the evening, her captors returned. Mike dropped a fast-food bag on the floor beside her.

"Well, untie her hands so she can eat," Jon told him. "Unless you want to feed her."

Mike snarled, but did as he was told. Jon held the gun on her while she ate two hamburgers.

She saw Jon glance at the marks on her wrists, but he made no comment. He released her long enough to go to the bathroom, but that was her only reprieve.

After Mike had left for the night, Jon refused to release her again for any reason.

She talked for hours, trying to persuade him to let her go and turn himself in. Each time she tried, she made a little progress. Since he'd slipped up earlier and nearly said something he didn't want her to know, he'd been more cautious. She felt certain he was trying to deal directly with the people who had been supplying the drugs to Brian.

"You have too much to lose, Jon. I've seen your school records. If you get out of this now, you can still salvage your future." She saw him considering.

At first, Jon didn't say much, but as the hours wore on, he began to ask questions. She suspected he was beginning to realize he was in over his head when he started asking her "what if" questions.

"What would happen to me if I did what you're asking?" Jon said.

She tried to sound as encouraging as she could without making him think she was snowing him. "That depends on the degree of your involvement and how much help you can be in apprehending the supplier. I'd do whatever I could to help you."

He gave her a doubtful look.

"I need your testimony about what went on in the alley the night Brian Delany died." She also needed to get out of this alive to benefit from that testimony. If Jon and Mike were holding the drugs or the money from Brian's deal, hoping to infiltrate the network, the suppliers would be after them, too. "To be honest, arresting two teenage boys isn't much of a collar. I want the guys at the top and so will the D.A., I can guarantee that."

She gave him a few minutes to think about what she'd said, then added, "You know they can't let me live. Are you ready to be an accomplice to murder?"

Jon turned out the lights and left sometime before dawn. It was late the next morning when he and Mike returned.

Laurel blinked at the sudden glare as she studied the boys. From their level of anxiety, she knew her time was running out.

Mike was really the giveaway. His glassy, fearful stare told her she had to convince them very quickly or make a play to overtake them.

The gun in Jon's hand made her decision more difficult. She doubted if he'd shoot her outright, but he might panic in a struggle, or worse, he might accidentally be shot.

They went through the same feeding ritual. She examined every possibility for escape as they released her hands. It was too risky. Besides, she needed their help.

They sat around staring repeatedly at their watches for a while. Then Mike left.

Laurel tried another tack. "I have a pretty good idea why you got involved in all this, but what about Mike? What's his story?"

Jon came and sat on the floor beside her. He looked older somehow. His eyes bored into hers with a new depth. "It's a way out for him. He's sixteen. His dad doesn't give a damn about him—beats the hell out of him for kicks."

"What about his mother?" Laurel kept all judgment from her voice.

"She doesn't sober up long enough to do anything permanent." He stared at Laurel. "Mike doesn't have a whole lot to lose, one way or the other."

"If you turned yourselves in, he could get the help he needs," she said.

He studied her face with the perception of someone far exceeding his years. "If we let you make a phone call, can you find out if they'll drop all charges against us if we cooperate fully?" Jon's eyes didn't move from hers.

Was he testing her? If Jon was as intelligent as Gary had indicated, he'd know the call would be traced.

"They would trace the call and have officers here before I got through to the captain." She kept her gaze steady. "I won't make promises I may not be able to keep. I will promise to do everything I can to help. Whether or not you can cut a deal with the D.A. will depend on how much information you can give him and how soon he gets it."

He studied her carefully. She didn't flinch under his scrutiny.

"What do you think we'll get?" he asked.

"Right now, with no priors, that could be a light sentence or even a suspended sentence with probation, but that's up to a judge to decide. I do know that at this time, no one believes Brian Delany shot me. Everyone thinks it was whoever else was in that alley that night. If it can be proven that you two were there—and it can, by the gun in your hand and the briefcase in the credenza—you could be charged with attempted murder."

Jon's eyes widened in surprise when she mentioned the briefcase, and she knew she'd guessed its location correctly. Still he didn't look convinced.

The outer door opened.

"Jon." She stared at him in earnest. "I know you're too smart to throw your life away like this. Time is running out. Untie me and surrender yourselves into my custody while you still have the chance."

"It's all set up," Mike said from the doorway.

Jon rubbed the palm of his hand back and forth over the knee of his jeans as he glanced from Mike to Laurel. "It's too late."

Scott made one last check of the gym for Laurel before heading to the station, as Captain Larson had requested. The captain promised he'd make a few phone calls and check out Scott's suspicions.

Scott caught Gary Boyd's gaze as he was about to serve. The ball slammed into the net. Scott didn't take the time to acknowledge or explain his anger. If Boyd had given the evidence to the captain instead of Laurel, she might not be in danger now.

At the station, a uniformed officer ushered Scott directly to the captain's office. Fearing for Laurel's safety, he tried to explain as quickly as he could.

"Slow down, Mr. Delany." Captain Larson stood behind his desk with a placating look Scott recalled seeing many times in his role as a judge's son.

He took in a couple of deep breaths as he looked out the open blinds of the captain's window into a large room filled with desks and computers. A mere handful of officers remained. A huge banner hung on the wall that read Beat H.B. He recalled the crowd that had turned out at the volleyball game, and his temper flared. "Why aren't you doing anything? Sergeant Tanner is in trouble and all anybody has on their mind is a damn volleyball game."

"I can assure you, Mr. Delany, I have people looking for her even as we speak," Captain Larson said.

Scott should have been comforted. He wasn't. If the captain already had officers out looking for Laurel, he must also believe she was in danger.

"If you have information that might expedite our search, I want to hear it." The captain tossed his pen on the desk, leaned back in his chair and stared at Scott.

"I know something is wrong. She hasn't been home in over twenty-four hours. The last time I talked to her, she'd found a picture of one of the kids from the alley—"

"She didn't see anyone else in the alley the night she was shot," the captain said impatiently.

"Not the night she was shot. Weeks later. We were both there and these two teenage boys saw me and panicked. If you don't believe me, ask her partner." Scott watched the captain's chest expand sharply at the mention of Gary Boyd, but he continued. "Laurel figured it was because they thought I was Brian and they knew he was supposed to be dead. They also knew they had his . . . property—the briefcase and the gun." He could see the captain's face taking on a new look of not only keen interest, but barely controlled rage.

Captain Larson picked up his phone. "Is Boyd here yet?" he screamed into the device. "I want him in my office the minute he shows up." He slammed the phone down.

"I don't know what information her partner gave her, but she already knew one of their names and had a picture of him and Brian together at the high school a couple of years ago," Scott added.

The captain's gaze fixed on something beyond the window. Gary Boyd stood in the squad room, bending over an open desk drawer. Captain Larson summoned Gary into his office with a curt toss of his head. Gary pulled out a manila folder and headed in their direction.

"What the hell have you and Tanner been up to?" Captain Larson demanded the moment Gary shut the door. Larson quickly interrogated the officer. When Gary affirmed the captain's suspicions, Larson let him have it in a tone that turned every head in the outer room in their direction.

Scott's patience snapped. "Why are you arguing over proper procedures when Laurel's life may be in danger? If Officer Boyd knows where she might be, I would think a reprimand could wait." Scott struggled to rein in his temper. He knew yelling at the captain wasn't the smartest thing to do right now, but with each minute that passed he feared more and more for Laurel's safety.

Captain Larson turned his sharp gaze on Scott. "Mr. Delany, you haven't told us exactly what your interest is in all of this."

Scott ground his teeth, unwilling to say the real reason. Instead, he said, "I've done some investigating on my own. I believe my brother shot Sergeant Tanner as she claims."

Captain Larson shook his head slowly from side to side. "What evidence do you have?"

Gary eyed him with suspicion.

Damn. He didn't want it to come out like this, but his concern for Laurel's safety forced him to continue. "I found documents in a second hidden safe." He summarized the contents and what his investigator had turned up on Stanley Murdock and Raul Ortiz. Scott looked over at Gary, who told them what he'd given Laurel and added new evidence he'd gotten.

"That's enough for me," the captain said. "We'll get a search warrant for Dever's home."

"Will we be able to get one based on that?" Gary nodded at the file.

The captain tugged at his mustache. "There's something else you should know." He looked solemnly from Gary to Scott. "We found Laurel's informant, Donald Cooper, a little while ago."

Gary leaned forward in his chair.

Scott felt a tightness in his gut.

"The coroner estimates he's been dead for at least three weeks," the captain said.

"Damn!" Scott slammed his fist on the captain's desk.

Gary slumped despondently in the chair.

Scott fought a horrifying sense of dread. If the same people who had killed Cooper had Laurel, she faced greater danger than he'd imagined.

"We've got to try for the warrant on what we've got. I don't think we've got much time to spare." Captain Larson instructed Gary to proceed.

"How long will that take?" Scott asked. He didn't like the answer he got. He could make it to his father's house in less than half the time. "Any reason my father can't sign this thing?"

Both men looked at him as if he'd lost his mind. The captain shook his head, but picked up his phone. He pushed a button, then handed it to Scott. "You can try."

Scott said, "Give me a minute alone."

The captain frowned.

"Please," Scott added as an afterthought.

The captain nodded. He and Gary stepped outside, shutting the door behind them.

Scott knew his father would be home and near a phone because of his mother. He quickly explained the situation.

"You've got to be joking," his father replied.

"I've never been more serious." Scott clenched his fist.

"Why, Scott?" His father's voice was raw with the pain of betrayal. "How could you even ask me to do this?"

"Because I think you're smart enough to realize this is all your fault, and honorable enough to do the right thing." He heard his father sigh. Time was wasting. He agonized over what he had to say next, knowing it would forever destroy his relationship with his father. "Laurel wouldn't have gone after these guys on her own if it wasn't for your threat. If you don't agree to sign this warrant, I swear I'll nail you to the wall."

After a brief pause the judge spoke without emotion. "Bring it here. I'll sign it."

"Thank you," Scott said, motioning for the captain. He handed over the phone. Gary was already at his desk, typing up what had to be the warrant. When he finished, he ripped it out of the typewriter.

"Come on," Scott said, hurrying Gary when he stopped to whisper something to another officer on his way out the door.

At his father's house, they got the warrant signed quickly. "Thank you, Father." Scott extended his hand, hoping. After a brief hesitation, his father accepted it. "I'll call as soon as I can," Scott promised.

They hurried to the designated meeting place a block from Dever's house. Gary's threats to have Scott arrested didn't dissuade him from getting involved. He had to know Laurel was safe.

"You're not trained," Gary argued more effectively. "You could cause her to be hurt unnecessarily." He knew right where to hit him.

Scott promised to stay in the car.

"I think there's more going on between you and Laurel than your brother's illegal activities," Gary challenged.

Scott hesitated, feeling the weight of guilt on his shoulders for the additional trouble he'd caused. She deserved to be fully exonerated, not to have shadows of doubt hanging over her for the rest of her career. "I said some pretty stupid things the last time I saw her."

"Don't underestimate Laurel," Gary said.

He looked at Gary more closely, but didn't have time to pursue the questions the man provoked. The other officers were all assembled.

"We'll find her. She's going to be all right," Gary said as he left Scott alone in the car.

Scott wondered which one of them Gary was trying to convince.

He waited impatiently while six officers entered the Dever home. He couldn't stand not knowing if Laurel was inside or not. After an unreasonably long time, he went to the front door. An officer was coming out carrying a plastic bag, which held a pair of black leather driving gloves.

"Where's Laurel? Is she all right?" His voice sounded high and unfamiliar.

"Not here," the officer said solemnly.

Scott ran inside. To his surprise, Gary sat casually on the sofa talking to a child, a boy of about twelve or thirteen. Two uniformed officers stood in intimidating poses with feet apart and arms folded across their chests.

The boy turned to look at Scott and his gasp of surprise was audible to everyone in the room. He edged back on the couch as if a monster from his nightmares had just walked through the door. Perhaps he had, Scott thought.

Gary caught on immediately and began to use the information. "Mr. Delany, this is Jon Dever's brother, Galen. We found the black gloves, just as you said we would."

Gary continued to try to coax the boy into telling them what he knew, but the kid was scared—too scared, Scott thought.

Scott squatted down to the boy's level. "Listen, Galen, we don't want to hurt your brother. We know he's in some trouble, big trouble, but not so much with the police as with the people whose things he has taken. He could get hurt real bad if the police don't find him first."

"He's at my dad's warehouse," the boy began. The information came out in such a rush, Scott had difficulty understanding him. Galen said he remembered seeing the lady cop at his school with Officer Boyd.

In minutes, they had all the information they needed. Gary called it in and they headed for the new location. It was a warehouse not far from where Laurel had been shot. Scott thought of her going there alone and how hard it must have been for her. He wished that her fellow officers had been more supportive during the past weeks, but he, more than most, knew what it was like going up against the edict of his father.

"Do you think you'll have enough men to pull this off safely?" Scott asked, thinking angrily about the final game of the interdepartmental volleyball tournament and how many of the officers would at this very moment be laughing and playing, oblivious to the fact that Laurel's life might be in danger.

"We'll have enough," Gary said distractedly.

Gary's apparent lack of concern made Scott turn in his direction, temper flaring.

Before he could say anything, one of the other officers came up beside the car. "The yellow Camaro is parked behind the warehouse, and the engine is still warm."

Gary picked up his radio and called the station. He relayed what they'd just been told, then listened to the captain's reply.

As Gary spoke into the microphone, he looked directly at Scott. "The sergeant's car is parked across the street."

Scott felt something explode inside his chest. He shifted in the seat and looked over his shoulder. Gary was right. They had Laurel. The need to do something overpowered him. As he reached for the door handle, Gary's hand clamped down on his shoulder. He turned on Gary, grabbing his wrist with a speed that startled them both. "I'm not going to sit here while you go after her with only a handful of men. You're going to need help."

Scott turned his head at the sound of squealing tires. Within minutes, the parking lot filled with police officers, both on and off duty, some still in their volleyball jerseys.

Her friends had come through for her. He hoped it wasn't too late.

Gary laid the folder on the seat and got out to confer with a lieutenant. Scott couldn't just sit there. The file on the seat caught his attention. Clenching and unclenching his fists, he picked it up and started looking through it. He found all the information Gary had disclosed, but something else caught his eye. "The *Mary Clare*," he muttered aloud, thinking. It was a boat docked at the marina directly across the bay from Brian's house.

Scott looked up to find the officers ready for their assault on the warehouse. Gary glanced at him and nodded. Scott held his breath as the special team of officers simultaneously pried open the big rolling doors and small side door to gain entry into the building. Gary and several other backup officers followed them inside while others stationed at points outside radioed information to the lieutenant in command.

Scott couldn't stand it. He got out of the car and stepped over to wait behind the lieutenant's car, where he could hear the communication with the officers inside.

It felt like hours had passed before Gary came back out. "It's empty. Looks like they've taken her with them." Gary grabbed the mike to speak directly to the captain. "There's fresh blood on the floor. Not a lot, but enough to indicate a struggle of some sort."

Scott recoiled at the news. He had a terrible feeling in his gut. As they discussed where to look next, a compelling thought struck him. "Try the marina. Dever's dad has a boat there."

The captain insisted they'd have taken her someplace less populated where they wouldn't have as great a risk of being caught. "This kid is clever."

An officer stepped up to the car. "I'm heading back to the station," he said to the lieutenant.

"Can you give me a lift back?" Scott asked.

He rubbed a hand across his jaw. It might be illogical, but the gnawing in his gut told him the captain was wrong.

Chapter 16

"It's not too late," Laurel insisted. "But time is running out." She sat with her back against the wall in the windowless cargo area of Mike's van. Jon sat beside her on the carpeted floor. She spoke to him in a low, even tone, aware of the need for urgency, but not wanting him to panic. "You must have figured out I didn't get this far on my own. My partner has a whole file on you. It's only a matter of time before he discovers I'm missing and puts two and two together."

"We can handle Officer Boyd," he said with a confidence that didn't quite ring true.

Surprised Jon had come up with the name of her partner so easily, Laurel pressed to see how much he really knew. "He's not the only one who knows I went out looking for you and never returned."

This time, a look of genuine confidence appeared on Jon's face. "If you mean the twin—" he paused, grinning with relief "—he's not my problem anymore."

Laurel's heart thundered in her chest. "How do you know—"

"Man, he scared the crap out of us when we saw him that day in the alley," Jon went on and actually laughed. "I thought we'd been had royally by the D.A. I even got a speeding ticket on my way home."

"What did you mean, he's not your problem anymore?" Laurel intruded on his boasting, concern for Scott's safety paramount in her mind.

He met her gaze. "Murdock said to leave the twin to him. He'd handle him personally when he got in today."

Stanley Murdock was after Scott. Laurel's mouth went dry. Her heart pumped dread through her body. Her anger at his betrayal had mellowed into pain, regret and, finally, understanding. She couldn't bear the thought of something happening to him.

After thinking about her own family and how much they'd meant to her, she could empathize with Scott's need to preserve his relationship with his father. There would never be a place for her within that family because his father would always put Scott in the position of having to choose between them. Even if Scott chose her, she couldn't let him sacrifice his relationship with his father, because she knew how much that would hurt him in the long run.

Laurel looked up to see Jon still staring at her with the gun in his hand. She didn't want to die without talking to Scott. Too many people had died with feelings left unspoken.

During the night she'd thought of Scott and the angry words she'd hurled at him. She had allowed her expectations to soar and she'd been disappointed when he'd turned out to be so much like Dan. If she was being selfish, it was out of desperation at the very real threat of going to prison.

As she watched Jon turn the gun over in his hand, she prayed with all her heart she'd made Scott as angry as he'd made her—angry enough to get on a plane and go straight back to London, where he'd be safe.

Murdock's direct involvement in the drug trafficking didn't surprise her. She wondered if he would be waiting for them when they reached their destination. She had to find out.

"I have to give you credit, when you turn to crime, you do it in a big way. Your list of offenses is adding up fast. If Murdock gets to Scott Delany, he'll kill him." A shiver traveled down her spine in the hot, stuffy van. "That will make you an accomplice to murder."

"Shut up," Jon said, pointing the gun at her midsection.

She fought to overcome her fright. "You have to know it will go much more easily for you if you surrender into my custody."

They hit a speed bump and the barrel of the gun rammed against Laurel's ribs. She gasped.

"Watch what the hell you're doing," Jon yelled to Mike.

Fear soaked into her skin, but she didn't let up. "You may as well shoot me now. They won't let me live. They can't afford to. If you turn me over to them, it will be just as if you pulled the trigger yourself."

"Shut up! Just shut the hell up!" Jon shouted.

The van stopped and Mike came around to open the side door.

"Get in and close the door," Jon said. He handed Mike a roll of duct tape. "Tape her mouth so she doesn't scream while we move her to the boat."

Laurel struggled to stop him from covering her mouth. Jon jabbed the gun into her back, making her reconsider. Diesel fumes mingled with the salty marine air as she inhaled through her nose.

Mike opened the door again, and Jon pulled her to her feet. They tossed a large raincoat over her shoulders to hide the straps binding her wrists and the gun pointed at her side.

"Come on." Jon nudged her forward.

If not for the gun, she would have made a break, even with her hands tied behind her back. She followed Mike down the walk to the docks.

At a chain-link gate, Jon slipped a plastic card key into the slot and a green light flashed. She also noticed an electronic eye mounted inside a security gate, monitoring people going in and out. She wondered if anyone monitored the monitor. Jon opened the gate and proceeded down the narrow dock to a large cabin cruiser. Painted on the back of the yacht were the words *Mary Clare, Newport Beach, California.* The name reminded her of that ship that had become famous because all the passengers mysteriously disappeared from it, the *Mary Celeste.* She shuddered at the thought.

Unfortunately, Laurel saw no other boaters on the docks to whom she might run for help. Mike carried the briefcase down the dock. The three of them looked so incongruous that anyone witnessing their move would surely have been suspicious.

A mild ocean breeze cooled her sweat-dampened skin. Jon kept the gun against her side as she boarded the *Mary Clare.* He pulled a key from his pocket to unlock the cabin. Inside, he ushered her through a well-equipped galley, down a narrow companionway to a large forward sleeping cabin. Mike yanked the tape off her mouth before Jon could protest.

Laurel silently endured the flash of pain, breathing deeply through her mouth. She sat on the edge of the bunk, closely watching Jon while Mike went back on deck. "Once they get here, there's no turning back, Jon. Your life, your whole future, will be determined at that moment. You're the only one who has the power to change that, but you've got to do it *before* they get here." Desperation filled her plea.

Jon nervously ran his fingers through his dark hair. He appeared to be on the verge of making a decision.

Mike burst into the room. "Murdock's here and he's got someone with him. Looks like it might be that Colombian guy."

Jon looked startled. "Ortiz?" He shoved the briefcase into a drawer beneath the bed and opened a tall, narrow wardrobe beside the cabin door. "Get in here and be quiet until I check this out," he ordered Laurel.

A moment later Laurel heard muffled voices in the other room. She heard one of the men say, "Did you bring the briefcase on board?"

Mike answered in the affirmative. As they talked, minutes seemed like hours in the stuffy closet. She heard the soft hum of an engine starting, then suddenly angry shouts echoed through the boat. The sound of heavy footsteps in the cabin filled her with dread, and then the wardrobe door swung open.

The dark man standing in front of her studied her for all of one second. In his black eyes she saw a ruthlessness that chilled her clammy skin. The man glanced back toward the companionway. In a low, menacing voice, he said, "You bring me here to talk with children and now I have this woman to—"

"Someone's snooping around outside," Mike cut in nervously.

"If you've double-crossed me . . ." The dark man didn't finish his threat, but turned aft. "Keep her quiet."

A blond man with a fair complexion stepped up and pulled her from the closet. "Facedown on the bed," he ordered in a low voice that betrayed his New York accent.

Murdock, she thought, both repulsed and alarmed.

He took the pillow from under her head, folded it in half and shoved it at Jon. "Use this if you have to shoot her," he said. "We don't want to attract any more attention."

Laurel swallowed. If Murdock was here, did that mean he had already taken care of Scott. She knew she couldn't ask—and it was killing her.

After Murdock left the room, she turned to Jon. "Please, untie me and give me the gun. Now. Hurry, Jon." She saw the indecision play on his face. "I don't know what those two are up to, but I'd bet their plans don't include you and Mike. They'll probably take whatever is inside that brief-case and stage an accident for all of us while they walk away unscathed."

Jon dropped the pillow and shoved the gun into the front of his pants. He reached for her arm as a ruckus broke out in the other room. Laurel heard a short series of blows and grunts. She gasped with alarm.

"Well, I'll be damned. Look who we have here," Murdock chuckled.

"Go to hell, Murdock."

Scott's labored voice caused Laurel's breath to catch. She tried to twist around.

"Don't move," Jon whispered.

The voices continued in the other room, and she strained to hear them. "What the hell's going on here, Murdock? What are you trying to pull?" Ortiz said.

"Señor Ortiz, let me introduce you to Scott Delany, your former associate's identical twin brother." After a short pause, he turned very serious. "What brings you here? Certainly not any sense of duty to your poor brother."

When Scott didn't answer, Murdock said, "I never will understand why Brian was so damned jealous of you."

Scott didn't say anything. She heard the sound of a blow and could not hold the cry in her throat. *"No."*

A brief silence followed. She regretted her outcry immediately.

"Well, well," Murdock said in a decidedly evil tone. "Perhaps I was wrong. Maybe you did come after your brother's killer, after all." He gave another low chuckle.

"Excellent idea," the other man said. "We can solve all our problems at once. Take our guest to the forward cabin."

Laurel understood exactly what they had in mind. She looked at Jon, all the while praying he was as intelligent as his teacher had said. One look at his face told her it was so.

"What should I do?" he whispered urgently.

"My hands."

Jon had his pocket knife out when they heard footsteps approaching from the companionway. He didn't have time to cut her restraints, so he passed the knife to her instead. She quickly sat on the bed with her hands behind her, trying to conceal the weapon.

The sight of Scott walking through the door nearly made her drop the knife. A disheveled lock of hair fell onto his forehead and blood dripped from the side of his lip. He made no outward sign that he recognized her. He, too, was bound at the wrists.

"You. Come here," Ortiz said to Jon. "Where is the briefcase?"

Jon hesitated.

"Under here." Mike jumped in and pulled it from the drawer.

Ortiz smiled wickedly at Jon. "There must be a portable propane tank on board."

Jon said nothing.

Ortiz turned to Mike. "Get it."

They took the briefcase and left Laurel and Scott alone in the locked cabin. Laurel wanted to reach for him, but knew there wasn't time.

"Laurel, I want to tell you—"

"Not now." Her heart ached with wanting to know what he'd felt so compelled to tell her, but she had to cut him off. Time was against them and their lives depended on her getting them free before someone returned. She turned and showed him the knife. He started to speak, but she shushed him. "Help me open it," she whispered, aware of the bossiness in her tone.

Together they opened the knife and Laurel was able to free their hands. Scott quickly pulled back the big rectangular window curtain, searching for another way out. The heavy fabric covered a tiny round porthole.

She heard footsteps coming down the hall toward them. Stepping to one side of the door, she nodded for Scott to take the other side. She knew this might be their only chance to surprise and overtake their adversaries. The lock turned in the door.

Suddenly, bright lights lit up the night sky and spilled over into the interior of the yacht. Scott looked startled, but Laurel felt a surge of hope.

Captain Larson's voice resounded from a bullhorn. She heard the sound of movement on the deck surrounding them. A volley of gunshots exploded. From inside, she heard another sound. The door opened and Jon crawled in on his hands and knees. He gave her his gun.

"Stay here and stay down," she told Scott.

"No. There's two of them out there. I'm coming with you," he insisted.

Ortiz called out from the other end of the yacht. "We have hostages and we'll kill them if you don't back off." To

Murdock, he said, "Go get the woman and show them we mean business."

Now was their chance. Laurel shot a glance at Scott, who nodded his head in understanding. She stood to the left of the cabin door, the gun clasped tightly in her hands, barrel pointing upward. Scott braced himself against the side opposite her, ready to jump Murdock when he came through the doorway after her.

Murdock rushed through the door in a crouched position. Scott grabbed at the hand in which Murdock held the gun. At the same time, he landed a crushing blow to Murdock's jaw. The gun flew from Murdock's grasp and landed on the bed. Jon grabbed the gun, while Scott continued to pummel Murdock with his fists. Laurel crept aft to where Ortiz waited. She heard Gary Boyd's voice coming from somewhere close by and hurried on. As she reached the main cabin, Gary breached the doorway. A shot rang out. She saw Gary's body flung backward by the impact of a bullet. Her chest tightened with horror. The shot came from the left side of the galley.

Ortiz.

She had a clear shot. Her heart pounded so hard she could barely speak. "Drop your weapon."

He turned, swinging his gun in her direction.

She fired.

The gun dropped from his hand as he stumbled backward. She held her gun on Ortiz as he writhed on the floor. Silence hung in the air, mingling with the scent of gunpowder.

"Scott?"

"I'm okay," he said. "Are you all right?"

Laurel reassured him, then blew out a huge breath. "Captain," she called out. "Hold your fire."

Relief overwhelmed her when the officers stepped inside and took over. Her whole body was shaking. Scott came down the companionway lugging Murdock, whose face was battered and bloodied. He handed Murdock to one of the officers and pulled her into his arms. As good as his embrace felt, she had to dislodge him. Tears blurred her vision as she walked over to where Gary had gone down.

Gary was moving when she knelt down beside him. She saw the vest sticking out from under his shirt and she breathed a tremendous sigh of relief. He was dazed, and the breath had definitely been knocked out of him, but he was all right. She was thankful he had learned from her mistake and had worn his body armor—and thankful Murdock and Ortiz had not used the cop-stopping bullets designed to penetrate the protective Kevlar.

Two officers took Jon and Mike away in handcuffs, as the captain stepped on board wearing an anxious expression. "Are you okay, Laurel?"

She nodded to the captain, then turned back to Scott. He stared at her as if trying to read her thoughts. She wished she could read his. Her breathing had calmed, but her pulse raced once more. His lip was bleeding again, but he was all right.

"You came after me," she said softly, still finding it hard to believe.

"I had to," Scott said just as quietly, his eyes delving deep inside her. "I've got something to say. And this time, I'm not going to let you out of my sight until I've said it."

Chapter 17

Captain Larson had other plans for Laurel. Before she could say another word to Scott, she was whisked off to the police station, where she spent two hours in debriefing. Jon Dever admitted he'd taken the briefcase, gun and gloves after Brian Delany had been shot. Jeffrey Hays showed up and informed her the district attorney's office would formally drop all charges against her. She sighed heavily with relief that she was no longer facing the threat of a prison sentence. Knowing her name and reputation would be cleared brought her a lesser measure of satisfaction. The cost had been dear.

Sitting across the desk from her captain, she waited anxiously while he finished with his call to the chief.

His face gave nothing away. "Sergeant Tanner, you'll be reinstated with full back pay, but there's a problem."

She held her breath, waiting.

"Because you were involved in another shooting tonight, I'm forced to put you on another three-day administration leave.'' A hint of a smile tipped at the corners of his mustache. "And, of course, you'll be encouraged to seek counseling with the department psychologist, Dr. Perry."

Laurel felt her own smile tug at her lips. "Yes, sir. I can live with that."

"Now, why don't you go home and get some rest?" he said.

Wearily, Laurel rubbed her hands down her face. She'd been holding on to her emotions by a thin thread.

In clearing her name, she'd driven an irrevocable wedge between her and Scott. By morning, Brian Delany's name and reputation would be thoroughly decimated by the media. She knew what effect that would have on Judge Delany's already low opinion of her. She wondered what effect it would have on Scott. She knew he'd risked his life to come after her tonight because he'd felt responsible for escalating her problems. He'd helped her find the truth because it was the right thing to do. She had no idea what he'd do now.

She thought he genuinely cared for her. But caring for her wasn't enough. When the shooting started on the yacht, she'd done everything Scott had accused her of doing the day before. She had been bossy and she'd refused to listen to him yet again. But she'd responded as she'd been trained to do. She knew she couldn't ignore her training—and she didn't want to. After tonight, she wouldn't be surprised to find Scott on the next flight to London.

"Perhaps you didn't hear me, Sergeant?" Captain Larson said, his voice showing concern.

Laurel glanced up at him and pulled her thoughts together. "Yes, I did. Thanks. I'm more than ready to go home."

Gary stood outside the captain's door. Assembled behind him in the squad room she noticed a large gathering of both on-and off-duty officers. Gary stepped forward. "Well, are you back to work, partner?"

Laurel's throat tightened. She nodded. "As soon as the charges are formally dropped." Tears welled up in her eyes as Gary opened his arms for an embrace. "Oh, Gary." She hugged him tightly as her friends applauded her news. "You just want someone to help with all the paperwork."

"That's right." He laughed as he hugged her back.

"Way to go, Sergeant," Malone chimed in.

"I knew you'd make it," Alice Johnson said, giving her a hug.

Pete Dickson shook her hand while Sam Ladd gave her a hearty pat on the back. Laurel relished the warm affection of her friends.

Her eye caught the banner on the far wall. She turned back to face Gary. "Sorry I missed the volleyball game. How'd it go?"

Gary smiled. "We walked out in the first half and told Huntington Beach we'd forfeit the game."

"Oh, no," Laurel groaned.

"We told them what was going down," a voice said from behind her.

"They wouldn't let us forfeit," Alice said. "They're giving us a rematch next week."

Gary's smile broadened. "They even volunteered to go with us as backup. Of course, I told 'em there was no need. Hell, you probably didn't even need us, but we didn't want you to think we didn't care."

The emotional ups and downs finally got to her and the tears spilled down her cheeks. "I'm sorry." She sniffled and accepted a tissue. "I guess I'm really worn-out."

Her friends muttered words of understanding and the group dissipated. Only Gary remained at her side.

She thanked him, then glanced around the room, her eyes automatically searching for Scott. "I hate to ask for anything more, but I think I need a ride home."

Gary hesitated. "I'd be happy to give you a ride, but Scott Delany is still here. He's waiting for you."

Laurel drew in a deep breath as a tingle raced over her skin. She squelched the hope blossoming inside her. She felt torn between a burning need to seek comfort in his warm embrace and to make a clean break as quickly as she could before his withdrawal tore her apart. She couldn't take any more disappointment. He'd said he wanted to talk, but that could mean anything. After what happened on the yacht, he was probably anxious to have it over and done with, to say a proper goodbye. "Where is he?"

"Out front," Gary replied.

Laurel walked out to the lobby. Word of the night's events had already leaked to the media. As soon as she stepped out the door, newspaper and television reporters fired questions at her from all directions. "I have no comment at this time," she told the group.

She glanced up and saw Scott step out the front door of the building. Gary tried to clear a path for her to the same door, but Caroline Endicott, a local TV correspondent, brought Laurel to a halt with her first question.

"Do you feel resentment for the way you've been treated and wrongly accused, Sergeant Tanner?" Endicott asked.

Laurel stared into large blue-gray eyes while the assembled crowd fell silent. She carefully considered her reply. "Everyone was doing his job as expected. It's especially tough when the people whose conduct is in question are representatives of law enforcement and the judicial system."

"That's the sergeant speaking. What about the woman, Laurel?" Endicott pressed.

"I'm one and the same." That particular truth weighed heavily on her heart at the moment. "The people who matter stood by me when it counted. No one could ask for more than that."

"You must be thrilled by the turn of events tonight," the reporter probed.

"I am not thrilled by any of this." Laurel struggled to hold on to her composure. "I'm relieved because it looks like I'll be able to go back to work soon, but I'll never be able to forget that a man has died." She felt the truth of that statement more than she could ever explain.

If there were any possible way to bring Brian back to stand trial, she'd do it in a second. The two teenagers would be given the chance to pay for their mistakes and learn from them. Brian Delany would never have that chance.

No one tried to follow her when she turned and walked out the door. At the foot of the steps, Scott stood beside his rental car with the motor running and the passenger door open.

"Are you sure you're okay? That cut on your lip might need stitches." Laurel looked across the seat to Scott.

"I'm fine. It's not bad." He turned the corner and headed for her apartment.

"I want to thank you—"

"Just sit back and relax, Laurel," Scott interrupted. "We can talk later, after you've rested."

She started to protest, then reconsidered. He was right. Exhausted, she leaned her head back against the headrest and closed her eyes until Scott turned off the engine in front of her apartment.

Apprehension tightened the muscles at the back of her neck as she let him usher her inside. She didn't know if she was up to facing their problems after all she'd been through tonight, but she doubted she'd get very much sleep if she put it off.

"Come on." Scott guided her into the bathroom, where he started filling the tub with water. "You'll feel better after a hot bath."

The bath sounded wonderful. How did he always know what she needed?

Scott stepped back into the hall. "Take your time." The low rumble of his voice made her ache from the wonderful memories it evoked.

In her present condition, the temptation to postpone their talk, to take him in her arms and to her bed for one last night of loving was far too great. Biting down on her lip, she shut the door behind her.

Twenty minutes later, Laurel stepped out of the bathroom wearing a pink chenille robe and matching slippers. She paused at the doorway, studying Scott as he sat on the sofa.

Finally he looked up and caught her staring. He smiled at her in that familiar way, causing a wave of longing to sweep over her.

He patted the cushion next to him. "Feel better?" The husky timbre of his voice did little to hide his tension.

She nodded. "Much."

"Can I make you something to eat?"

She shook her head. "I'm not hungry."

"It's been quite a day, hasn't it?"

"The worst," she said truthfully.

The look on Scott's face could have been regret or commiseration. To break the awkward silence, she said, "There's one thing I don't understand. How did you know to look for me at the marina?"

He met her gaze. "I saw the boat registration in the file Gary had in his car. I knew the marina was directly across the bay from Brian's. It was just a hunch that you'd be there."

"You mean you've learned to trust your instincts?" she said with mock disbelief.

The tender expression Scott wore said more than any words could convey.

She looked down at the pink fabric twisted between her fingers. "Thanks for coming after me. You probably saved my life as well as the lives of those boys. I heard that when Ortiz got to the hospital, he admitted he'd intended to set the yacht on fire."

"I could have gotten us both killed," he admitted.

"You're not a trained police officer. I appreciate what you did, even if it was dangerous to go off on your own," she admonished.

After a few moments of silence, Scott reached for her hand. "Laurel, I still owe you an apology," he began. "And an explanation."

Her pulse skipped with anticipation.

"I'm sorry I hurt you. I didn't mean the things I said. At least, not after I'd gotten some sleep and my brain started functioning again." He brought her hand over to his lap and rested it on his thigh.

Warm memories returned as the firm muscle beneath her fingers tightened.

"There is so much I didn't tell you, so much I need to explain. The other morning when I came here, I'd been up all night. My mother had had a heart attack."

"Oh, no," she gasped, squeezing his fingers.

"I broke one of her ribs when I was doing CPR. Then she had to have emergency heart surgery. When she came out of it, my father wouldn't let me see her because he blamed me for causing the attack in the first place. She'd overheard my father and me arguing. I guess I blamed myself, too. I was so upset and confused, I wasn't thinking straight."

After he'd confided his guilt about Brian to her during their walk in the mountains, she knew how deeply his father's accusation must have stung him. "I'm so sorry, Scott. How is she doing?"

His answering smile filled her with relief.

"Thanks. She's going to be fine. I finally got to see her, and she said the heart attack had nothing to do with the fight she'd overheard between me and my father," he explained. "She'd been hiding her symptoms from us for months."

"While I was searching for you," he continued, "I had a lot of time to think about what else you said that day and what you were doing. You never walked away from your problem or gave up the fight, no matter how unsolvable it seemed at the time." His eyes sparkled with admiration. "All this time, I've tried to apply the same principles I use in business to my personal life. When I came up against a problem I couldn't find a solution for, I simply decided to cut my losses and move on. Now I know that's not the way to deal with problems—or with the people I care about."

Scott ran his fingers lightly over her knuckles, tickling her senses with his warm touch. She remained silent, but cautiously allowed hope to grow inside her.

"Anyway, you were right about my still trying to protect Brian. Not many people have the guts to stand up to my father. I'm proud of you for sticking by your word in the face of so much pressure."

Laurel shrugged off his praise. She could understand what he'd been going through and she remembered their conversation clearly. She'd had plenty of time to relive it while tied up in the warehouse. "I'm sorry, too. I was in such a hurry to meet Gary, I didn't give you a chance to tell me about your mother or explain anything. All I could think about was going to prison."

"I realize that now," he said.

"But, Scott, it's not just what happened that morning." Laurel knew she couldn't risk a misunderstanding at this point. She had to tell him how she felt. "You have to understand, the work I do is more than a job or even a career. For me it's a way of life. It's who I am."

Scott stared intently at her. "I'm not asking you to change. I love who you are."

He brought her hand to his mouth and touched his lips to her knuckles. The warm sensation caused by his gentleness filled her with longing. "Then what are you asking?"

The intensity of his gaze held her spellbound for what seemed like an eternity. "I'm asking you to share my life. I'm asking you to marry me."

Marriage. Her pulse leaped. Her heart ached with longing and frustration. It would be so easy to say yes and damn the consequences, but she'd preached too much to Jon Dever about people taking responsibility for their own actions not to accept that responsibility herself. "What about your family? I know how much your parents mean to you. I don't want to destroy what you've worked so hard to rebuild."

He sighed. "Look, I know there's a lot of details to be worked out, but we can work them out." He took both her hands. "Laurel, I love you."

She bit down hard on her lip to keep from crying. The words should have been enough, but she knew they weren't. She loved him, but that love would destroy him if it kept him from his family. She swallowed. He wasn't going to make this easy on her. "I love you, too, but it doesn't change anything."

Scott's face brightened. "Yes, it does."

"What do you mean? Think about it. When your father hears what happened tonight—that I found the proof that incriminates Brian—he will despise me even more. He'll—"

Scott gave her a knowing smile, which caused a flutter deep inside her. "He already knows."

"But how could he?"

"Who do you think signed the warrant to search the boy's house? Who do you think, after hearing the whole story from Captain Larson, signed the warrant that allowed all those friends of yours to go into the warehouse after you?"

"Your father did that?" Laurel couldn't believe it.

"Well, it did take a little effort on my part to convince him. But despite all his faults, he does believe in the truth. And justice." Scott brought her hand to his chest. "What really counts is what's in here." His heart hammered beneath her fingers.

"You taught me something important," he continued. "For so long, I took responsibility for Brian's actions. Then I tried to take responsibility for my father's, as well." He shook his head gently. "When I talked to my mother last night at the hospital, I told her I loved her and I would never shut any doors between us again. I'm going to tell my father the same thing. If he chooses not to see me or talk to me, it will be his decision and his responsibility."

A flicker of hesitation briefly dulled Scott's eyes. "Laurel, it doesn't matter if my father ever forgives you for shooting Brian. The only thing that matters is that you're able to forgive yourself."

Laurel thought about what he said, and her heart filled with new love and respect for him. He had changed since their first meeting such a short time ago. Had he not shown her how completely he trusted her when he'd followed her instructions on the yacht?

She realized she had to trust Scott in the same way. His relationship with his father was his responsibility. She had to trust his instincts and the decisions he made.

In admitting she loved Scott, she'd made herself responsible for her own emotional welfare.

"If we love each other enough, we should have enough faith and trust in each other to believe we can work out any obstacles that come up," Scott said. He brought her hand up to his lips.

Thoughts and feelings raced through her mind at an incredible speed. On a gut level, it felt right. She was afraid to believe it was real, but more afraid to let the opportunity slip by without giving it a chance.

"Scott, I love you so much." She lifted her other hand to his jaw. "I want it to work. More than anything."

Scott pulled her into his arms. He pressed her close, kissing her deeply. When he lifted his lips from hers, he was breathing hard. "Does that mean you'll marry me?"

She captured his face in her hands. "Yes, I'll marry you."

He released a warm breath of relief against her cheek. "I love you," he said softly before his mouth moved over hers. He kissed her again, slowly, tenderly.

Her eyes remained closed after the kiss ended. She felt his lips on her forehead. After a few moments, she lifted her head to look into his eyes. "Let's go to bed."

Scott continued to hold her and softly stroke her back as they walked together to the bedroom. She slipped off her robe and climbed into bed. Scott undressed and slid in beside her. He put his arm around her and brought her close.

She did have one more question that came to mind as she cuddled against him. "How do you feel about babies?"

Scott raised up and turned on the bedside lamp to study her expression. "I like babies," he said cautiously. "How do *you* feel about babies?"

She laughed. "I love babies. I'd like to have children someday."

Scott relaxed beside her. "Good. Me too." After a moment he added, "You know, if my father gives us any trouble, I do happen to know his one weakness."

Puzzled, she turned on her side and studied him more carefully. "What do you mean?"

"He has wanted grandchildren for as long as I can remember. If we have babies, we might never be able to get rid of him."

She chuckled. "Then let's not have babies right away. I want you to myself for a while."

Scott smiled down at her. She could see the desire in his eyes before he turned off the light. "I love you," he said, his voice thick with emotion. He kissed her lightly.

She stroked his chest.

"You should get some sleep now," he said.

"I don't want to sleep." She wanted Scott with an intensity she knew would never wane. Her fingertips found and circled his nipple. It formed a pebblelike hardness beneath her touch. She felt his chest rise sharply with the air he drew into his lungs.

He trembled at her touch. "You really should try."

"Do you really love me?" She let her fingers ease down his abdomen.

"I wouldn't have said it if I didn't mean it." The muscles in his abdomen tightened. His hand cupped her breast.

She slid her hand over his hip and gently stroked his inner thigh. The longing she felt was more than physical. She knew he felt it, too, the need for closeness, the need to consummate their vows. "Show me."

Breathing fast and hard, in a voice tense with restraint, he said, "You need proof?"

"You know how it is with cops—we need evidence." She moistened her lips and ran them lightly over the pulsing artery in his neck.

Laurel became acutely aware of the changes occurring in her own body; the tightening of her nipples, the shortness of breath, and the warm moistness between her legs.

"But I already said—"

"Hearsay."

In the diffuse light from the window, his eyes sought hers. Slowly, he moved his lips over her cheek, her chin, her lips. "What kind of evidence do you need?"

Laurel felt the swirling, spinning sensation start in her head and work its way down to her toes.

He brushed her nipple lightly with his thumb. "I helped convince your captain you were in danger—"

"Circumstantial." She released a small gasp of pleasure.

Scott gently pushed her to her back. She surrendered to his urging. "What kind of evidence do you need?" he repeated.

She breathed deeply, savoring the scent of his body, the feel of his skin.

He nuzzled her neck, his warm breath tickling her skin. As he moved above her, his arousal pressed insistently against her.

She snuggled closer as her need grew.

"Laurel." He said her name in a throaty whisper. "What kind of evidence do you need, love?"

She smiled against his lips. "Hard evidence."

* * * * *

HE'S AN

AMERICAN HERO

He's a man's man, and every woman's dream. Strong, sensitive and so irresistible—he's an American Hero.

For April: KEEPER, by Patricia Gardner Evans: From the moment Cleese Starrett encountered Laurel Drew fishing in his river, he was hooked. But reeling in this lovely lady might prove harder than he thought.

For May: MICHAEL'S FATHER, by Dallas Schulze: Kel Bryan needed a housekeeper—fast. And Megan Roarke did more than fit the bill; she fit snugly into his open arms. Then she told him her news....

For June: SIMPLE GIFTS, by Kathleen Korbel: For too long Rock O'Connor had fought the good fight to no avail. Then Lee Kendall entered his jaded world, her zest for life rekindling his former passion—as well as a new one.

AMERICAN HEROES: Men who give all they've got for their country, their work—the women they love.

Only from

MILLION DOLLAR SWEEPSTAKES (III)
AND
EXTRA BONUS PRIZE DRAWING

ℐINTIMATE MOMENTS®

™ Silhouette®

CONARD COUNTY continues...

Once again Rachel Lee invites readers to explore the wild Western terrain of Conard County, Wyoming, to meet the men and women whose lives unfold on the land they hold dear—and whose loves touch our hearts with their searing intensity. Join this award-winning author as she reaches the POINT OF NO RETURN, IM #566, coming to you in May.

For years, Marge Tate had safeguarded her painful secret from her husband, Nate. Then the past caught up with her in the guise of a youthful stranger, signaling an end to her silence—and perhaps the end to her fairy-tale marriage.... Look for their story, only from Silhouette Intimate Moments.

ROMANTIC TRADITIONS continues in April with Carla Cassidy's sexy spin on the amnesia plot line in TRY TO REMEMBER (IM #560).

"Jane Smith's" memory had vanished, so when Frank Longford offered her a safe haven and a strong shoulder, she accepted. Then the nightmares began, with memory proving scarier than amnesia, as Jane began to fear losing the one man she truly loved.

As always, **ROMANTIC TRADITIONS** doesn't stop there! July will feature Barbara Faith's DESERT MAN, which spotlights the sheikh story line. And future months hold more exciting twists on classic plot lines from some of your favorite authors, so don't miss them— only in INTIMATE MOMENTS ™ *Silhouette*®

**And now for something
completely different
from Silhouette....**

SPELLBOUND
R O M A N C E

**In May, look for
MIRANDA'S VIKING (IM #568)
by Maggie Shayne**

Yesterday, Rolf Magnusson had been frozen
solid, his body perfectly preserved in the
glacial cave where scientist Miranda O'Shea
had discovered him. Today, the Viking warrior
sat sipping coffee in her living room, all six feet
seven inches of him hot to the touch. His heart,
however, remained as ice-cold as the rest of him
had been for nine hundred years. But Miranda
knew a very unscientific way to thaw it out....

Don't miss MIRANDA'S VIKING by
Maggie Shayne, available this May,
only from

IT'S OUR 1000TH SILHOUETTE ROMANCE,
AND WE'RE CELEBRATING!

JOIN US FOR A SPECIAL COLLECTION OF LOVE STORIES
BY AUTHORS YOU'VE LOVED FOR YEARS, AND
NEW FAVORITES YOU'VE JUST DISCOVERED.
JOIN THE CELEBRATION...

April
REGAN'S PRIDE by **Diana Palmer**
MARRY ME AGAIN by **Suzanne Carey**

May
THE BEST IS YET TO BE by **Tracy Sinclair**
CAUTION: BABY AHEAD by **Marie Ferrarella**

June
THE BACHELOR PRINCE by **Debbie Macomber**
A ROGUE'S HEART by **Laurie Paige**

July
IMPROMPTU BRIDE by **Annette Broadrick**
THE FORGOTTEN HUSBAND by **Elizabeth August**

SILHOUETTE ROMANCE...VIBRANT, FUN AND EMOTIONALLY
RICH! TAKE ANOTHER LOOK AT US! AND AS PART OF THE
CELEBRATION, READERS CAN RECEIVE A FREE GIFT!

YOU'LL FALL IN LOVE ALL OVER
AGAIN WITH
SILHOUETTE ROMANCE!

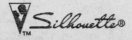

CEL1000

 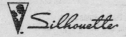

SILHOUETTE... Where Passion Lives

Don't miss these Silhouette favorites by some of our most
distinguished authors! And now, you can receive a discount by
ordering two or more titles!

D#05706	HOMETOWN MAN by Jo Ann Algermissen	$2.89 ☐
D#05795	DEREK by Leslie Davis Guccione	$2.99 ☐
D#05802	THE SEDUCER by Linda Turner	$2.99 ☐
D#05804	ESCAPADES by Cathie Linz	$2.99 ☐
IM#07478	DEEP IN THE HEART by Elley Crain	$3.39 ☐
IM#07507	STANDOFF by Lee Magner	$3.50 ☐
IM#07537	DAUGHTER OF THE DAWN by Christine Flynn	$3.50 ☐
IM#07539	A GENTLEMAN AND A SCHOLAR by Alexandra Sellers	$3.50 ☐
SE#09829	MORE THAN HE BARGAINED FOR by Carole Halston	$3.50 ☐
SE#09833	BORN INNOCENT by Christine Rimmer	$3.50 ☐
SE#09840	A LOVE LIKE ROMEO AND JULIET by Natalie Bishop	$3.50 ☐
SE#09844	RETURN ENGAGEMENT by Elizabeth Bevarly	$3.50 ☐
RS#08952	INSTANT FATHER by Lucy Gordon	$2.75 ☐
RS#08957	THE PRODIGAL HUSBAND by Pamela Dalton	$2.75 ☐
RS#08960	DARK PRINCE by Elizabeth Krueger	$2.75 ☐
RS#08972	POOR LITTLE RICH GIRL by Joan Smith	$2.75 ☐
SS#27003	STRANGER IN THE MIST by Lee Karr	$3.50 ☐
SS#27009	BREAK THE NIGHT by Anne Stuart	$3.50 ☐
SS#27016	WHAT WAITS BELOW by Jane Toombs	$3.50 ☐
SS#27020	DREAM A DEADLY DREAM by Allie Harrison	$3.50 ☐

(limited quantities available on certain titles)

	AMOUNT	$ _____
DEDUCT:	10% DISCOUNT FOR 2+ BOOKS	$ _____
	POSTAGE & HANDLING	$ _____
	($1.00 for one book, 50¢ for each additional)	
	APPLICABLE TAXES*	$ _____
	TOTAL PAYABLE	$ _____
	(check or money order—please do not send cash)	

To order, complete this form and send it, along with a check or money order
for the total above, payable to Silhouette Books, to: **In the U.S.:** 3010 Walden
Avenue, P.O. Box 9077, Buffalo, NY 14269-9077; **In Canada:** P.O. Box 636,
Fort Erie, Ontario, L2A 5X3.

Name: _____

Address: _____ City: _____

State/Prov.: _____ Zip/Postal Code: _____

*New York residents remit applicable sales taxes.
Canadian residents remit applicable GST and provincial taxes.

Silhouette®

SBACK-AJ